PRAISE FOR J. A. LUDWIG

"A strong debut for both genre-lovers and people who want to see someone with Aya's heart in the hero's role for a change."

— NICHOLAS THURKETTLE, AUTHOR OF
STAGES OF SLEEP

"A great read with action that keeps you turning the page."

— RJ JOHNSON, AUTHOR OF *THE
TWELVE STONES*

"An excellent novel with great character development and world building."

— D. FISCHER, AUTHOR OF RISE OF THE
REALMS SERIES

"The best books present as many questions as they answer, leaving us hungry for more. This is one of those!"

— S. JOHNSON

"An exciting, action packed story!"

— G. MORALES

BLOOD EMBERS

BLOOD EMBERS

BOOK TWO OF BLOOD MAGIC

J. A. LUDWIG

Fiction is the truth inside the lie.

— STEPHEN KING

I

FLAMES IN THE DARK

1

"How much longer do we wait?" Aya asks, anxiously playing with the silk bracelet on her wrist.

"Until Elder Mirrah gets here. She wants to see us off. Whether your fellow former-slaves and the Arena workers are with her or not." Jaxon Parth takes a deep breath and releases it slowly. "We'll have to wait and see."

"No rush," a voice says a short distance to the right. Aya leans forward slightly to spy the two men sitting on boulders.

"I'm not exactly excited to go into that creepy cave," Kylii Lakiin says, his golden eyes staring up at the sky.

"Agreed." Daniil, Kylii's brother, sits on a lower boulder, his pale blue eyes locked onto the animal sitting beside him.

The beast, a female Khorgoi named Tanith, yawns. Rows of tiny, sharp teeth flash white standing out against the dark, red scales covering her body. The brown mane on her back and chest moves with the breeze. Stretching her front paws forward, her curved claws dig into the earth.

A fascinating and intelligent creature, Tanith is accompanying them because she wishes to. She has communicated that through Daniil, with whom she became bonded while fighting beside him in their final battle in the Arena against the Blood King's strongest warriors, the Brüdel. The Brüdel made the fatal mistake of believing that they controlled her fiercely independent spirit.

Raising a hand to block the morning sunlight, Aya Flandeen glances behind her at the dark maw of the cave. The blackness swallows the warm light, making it impossible to see within; as though afraid of the unknown shadows, vegetation ceases growing close to the cave's entrance. Only a few vines dare climb the surrounding walls, adding vibrant splashes of green against the stone. Aya's chest tightens, and her heart pounds the longer she stares at the unnerving cave mouth.

The small group waiting at the entrance sits in tense silence. Most are former slaves of Bloodfall Arena, the ones who managed to escape with Aya. Some sit around a pile of supply bags. Some inch farther from the opening as time passes, afraid something will emerge from the depths to drag them inside. Some struggle to remain awake at the early hour. Others try to keep themselves distracted, playing cards or checking their bags for the umpteenth time.

Two men lean against the walls of the cave behind the group, unafraid of the scar-like opening. These men weren't victims of the Arena but former slave traders who abandoned their trade to help those they once sold.

Aya lowers her arm, facing away from the cave. The two men standing on either side of her impatiently shift their weight. Jaxon's blue eyes focus on the forest in front of them, each movement catching his attention. His black hair is combed back out of his face and stubble grows on his chin.

Standing with his arms crossed over his chest, Yme Gurek searches the forest with his silver eyes. Each breath he takes fills the air with more magic, creating wind. The hair on Aya's arms stands as the breeze brushes against her skin. Magic mixes with the air, the gentle touch awakening her own. Deep inside, she feels her Life Healer magic uncurl, wishing to mingle with the familiar feeling washing over her.

"Will many stay behind?" Yme asks.

"That depends. If you want my honest opinion, I believe some won't be joining us," Jaxon answers. "Hopefully, Aya's words convinced most otherwise."

Aya's thoughts flash back to the night of their escape from Bloodfall Arena. She can still hear the fighting, the screams, and the fresh, open air on her skin after so many months inside.

And *his* voice. She still hears *his* voice.

We haven't tasted Life Healer in so long. The Blood King's words echo in Aya's head, reminding her that time is ultimately slipping away from them.

If the Blood King's men catch up to them, they'll all be dragged back into the Arena. They'll be forced to fight for their lives once again for the entertainment of a man who enjoys bloodshed and death.

They would've been caught already if Jaxon hadn't surprised them outside the Arena with a place to go.

Four Days Earlier

"There's an oasis town at the end of this canyon that the Blood King doesn't know about," Jaxon says. "Or if he does, he doesn't care enough about it to station any of his soldiers nearby. The town will give us shelter, food, maybe clothes."

Hushed whispers rise from the recently escaped Arena slaves. None are sure whether to trust this man they knew as a slave trader. Many, including Aya, were victims of his Black Caravan, brought to Bloodfall Arena to fight in the Blood King's deadly games. Jaxon may have helped with their escape, but Aya knows it isn't enough to gain their full trust.

"How far?" Aya asks.

"Two days on foot."

"And after that?" Yme inquires.

"We'll talk about that after we get there."

"Why should we listen to you?" a voice demands from the

crowd. Aya's attention is pulled to two women, sisters who were brought to the Arena the same time as Aya. The one who spoke is Rava. Her sister, Mava, struggles to hold her back from attacking Jaxon. "How do we know this isn't a trap?"

A man standing beside them nods his head in agreement, another who was brought to the Arena along with Aya. "Maybe Seera planned this in case we *actually* made it out," Bern chimes in. "You and Dolus are probably working with her. How do we know there aren't soldiers waiting for us?"

Hearing his name, Dolus Otho, the former Voice of the Arena, scuttles closer to Jaxon and Aya. "I have nothing to do with this. Tell them!"

"Even if he and I *were* plotting, I don't think my stabbing of the Blood King would be considered part of the plan," Jaxon points out.

Murmurs rumble through the group. Daniil and Kylii Lakiin move to either side of Aya, the brothers both bearing impressed expressions. Tanith watches Jaxon with her strange, white eyes.

"Did he actually—?" Kylii starts.

"Twice," Aya confirms. "We can trust him. *And* his men."

"We've wasted enough time arguing," Yme says. "If it's going to take us two days to reach this town, we should move."

"The sun won't be rising for many hours, and we should make it our goal to get as much distance as possible between us and the Blood King before dawn," Jaxon adds.

Jaxon begins to lead the weary group away from Bloodfall. Aldur and Fleance, Jaxon's men from the caravan, walk on either side of their leader. The canyon walls remind Aya of the Arena's walls. Though not as high, there is still an oppressive feeling as the group of nearly eighty men and women trudge forward.

The excitement from the escape fades. Replacing it, exhaustion and the strong desire to sleep. The rough terrain adds to the group's tiredness, reminding many of the treacherous journey they suffered to reach Bloodfall.

"We should stop and rest," Skara, a healer, mentions to Aya. "None of us have slept in over a day now."

"It's better to keep moving," Jaxon says. "The Blood King will send his men after us, but it will take time for them to organize and find our trail. If we can put enough distance between us and the Arena, then we will rest."

"Says a man who wasn't forced to fight a major battle several hours ago," Skara complains, referring to the fight against Blood King Klaeon's private assassins, the Brüdel.

"You're wasting energy talking," Yme snaps. "I for one want as much distance between me and Klaeon as possible. I won't feel safe to sleep until then."

Others in the group mumble their approval and Skara, dejectedly, falls silent.

Aya leans close to her. "They don't understand how we healers think. They seem to forget who saved their sorry asses during the battle," she whispers to Skara.

A small smile forms on the healer's face. "He's right, but I'm worried about the children and the older slaves."

"We're no longer slaves, Skara," says Tristan, another healer.

"Right. The older... folk."

Aya glances behind at Bon and Cal, the youngest of the group. Their pace is slower than the others and behind them the older people limp as their aged bodies feel each incline.

The former Arena workers hang back, bringing up the rear of the group. If soldiers did manage to catch up, they plan to give the rest time to escape while they fight. A few also assist those struggling to walk, ensuring no one is left behind.

Dolus stays close to Aya, sensing the angry, distrusting looks all around him. Aya catches him staring at Jaxon multiple times, a haunted look always falling over his expression.

"You seem to know Jaxon well," she asks, startling the older man. "Why are you afraid of him?"

Shaking his head furiously, Dolus waves his hand at her. "I can't say. That man is dangerous. Always has been. I never liked him or his caravan. Too many strange stories coming out of those who managed to leave his employ alive, or what constituted *living*."

"What do you mean?"

"Men who become slavers only have two reasons to do so," Dolus continues. "One, money. Or two, to keep from becoming slaves themselves. Do you know why *he* became a slaver?"

"The money?"

Dolus snorts and moves closer to her, his hot breath on her face. "He became a slaver for the third reason a man becomes a slaver."

"Which is?"

"Aya?"

Jaxon's voice makes Aya jump. Dolus jumps higher, shrinking away from the sudden appearance of the former leader of the Black Caravan.

"Could you ask... Daniil if that beast of his can travel to the higher canyon walls and see if it spots anyone following?"

"Why me?"

"I don't think he'll listen if I ask." Jaxon looks past Aya. "Dolus."

"Jaxon," Dolus squeaks.

"I'll ask," Aya says, pulling Jaxon's attention away from the shaking man.

"Thank you." Jaxon heads back to the front of the group.

Aya turns back to Dolus, but the man is already scuttling

away, suddenly less fearful of the former slaves. She tries to imagine a third reason to become a slaver, but all she is left with is the haunted look in Dolus' eyes.

3

Aya watches Tanith leap effortlessly up the canyon walls. The Khorgoi's movements are graceful, each step confident and strong. *How did she ever get captured by Klaeon's men?*

The ground shakes beneath her feet, and magic fills the air. Behind the group, Yme and two other mages stand in the middle of the canyon path. Yme squats and holds his arms in front of him, forearms touching. He slowly stands straight, holding his arms together. The earth rises with him, creating a pillar in the middle of the path.

The two mages standing on either side of Yme move to the walls of the pathway and place both of their hands on the walls. They carefully move one hand as though pulling something from the thick earth, and the walls of the canyon move inward, meeting the pillar, and blocking anyone who might be following.

Finished, the three men catch up to the still walking group, as Tanith returns from her venture to the top of the canyon.

"Doesn't seem like anyone's following—yet," Daniil reports.

The news is welcome, but also reminds the group of the possible danger behind them. A rush of energy fills everyone, and exhaustion is momentarily forgotten.

Every hour, Daniil sends Tanith up the sides of the surrounding slopes and Yme and the two earth mages close off the path behind them.

After Tanith returns from a fifth scouting without spotting anyone, the Khorgoi's movements are noticeably slower. Yme and the mages take longer to build the earth wall, slowing the group as it waits for the three to finish each block.

Aya wanders towards the front, next to Jaxon. "It's been five hours with no signs of anyone following us. If we're not planning to stop soon, everyone is going to need as much energy as they can get to continue on."

"I agree." Jaxon motions to Fleance, who quickly approaches. "Let Yme and the earth mages know they can stop blocking the path." Without a word, Fleance hurries to the back of the group to convey the order.

"And Tanith?" Aya inquires.

"She doesn't need to go up anymore. We still have about two more hours to go before I feel confident there's enough distance. You can pass that message on or not."

Aya slows her pace until Daniil and Kylii are within range. "Tanith doesn't have to go up top anymore."

The Khorgoi huffs her breath and shakes her head, a thin layer of dirt flying into the air.

"She's appreciative," Daniil confirms. "Though she'll be ready to start again if needed."

"How much longer?" Kylii whines. "I've lost the feeling in my feet."

"Earlier, he lost feeling in his toes. If we walk long enough, he'll lose feeling in his head," Daniil jokes.

"I think someone has already lost that," Kylii retorts, anger filling his tone.

"Jaxon thinks two more hours at least," Aya says. Kylii's groan echoes her own feelings, but she understands Jaxon's overcautiousness.

The self-proclaimed ruler who orders the bloody battles and twisted tournaments of Bloodfall Arena, who finds enjoyment from the death of many innocents, mainly mages, is a magic user himself; and Aya worries about what else the Blood King is hiding.

And he uses forbidden Blood Magic. He can take away another's magic, like Yme's fire. Because of him, I was taken from my home.

If there were no Blood King, Jaxon wouldn't have been a slaver. He wouldn't have taken so many from their homes. He would've never come to Aya's village in Foula Valley, and she would've never been taken to the Arena.

The sky lightens above, the dark night becoming a calming blue as the sun ascends. The group's pace slows, a few leaning on one another to keep from collapsing. Aya's eyes droop, and her head nods forward. Jerking her head up, she tries to shake the sleep away, but she knows it's a losing battle. She's unsure how many hours have passed, but she knows the group can't go on much longer.

"We'll rest here," Jaxon announces. "Get some sleep if you can."

It doesn't take much encouragement, the hard earth doing little to impede sleep. Even the brightening sky doesn't keep Aya awake, and she falls deep into nightmares filled with Klaeon's strange eyes. The strange presence she felt try to steal her magic from her takes shape in her nightmares as a shadow covered in spiked chains.

Waking from the nightmare, Aya winces at the sun high in

the sky. She sits up, shaking with chills left over from her nightmare. It reminds her of the recurring dreams she had back in her village. The dark figures in shadow, the chains drenched in blood... she knows now, Klaeon is that figure. *Does that mean Yme was one of the other figures? The figures in light?*

Movement catches her attention, and Aya spies Jaxon standing watch at the far end of the group. She carefully moves away from the sleeping figures around her and stands next to him.

"Still don't sleep?" she asks, referring to rumors she heard from other members of the Black Caravan. Many of the men believed Jaxon was more than human. None ever saw him sleep and he seemed to have unnaturally high luck.

Crossing his arms over his chest, Jaxon chuckles softly. "Old habit. You're not the first to wake, though." He motions his head in front of them.

Yme sits alone a short distance from the group, his back to Aya and Jaxon. His hands move slowly across the ground at his sides.

"What is he doing?" Aya plays with the bracelet tied to her wrist. Each colored, woven silk strand represented the four rulers of nature. Green for the earth, blue for the sea, white for the sky, and red for the sun. It was one of two gifts her parents left her after their death. The other, a black-bladed dagger, is crudely tied to her thigh.

"I have no idea, but he's been sitting there for almost an hour." Jaxon turns away from her.

She catches a brief flash of shame in his eyes as he walks away. "Where are you going?"

"Need to talk to Fleance. We should move soon."

Rushing to him, she grabs his arm. "Just a little longer. Some haven't slept in over a day."

Gently pulling his arm free, Jaxon reluctantly nods. "Two

hours. Any more and we risk anyone following us catching up." He leaves her alone.

Aya carefully approaches Yme. She waits for him to notice her, but after a minute she asks, "What are you doing?"

"It's been a long time since I was outside. The earth feels different without the Arena's influence." Lifting his head, Yme takes a deep breath. "The air, too. It's clearer."

"I bet if you had some water, it would be... wetter."

"Cleaner. But thank you for mocking me," he says, sarcasm thick in his tone.

"Sorry." Aya sits on the ground next to him. "Now that we aren't in the Arena, what are your plans?"

"I don't have any plans."

"I don't believe that."

Yme raises his hand and stares at his palm. "I want my fire back. I want to stop Klaeon from destroying any more lives." He clenches his fist. "What about you?"

"I don't know. I could try to find my way back to Foula Valley, but I'm not even sure which direction to go. I don't think I'd get very far before another slave trader picked me up."

"You know how to fight. And there are people who would be eager to escort you back."

Biting her lower lip, Aya thinks about Mava and Rava. Their village is close to her own village of Oula, but could she risk any more lives trying to get home? "I don't know. Maybe I can convince Jaxon to take me home."

"You have an odd tendency to trust untrustworthy people," Yme states.

"What do you mean?"

"Leid. Dolus Otho." Yme eyes the Voice of the Arena, asleep nearby.

Aya's thoughts flash back to Leid. The killer in Bloodfall Arena who turned out to be a mage. His cold-hearted approach to fighting still sends a shiver through her. He chose to stay behind, but she remembers how he helped her and Yme in the fight against the fire-breathing volacerta.

"Jaxon was the one who brought you to the Arena, wasn't he?" Yme brings her back to the present.

"Yes."

"Do the others you came with trust him?"

"No."

Yme leans close. "Maybe you should ask why."

4

Two hours pass and Jaxon rouses the group. They continue through the canyon path, but Aya notices Fleance is nowhere to be seen. *Must have to do with whatever Jaxon needed to talk to him about... I wonder what it was?*

The Earth mages return to blocking the path behind, and Daniil sends Tanith up the canyon sides a few times to ensure they're still not being followed.

As Tanith returns to Daniil's side, she rubs her muzzle against his hand. He nods as though hearing a voice and Aya's attention is pulled to Kylii's annoyed face. The fiery brother whispers something quickly to Daniil before storming ahead to walk with Aldur, the larger man visibly tensing at his new walking companion.

Quickening her pace to walk beside Daniil, Aya hesitates when she sees the large frown on his face. "Is everything okay?"

Refusing to look at her, Daniil glowers at Kylii's back. "It's nothing."

"You want to try saying that without the frown?"

"It's *nothing*."

Aya slows her pace to give him space, Yme appearing at her side. "What's the matter?"

"I think something's wrong between Daniil and Kylii."

"They'll be fine. Fighting is part of being siblings."

Turning to him, Aya smiles. "Are you speaking from your own personal experience?"

A dark expression crosses Yme's face, and he doesn't answer. Aya remembers a similar expression on his face when they fought an illusion mage together. Whatever the mage showed Yme must have been something painful because once he was free of the illusion, he crushed the mage's head into nothing. She didn't want to ask what he saw until he was ready to tell her.

She doesn't believe Yme's explanation that this is a simple spat between siblings. She witnessed the brothers argue in the Arena, but there was always a playfulness to it. Something else is happening, creating a strange air of distance.

The group walks in silence the rest of the day, still fearing at any moment Klaeon's soldiers will appear. Aya overhears some whispering of how they're reminded of the long journey that brought them to the Arena. Unlike that journey, Jaxon allows time for rest, but there is no food nor enough water to go around. What little they have is relegated to the weakest in the group.

As the sun lowers in the sky, grass grows in larger clumps until it covers the entire ground, adding vibrant green to the otherwise monotone landscape. Plants grow on the sides of the path—plants familiar to Aya. Similar to those found in Foula Valley, they stand out against the gray mountains towering above them.

The softer earth is welcome as they walk long into the night. When they finally rest, the thick grass is more comfortable than the beds of the Arena. The smell of plant life is calming, and the group has no trouble falling asleep.

The morning brings dew and a light fog. As the group wakes, Aya realizes Fleance is still missing. She doesn't know if anyone else has noticed. If they have, they keep it to themselves.

The vegetation grows thicker the longer they walk, and the mountains disappear amongst trees towering above. Small streams fill the air with moisture and many in the group stop and drink from the clear water. The hours pass faster as the fear fades from the former slaves. The only reminder is the grumbling of starving bellies.

Jaxon slows them as they approach a cliff edge. He motions towards a sloping path leading down into a canyon. Entering the deep canyon, Aya spots a small patch of forest nestled between the steep canyon walls. At the center sits a small town, the roofs of the buildings blending with the green of the trees. A waterfall from the top of the canyon feeds a river passing directly through the town. Bridges cross the river and boats move slowly through the water. Men throw nets into the river, pulling up fish with ease.

Every building is built on top of wooden beams above the forest floor and has a deck with railing around the perimeter. Boats are tied to the railing or sit on two logs beside the homes. Aya remembers stories Elder Mircien told her of villages built close to the Garen River in Foula. Building above the ground protected the buildings when the river flooded.

Entering the town, Aya notices a strange sense of calm throughout. None of the locals seem particularly surprised by the sudden group of strangers walking past. Children hide behind their parents, curious about the group, but are the only ones to show any fear.

Jaxon stops the group before one of the bridges crossing the river. Five people stand in the middle of the bridge, three women and two men. Aya recognizes Fleance standing at the head of the small group next to a woman dressed in elegant robes.

So that's where he was. Jaxon sent him ahead to warn of our arrival.

"I see this young man was speaking the truth when he arrived yesterday," the woman says. "Though we weren't given *much* warning, you are welcome here. You're all very fortunate to be alive. Few, if any, can say that after having been slaves of Bloodfall Arena. In honor of your escape, we offer our homes and food. Some may even have fresh clothing for you, if you so choose. And tonight, we will have a feast to celebrate."

Townsfolk approach the group and greet the former slaves and Arena workers. Many are led off to be fed and rest. The only ones who stay behind with the woman who spoke are Aya, Yme, Daniil, Kylii, Tanith, Aldur, Fleance, and Jaxon.

"This way," the woman urges, heading across the bridge. They follow quickly, Jaxon walking beside Mirrah as Fleance moves to Aldur's side.

Glancing into the water, Aya sees schools of fish swimming against the current. Their silver scales catch sunlight, making the river sparkle. Larger fish swim through the schools, varying in colors, but mainly a dark brown. Long whiskers trail behind them as they move.

"I'm sorry I didn't send word sooner, Elder Mirrah. Once the escape happened, we had to move quickly," Jaxon says as they reach the opposite bank.

Mirrah fights a smile, reaching her hand towards him before catching herself. "It's been many ages, Jaxon. I wondered if the Arena had taken you. But I've heard more recent rumors about a black-blooded slave trader who sounded a little too familiar."

"I had hoped none of those rumors would reach you."

"How do you know Jaxon?" Aya blurts out.

"It's not my place to answer personal questions about Jaxon. Though if he's in a sharing mood, which is a rarity I'm sure you're aware of, then I don't mind talking about history." Mirrah stops the group in front of a large hut, her home Aya assumes.

Turning to the group, Jaxon avoids their eyes, a slight flush on his cheeks. The usual façade of a leader is gone, leaving behind something reminding Aya of an embarrassed child.

"This town is where I was born. Elder Mirrah... is my mother."

The shock is palpable. Even Aldur and Fleance have expressions of genuine surprise. But Aya feels not only shock but hurt. He told her he came from a land dry and cracked...it had been a lie. *Another lie to add to the growing list.*

"You left to become a slave trader?" Yme asks.

"He left because he was unhappy," Mirrah corrects him.

Jaxon's expression is guarded, but he meets the elder's eyes with a look of hurt hidden beneath. "I left to protect this town. If I became a slave trader, if I provided enough slaves to the Arena, the Blood King would have no reason to send his men."

"So, it was selfishness, then," Kylii says, anger clear in his voice. "You ruined other homes to save your own."

"To protect your family, you destroyed others," Daniil adds.

"I did what needed to be done to survive."

Doing what needs to be done to see the light of the next day rules all our lives. Aya remembers the words Jaxon told her so long ago.

"Jaxon has done things many will never agree with," Mirrah interjects. "But what about all of you? When you were in that Arena, you did things you never thought yourselves capable of, I'm sure."

"*We* had no choice." Kylii motions to his brother and Yme. "We were taken from our homes. We did not *choose* to be part of the Arena."

Mirrah faces Yme. "Let me ask you, champion of the Arena. When you were taken from your home, who in your village spoke against it?"

Yme's jaw tightens and he shakes his head. "No one. My family was too afraid of Klaeon. Everyone else... believed I deserved it for what I did."

"What?" Aya gasps.

"I assume you, healer, and you two," Mirrah points to Daniil and Kylii, "are from lands the Blood King has no influence in. You think it is easy to denounce his actions, denounce his Arena. But you can't see past those walls, even when you stand outside of them."

"What is that supposed to mean?" Daniil demands.

"You think the Blood King's entire world is the Arena. That is not even a piece of the same puzzle. He is a King. He rules many lands. And there are many more people than Bloodfall who cheer when he waves his hand. And they will never see the evil you see in him. They will only see it in you."

Silence falls over the group as Mirrah's words fill them with doubt.

"And what of this town?" Yme asks, softly. "Do you only see evil in us?"

"No. What I see, in all of you, is pain. Deeper in some than others."

Aya squeezes her wrist, feeling the silk of her bracelet against her palm. *Is this the world my parents left? Is this why they hid in Oula?*

"I apologize for bringing the mood down," Mirrah says, her tone bright. She climbs the steps to the door of the large hut.

"But you are all welcome to stay in my home. Though it may be a little crowded with eight of you."

"Daniil and I will stay outside... with Tanith." Kylii nearly spits the Khorgoi's name. "We'd like to enjoy the outside air as much as possible." He places his hand on his brother's shoulder. Daniil visibly tenses at the touch but remains silent. Tanith glances up at him, cocking her head to the side.

"The deck is fine for us," Aldur says. Fleance nods his head in silent agreement.

"Very well. If you need anything, don't hesitate to ask," Mirrah says. "And I wish to assure you all. The Blood King inspires no love here."

The brothers nod and wave their hands in thanks as they walk towards a small collection of trees. Tanith follows close, shaking her head as insects fly in her face. Aldur and Fleance climb the stairs and find a spot on the deck in the corner, leaning against the wall of the hut. Fleance immediately falls asleep, but Aldur takes out his knife and grabs a fallen stick. He carves into the thin wood carefully.

Yme and Jaxon climb the stairs, following Mirrah inside. Aya stares at the dark doorway of the hut. The dark opening grows larger, shadows swirling inside. Pounding in Aya's ears overpower the sounds of the forest and town. Her chest tightens, and she finds it hard to breathe. She takes a hesitant step back.

"Aya? Are you all right?" Yme appears from the darkness, his brows furrowed in concern.

Shaking her head, Aya plays with the silk bracelet on her wrist. "I-I can't. It's... I can't explain." *I can't be surrounded by walls again.*

"If you need a minute, that's fine."

Nodding, Aya gives him what she hopes is a reassuring

smile. He heads back into the dark hut and Aya takes deep breaths, trying to calm her pounding heart. She appreciates the understanding but worries what this new anxiety means.

5

Aya swings her legs, sitting on the edge of Mirrah's house deck. She leans on the railing's post, watching the people of the town. The men fishing on the river sleep in the boats as they wait for the nets to fill. Children play on the shore, splashing in the water and try to catch fish with their hands.

Short docks are built in the river with more boats tied to posts. Several former slaves sit on the ends of the docks, enjoying the fresh air. Sitting together are Bern and Eka. Since Aya saved Bern's life, he'd been growing braver. When she first met him, he'd been more likely to run from a fight than help. Somehow, Aya changed him and he went on to save Eka's life. Now the two are near inseparable. They dip their feet into the river water and Aya sees a large smile on Eka's face.

The calmness of the town is intoxicating, but a constant shadow at the back of Aya's mind keeps her from truly enjoying it. The shadow of Klaeon.

"Are you feeling better?" Jaxon leans against the railing next to Aya.

"Yes. How about you?"

"Am I feeling better?"

Leaning back on her hands, Aya looks up at him. "Being home. Are you happy to be back?"

"I left this town for a reason. Coming back was never something I intended to do. But I also never intended to be part of a daring escape, either." Turning away from her, Jaxon nods his head at Aldur. The larger man lifts his knife in acknowledgement before returning to his carvings. Fleance's soft snoring fills the air.

"What Elder Mirrah said—" Aya starts.

"I'm sorry she spoke so harshly," Jaxon interrupts. "It's how she expresses concern."

Shaking her head, Aya climbs to her feet. She grabs the railing tightly in her hands. "I've been thinking about it. When you took me from my home, you said the same thing."

"I did? I don't remember that."

"Not verbatim. But you did enjoy telling me I was ignorant of anything outside my valley. You're right." Taking a deep breath, Aya stares across the river at the townsfolk going about their day. "Mirrah is right. I could only think of Klaeon in terms of the Arena. But a king doesn't rule one city. He rules lands, people."

"He claims to rule the land south of the Great Mountains, but only because none challenged him." Jaxon rubs his chin, scratching the scruff of his beard. "Though I doubt his ego will keep him south of the mountains for long. Men who have power only want more."

Aya believes him. She believes Klaeon desires more power. But she questions whether it is for himself... or for what lives inside of him. She heard it. When she and Jaxon saved Yme from Klaeon the night of the escape, she heard the second voice when Klaeon spoke to her.

We haven't tasted Life Healer in so long. The forbidden magic inside of Klaeon is alive. It explains how it seems to fill the air and force its way inside those close to him. She felt it many times. She knows it took Yme's fire magic from him and would've taken his life.

But what did it mean when it said tasted? Aya wonders, chills running up her arms.

"You should rest. Feasts in this town are large events that last all night," Jaxon says, breaking Aya from her dark thoughts. "And there's a fresh change of clothes for you inside."

The idea of shedding the Arena's rags is a tempting offer. She glances at the door to the hut. The anxiety is still there, the fear of being surrounded by walls again, but it isn't as strong. "Are you going to talk to Elder Mirrah?"

Confusion crosses Jaxon's expression. "Why?"

"Through the harshness, I could tell she worries about you."

"She's old. Worrying is part of her daily routine."

Aya stands, playing with the silk bracelet on her wrist. "There may be less time than you think to talk. You never know what tomorrow brings." She hopes he hears the hidden meaning in her words. The sharp pain in her heart reminds her, even though she trusts this man, he is still the reason the elder of her village, Mircien, is dead.

"Never know when a group of men will set fire to this place and kill her." Jaxon pauses, turning to her. "That's what you mean, right?"

Meeting his eyes, she allows the pain to cross her face. "You don't want to leave anything broken that can be easily fixed."

A small laugh escapes Jaxon's lips and he shrugs his shoulders. "Or risk breaking things further. You should head in. I had Mirrah set up a second blanket next to Yme for you."

Blood rushes to Aya's face. "What? Why?"

"So, you won't feel uncomfortable in a strange place. Sleeping next to someone you trust will help bring a deeper, more restful sleep. Trust me."

"Fine. But please consider talking to Mirrah."

Jaxon turns away, waving his hand in response. Aya heads into the hut, a momentary rush of panic filling her as she enters the darkness of the doorway. Once her vision adjusts, the panic subsides, and she's greeted by a large, spacious room.

Walls stop short of the roof, wooden beams crossing haphazardly between multiple rooms. One room is blocked by a sliding door while the rest are separated by hanging cloth. Aya walks farther in, stepping down a solitary step and onto a rug covering the wooden floor. Wooden furniture fills the room, small trinkets placed carefully throughout.

Sitting at a large table in the center of the room is Mirrah. Her mouth is set in a hard line and her eyes focus on the cup in her hands. Memories flood Aya. Memories of Mircien waiting for her with the same expression. It usually meant Aya was about to be yelled at.

"Are you okay?" Aya asks, forcing herself to approach the woman.

Mirrah raises her head and her expression lightens, though the anger only cools slightly. "I'm fine, my dear. I've set you and..."

"Yme. And my name is Aya."

"Yes, sorry. I guess we skipped formal introductions."

"We did. But it was a shocking surprise Jaxon brought us to his hometown."

Mirrah squeezes the cup in her hand and shakes her head slowly. "I'd accepted the fact I might never see my son again and yet, here he is. Walking in as though twenty years hadn't passed. As though he were only returning from a visit to the market."

Hesitating, Aya tries to think of something to say, but nothing comes to mind. She slowly sits across from Mirrah and crosses her arms on the table. "He's a good man."

"Good men can still do bad things. He learned that long ago."

"What do you mean?"

Taking a sip from her cup, Mirrah leans back in her chair. "Jaxon's father was a good man. He took care of us, took care of the town. But he had one fault. He was too trusting. When men from Bloodfall came to our town, he welcomed them with his usual kindness." She pauses, clearing her throat as emotion fills her with tension. "They repaid his kindness with a threat. Provide bodies to the Arena or the town would burn. He refused, but then the men threatened to take Jaxon."

Aya listens in silence, afraid to interrupt. She knows Jaxon will never tell her and any new information is tantalizing.

"Jaxon was too young to understand. All he saw was his father betraying his home. It wasn't long after this, Jaxon left. The men returned a few times, but eventually stopped. I assumed Jaxon had something to do with it. Eighteen years ago, I received a message from him. It was short and blunt. We didn't have to worry about anyone coming to our town again. I sent a message back. His father couldn't take the guilt after his only son left and threw himself into the river. I wasn't sure if he ever received it. Though I didn't expect an answer even if he did."

"You should talk to him," Aya suggests. "Explain why his father did what he did. I'm sure he's ready to listen now."

"I would like to believe that." Mirrah leans forward, placing her hand on Aya's. "Thank you for listening. I've set you and Yme in the next room. Feel free to sleep as long as you like. The feast won't begin until sundown."

"Thank you for your hospitality." Aya heads towards a room separated by a cloth door.

"Do you know the name of the river that passes through our town?" Mirrah asks suddenly. Aya pauses, shaking her head.

"Massel. It means flooding tears. The legends say all rivers and streams are the tears of the goddess Lachryses. But when her unbearable sorrow becomes too much, rivers flood and won't recede until a greater sorrow occurs." Mirrah laughs softly, but her eyes water. "It's been eighteen years since Massel last flooded."

6

Yme rolls over, rubbing the sleep from his eyes. He freezes when he senses movement, drowsiness immediately gone, and looks at the figure lying next to him.

Still asleep, Aya adjusts to Yme's movement and takes a deep breath. Carefully sitting up, Yme tries not to disturb her. But the beating of his heart quickens as he watches her still form. Even though little light is in the room, he can still make out her face. The corners of her lips are turned up slightly, giving her face a childlike expression of ease. Yme wonders if her lips are soft to the touch.

"Yme! Aya! Wake up!" Daniil's voice calls from outside, tearing Yme from his thoughts.

"You two are gonna sleep through the feast! What're you doing in there?" Kylii adds.

Roused by the commotion outside, Aya slowly sits up. She yawns and her tired eyes seem to focus. Yme's heart jumps when she sees him, smiles, and murmurs, "Morning."

"Evening, I think."

Aya looks out the window and laughs. "It feels nice to sleep and not be woken up by annoying, unbearable—"

"Yme! Aya!" Daniil and Kylii yell.

"What was that about annoying and unbearable?" Yme jumps to his feet and crosses to the window. He throws the cloth covering the window open and glares at the two men standing outside. "We heard you the first time. What do you want?"

Daniil crosses his arms. He and Kylii are both wearing new clothes. Tanith is lying next to Daniil. Her fur, now clean, appears several shades lighter.

The town is alive with movement; townsfolk gather across the river in front of a large hut with no walls. Cloth is rolled up where the walls should be and inside a fire pit dug into the earth burns bright. Yme can barely make out the long tables slowly filling with people.

The former slaves have washed off the dirt and blood of the Arena and put on new clothes, provided by caring villagers. They look more alive, like different people. The younger slaves, including Cal and Bon, play with the children on the river's edge.

"Everyone keeps asking where you two are," Daniil says, drawing Yme's attention back to him. "We told them you were probably planning what to do next."

"And here we find you two still in bed. Doing only the gods know what," Kylii says.

"Sleeping! That's all!" Aya yells from inside.

Kylii lowers his voice and winks at Yme. "Don't worry. We're all adults. You don't have to speak delicately."

The flush on Yme's face brings eruptions of laughter from the brothers. Aya rushes to the window, not so gently shoving Yme out of the way. "I heard that! We were just sleeping!"

The brothers' laughter increases.

"You two look nice. You both almost look normal," Aya says.

Tanith snorts.

"You look beautiful, Tanith."

Tanith's tail pats the ground appreciatively. Daniil leans his head to the side. "Unlike some people, we've already washed up and gotten dressed."

"I think we've earned the extra sleep."

A snicker escapes Kylii's lips. "If that's all you two were doing."

"Why did we bring these two with us, again?" Yme asks Aya.

"Because you love us," Daniil and Kylii say together.

"We'll see you two at the feast," Daniil says. "Remember everyone is waiting for you." The brothers lope away with Tanith following.

"I see you two are finally up," Mirrah says, carrying two small piles of clothes. She places one pile on a chair against the wall and hands the other to Aya. "These clothes are for you. They were donated by a young couple and they'd feel honored to have you wear them."

"And, because you are both no longer barbarians, here's water to clean yourselves up," Jaxon grunts, carrying two large buckets of water and washcloths. He puts them at either end of the room, spilling small droplets onto the floor. He smiles and places his hands on his hips. "If you need anything, just shout. We'll be outside... reminiscing." He meets Aya's eyes before leaving.

Laughing quietly, Mirrah turns to Aya. "If you need privacy, that curtain will split the room in two." She points to a large cloth tied against the wall. She winks at Aya and follows after Jaxon.

"Did I miss something?" Yme asks, confused at all the secretive looks. "You three seem to know something I don't."

Aya shakes her head. "It's nothing. Those two just needed a little push to talk."

"You're good at pushing."

"Only against stubborn walls."

Shutting the window, Yme crosses to the pile of clothes left for him. He lifts up the clothes and sighs. Aya moves to the bucket of water, grabbing the washcloth and dropping it into the cool water.

Reaching for his bucket of water, Yme turns and sees Aya undressing. He stares at her bare back, his heart pounding in his chest. She moves the wet cloth across her skin, over her noticeably darker arms and lighter back. Yme tears his gaze away, grabbing the bucket of water without turning around. He calms his breathing, removing his shirt to wash the dirt from his skin.

Why is my heart beating so fast? I've seen naked women before. Though he's never seen Aya that way. He and the brothers were always very respectful when Aya needed to use the waste hole in their cell. Is he feeling differently now they're free?

Yme finishes washing the dirt and blood from his body and quickly dresses. He puts on the brown shirt with matching black trousers and boots, surprised at how relatively well the clothes fit. Unsure of how far along Aya is in getting dressed, Yme walks to the window and peeks outside. He watches villagers carrying large plates of meat and vegetables towards the large hut. Yme's stomach grumbles at the thought of food as he closes the cloth covering the window.

"Are you ready?" Aya asks.

Yme turns to her, his heart leaping into his throat. Aya wears a green dress, which brings out her emerald eyes. *Why don't I remember her eyes being that green?* Her hair is braided over one shoulder, her silk bracelet used as a hair tie. She awkwardly adjusts the dress.

"I guess I should've told them I'm more comfortable in trousers," Aya mumbles. She glances at Yme and gazes up and down his new clothes. "Well, look at you. There *is* a man under all that dirt."

Yme manages to keep the blood from rushing to his cheeks and motions to the door. "We should go. Before Daniil and Kylii hunt us down."

7

The large hut is filled with the delicious aromas of cooked food. The cloth walls have been lowered to provide some privacy, and the fire at the center provides enough light to fill the entire hut. Long tables are arranged to seat the entire group from the Arena as well as those brave enough to speak with the new guests.

Townsfolk at one end of the hut play music, while others dance gaily in front of them. Those not attending the feast peek into the hut as they head home for the night, curious to see the guests, but not eager to join in the festivities.

The fear of death seems a long-forgotten memory and many of the escapees are more outspoken. Laughter fills the large room. They talk openly with the locals, thanking them over and over for their kindness and hospitality.

One table is set slightly separate from the others along the wall of the hut closest to the back. Mirrah sits at the center with Jaxon, Aya, Yme, Daniil, and Kylii. Tanith is lying on the ground between Daniil and Kylii, staying relatively out of sight so she doesn't frighten the townsfolk.

A tense silence has fallen over the table after Yme and Aya described the fight and escape from Klaeon. The revelation of Klaeon's Blood Magic is a surprise to all.

"He sucks the magic right out of you. That doesn't seem fair." Kylii breaks the silence, leaning forward to see Yme.

"And then he can use your magic against you?" Daniil asks.

Shaking his head, Yme stares at his hand. "He uses something like it. But it wasn't my fire. It was filled with another magic."

"So, Blood King is more than a name. Very little is known about forbidden magics and any living who would know are less likely to speak on them."

"What makes a magic forbidden and not a rare kind?" Daniil asks.

"It's magic that shouldn't exist. That's really all anyone knows," Jaxon explains.

Mirrah shrugs her shoulders. "Perhaps you can find someone who knows more to help you."

"I'm only interested in getting my fire magic back."

"But what are your plans for them?" Mirrah nods her head at the group filling the hut.

Yme stares at the Elder, confusion furrowing his brow. "Why should there be any plans? The plan was to escape the Arena. We did that. Everyone is free now to do whatever they wish."

"Do you really think these men and women only wanted to be free?" Jaxon asks, taking a drink from his cup.

"Why else would they risk their lives to escape?"

Swallowing, Jaxon leans forward and whistles to the closest table. Sitting at it are Mava, Rava, Bern, and Eka. "What do you all want to do now that you're no longer slaves?"

The four eye each other before Bern slowly stands. "We

want to protect Aya. We'll give our lives to make sure she remains safe."

Aya's shoulders tense and Yme hears her breath catch in her throat. *Not exactly words a Healer wants to hear.*

"And, with the Blood King still alive, how long do you think they'll last?" Jaxon asks, facing Aya.

"Do you really think he'll come after us?" she asks.

"You escaped his Arena with his top fighter, a large number of slaves, and even some of his loyal workers." Jaxon points to Dolus Otho sitting at a table with the former workers. His expression since arriving to the town has remained sour. "Not many kings would allow such insults to go unpunished."

"What are you suggesting, then?" Yme asks.

"He can't be left to do as he pleases."

"You want us to kill him?"

"You *do* want to stop him, right? You understand that probably means killing him?" Jaxon asks.

"He has an army. We have a handful of mages and fighters."

"Us against an army? That's insane," Kylii adds. "Can't we just go somewhere he won't find us?"

"And where would that be?" Mirrah asks.

Kylii shakes his head, raising his hands defensively. "I don't know!"

"There are plenty of lands to the north we can go," Daniil chimes in. He awkwardly smiles at Yme. "Doesn't help with your fire, though. Do you really want it back that badly?"

Jaxon slams his hands on the table, standing so forcefully his chair falls to the floor behind him. The large hut grows silent as everyone is caught off guard by the sudden noise. "There is nowhere any of you can go where the Blood King won't find you! Why bother escaping Bloodfall Arena if all you choose to do with your freedom is run and hide? Where's the fire you showed in your fight against the Brüdel? Where's the defiance you so proudly wore on the Arena floor?"

The hut has gone silent. Every eye is on their table and the music has stopped. Jaxon searches the faces of the freed slaves, his anger growing at the confused and even fearful expressions greeting him.

"Some of you still don't understand. What do you think the Blood King has been doing while you all were in the Arena? When he wasn't watching you fight, do you believe he went back to his home and sat around? He's been building, he's been gathering, and he's been gaining power. All lands south of the Great Mountains are now his."

"What do you mean *all* lands?" Mava asks, slowly rising from her seat.

"Exactly what I said. All lands. Lands that were free of his influence have been invaded. Included Minn Fields, Vastry Plains, and Foula Valley."

Aya's face blanches and she grabs Yme's arm, though he isn't sure she even realizes she has. He sees her eyes darting back and forth as her thoughts race.

"Liar!" Rava roars, lunging for Jaxon. Mava grabs her sister around the waist, holding her back. "You're LYING!"

"I'm not lying. Dolus, am I lying?"

Dolus Otho's lips quiver as the entire hut turns to him. He glances at the surrounding workers, but they keep their eyes on the floor or their plates of food. "After the tournament, after Aya and Yme's defeat of the volacerta, there were rumblings of a major land grab farther south. Vastry was easily taken, not many live there. Foula resisted at first, but soon fell. Minn Fields gave the largest resistance, but as of the King's return to the Arena, they too were finally subdued."

"Why the sudden interest in those lands now?" Yme asks.

"Men who have power only want more," Aya says weakly.

"Do you all understand now? You can't return to your homes. They aren't yours anymore. Even if you did go back, how long do you think peace would last? How long do you think your villages or towns, or families would protect you? How long before the Blood King's army marches through looking for new soldiers? There are only two choices. Ignore the problem or solve it. But you're all free. I can't make that choice for you. Yme can't make that choice for you. Aya can't make that choice for you. You must all make that choice for yourself." Jaxon storms out of the hut.

Mirrah rises from her seat, watching Jaxon leave. "I wish for all of you to excuse him. This celebration wasn't meant for talks of such dark things. Please eat, dance, and forget about such heavy things tonight. This is a celebration of new life. Let the music play!"

The musicians resume playing, softly at first, but then with great fervor. Conversation slowly follows. But the room retains an enhanced air of gravity.

Yme leans close to Aya. "Was he dramatic like that when he brought you to the Arena?"

Aya stands suddenly, her chair falling to the ground behind her. "I need some air." Before anyone can say anything to her, she leaves the table and exits the hut.

8

"Aya!" Yme's voice calls from behind. "Aya! Wait!"

Aya quickens her pace, hoping to get away or for Yme to give up following her. She doesn't know where she is going. She remembers very little of how the town is laid out, but she knows she has to keep walking. She follows the river towards the mountain, remembering the waterfall they saw when they approached the canyon. She doesn't know why she wants to go there, but she won't stop until she reaches it.

She follows the river out of town, venturing into the surrounding forest. The sound of Yme's struggles to move through the dense vegetation reaches her ears. Soon the roar of a waterfall fills the night air. Aya moves faster, the wind bringing tears to her eyes.

Or am I crying?

Pushing through a dense line of bushes, Aya enters a large clearing. Beautiful, green plants surround the pool, and a mist rises where the waterfall hits the pool. The moon, high in the night sky, reflects from the pool.

Gasping for air, Aya stares around the clearing. Leaves

fallen from the trees float gently on top of the water, following the current towards the town. Large boulders sit on the edge of the water and Aya sees carvings in some of the stones and tree trunks. She walks towards a tree and touches the carvings with her fingertips. There are names, declarations of love, and drawings, covering the entirety of the tree.

How many generations had come to this place? How many major life moments were experienced or occurred in this clearing? How many more will there be?

How many of these moments had been stolen by Klaeon? How many homes were destroyed?

I told him where I was from. Aya's thoughts flash back to the first time she spoke with Klaeon. He asked her where she was from. *Why did I answer? Why didn't I lie?*

"Gods! You're fast when you want to be!" A gasping voice yells behind Aya.

Aya knows the voice is Yme but runs for the waterfall. She doesn't want to talk. She wants to be alone.

"Hey!"

Aya climbs a large boulder next to the waterfall, the mist of the water covering her. She turns and stares down at Yme. He stops before climbing up the boulder, confusion filling his face. His cheeks are flushed, and his chest lowers and rises quickly. The mist covers him, and water gathers in his hair.

"You should have stayed at the celebration. I want to be alone," Aya yells. She blinks the gathering water from her eyes, unsure if it is from the mist or her own tears.

Yme takes a step back from the boulder. His eyes reflect the moonlight, glowing silver. "Why did you leave so quickly? Was it something Jaxon said?"

A lump grows in Aya's throat. "I want to be alone." She turns away from him and sits down on the boulder, pulling her knees to her chest.

The sound of the waterfall covers any footsteps Yme makes, but Aya hopes he understands her request. She stares into the water, watching the ripples from the waterfall. A pebble flies into the water, creating more ripples fighting the larger ripples. Another pebble skips across the water before flying into the air and up the waterfall.

Slowly turning her head, Aya spies Yme sitting on the edge of the water. He uses his earth magic to raise another pebble. He shoots it out across the water and his fingers move with each skip. Aya watches the delicate movements Yme makes. The motions are calmer than any he did while in the Arena. Every few moves, he raises his other hand and lifts the gathering water from his hair, throwing it into the pool.

They sit in silence, Yme throwing pebbles across the pool and Aya watching. Aya's vision blurs and the lump in her throat grows unbearable. Turning her head away, Aya is thankful for the noise of the waterfall. Everything Jaxon said at the celebration. So much information thrown at them and without the fear of fighting for their lives... it hits Aya all at once.

"Where you're from," Yme asks suddenly, "are you familiar with the story of how the moon's reflection came to be?"

Aya is silent. She knows of the gods from Mircien and Iria. But her mind is too rattled to remember a tale about the moon's reflection.

"A priestess of Nuray, Goddess of the Moon, was thrown into a lake by followers of Poya, Goddess of Night. As she sank to the bottom of the lake, the priestess prayed to see her goddess one last time. Nuray, hearing her priestess's prayer, sent her daughter Aynur to the lake. Being the Goddess of Moon Light, Aynur could only pierce the darkness of the lake so far. To help her daughter, Nuray reflected the moon upon the water, allowing Aynur's moon light to reach the priestess, granting her final wish before she died."

Staring at Yme, Aya moves closer to the edge of the boulder. "And those who threw her into the lake? What became of them?"

Yme glances up at her. "Poya was punished for her followers' rashness. Though Nuray allowed the moon to be vacant from the night sky once every cycle, her anger at the murder of her priestess formed into not only the moon's reflection, but also the moonglow flower. A flower that blooms only when the moon is not in the sky. Legends say the flower shines as brightly as moon light and is an annoyance to Poya who prefers complete darkness."

Aya looks out into the pool. The reflection of the moon is distorted by the ripples from the waterfall. *Many of these stories don't end happily. Are the gods only ever cruel? Even when they honor final prayers, is there still vengeance within them?*

Yme climbs up the boulder and sits next to Aya. "I've never seen a flower that shines as brightly as the moon. But there are some who, though they too have never seen such a flower, still believe in it. Maybe it's blind faith or maybe deep down they know the flower is only part of a story." He looks Aya in the eye. "But right now, you and I are the moonglow flower for a lot of people. We're something they can believe in. Even if we are nothing more than stories in their minds, they've placed their faith in us."

"But does that mean possibly starting a war? Do we have no choice where our paths lead us now?" Aya asks.

Yme's silver eyes lowers and he turns to face the pool. "Do you trust Jaxon? He's the slave trader who brought you to the Arena."

The lump threatens to return to Aya's throat, but she forces it back. "We can trust him."

"You've said we could trust him before. I'm asking if *you* trust him."

Hesitating, Aya thinks carefully. She plays with the silk bracelet holding her braided hair together. All the times Jaxon was cruel, all the times he showed kindness fly through her thoughts. She knows the answer. She knew long before Yme asked her.

"I trust him completely."

"Then you know where our paths are heading," Yme says. "We're going to stop Klaeon."

9

"Aya! Yme! There you are!" Daniil's voice calls from the doorway of the large hut. Loud voices, coming from inside, signal the end of the feast and celebration.

"Where have you two been? Everyone's bugging us about the plan. What's the plan? Do you know the plan? What's Aya's plan? What's Yme's plan? Do they both agree on plans? Could you please tell them we don't have a plan!" Kylii yells angrily.

Aya and Yme look at each other. Yme nods his head at her, mouthing the words *moonglow flower*.

They walk past the brothers into the hut. The brothers follow and everyone inside the hut falls silent, turning to Aya. Taking a deep breath, Aya clenches her hands into fists to steel her courage. "I'm going to stop Klaeon."

The freed slaves and former Arena workers shout at each other. Some are for the plan while others voice their disagreement. The villagers move away from the arguments to avoid being caught in the middle.

Jaxon appears at the opposite doorway and leans on a thick beam. He watches Aya carefully.

"Jaxon is right!" Aya shouts over all the voices. The arguing stops and eyes return to Aya. "Jaxon is right. Even though we've escaped the Arena, Klaeon will still come after us, our homes, those we love. There's only one thing to do. Stop him."

The group hesitates. Anxious eyes look at each other and fear grows in others. Aya doesn't know what else to say. She only knows this is the correct path. Walking across the hut, she stops in front of Jaxon. "Do you have any ideas on how we can stop him?"

He smiles and pushes off the beam. "We gather an army."

"And where do we find this army?" Yme asks.

"When the Blood King claimed the lands south of the Great Mountains, the countries to the north were nervous he would venture into their territories. When he stopped his expansion and settled in the west, those same countries forgot about the threat." Jaxon holds up a single finger. "Except for one."

"Of the countries North of the Great Mountains there is one that may be willing to aid you," Mirrah speaks from her seat. "It's a city carved into the cliff walls of a canyon that spans the continent. The people of this city are powerful and know the way of war and magic. They've driven back many who would conquer the north."

"We start there," Jaxon says.

"Do you know the way?" Daniil asks.

Nodding, Jaxon walks to the table and clears a spot. Mirrah hands him a scroll from her cloak. Aya, Yme, and the brothers gather around the table.

Jaxon unrolls the scroll, revealing a crudely drawn map. "The fastest way is through the caves of these mountains to the Forest of Spirits. The canyon lies on the other side." As he speaks, he traces the route on the map with his finger. "There's an entrance to the caves located near here. No one knows of it besides Elder Mirrah and me. Even if the Blood King's men manage to find their way here, we'll block the entrance and make it impossible for them to follow us."

"Are these caves safe?" Kylii asks. "Some of your local friends said creatures live deep in these mountains."

"They said they used to be men but turned their backs on the sun for the protection of caves where they wait for any to enter so they can feed on their flesh," Daniil adds.

Jaxon waves his hand dismissively at the brothers. "I've never seen anything larger than a bat in those caves. We should be fine with the number of magic users we have. The creatures in the cave may be dangerous but using fire we can keep them away."

Aya places a hand on the map, following the crude hand drawn lines. "Will this city want to help us?"

"They will if we tell them the Blood King plans to invade the north."

"You want us to lie?" Yme asks.

Jaxon shakes his head. "It's not a lie. Not a complete lie. The Blood King may not be invading soon, but it's the ultimate next step for him. Why else would he conquer the rest of the lands in the south? We're simply being pre-emptive in gathering the north to defend itself."

"How soon should we leave?" Aya asks.

"Ideally, tomorrow. But we'll need supplies and that will take a day to gather."

"Then we leave in two days." She faces those who escaped Bloodfall Arena with her. "I'm going to the cliff city. Klaeon has taken too much from me to let him continue thinking there's no one willing to stand up to him. If it takes going to countries who think they're safe from his reach and proving to them they're wrong... then that is what we are going to do. Those who wish to join us may, but no one will be forced to come. If this is the end of your journey with us, I wish you the gods care to make it wherever you wish to go."

Mumbles fill the hut. Several eagerly agree to follow Aya while others wear expressions of fear. Dolus Otho and the workers around him argue about their choices, the former Voice of the Arena apparently losing.

Aya taps the map and stares into Jaxon's blue eyes. "Your map better be right."

Smiling, Jaxon responds, "We'll find out together."

10

Present Day

Aya yawns, stretching her arms over her head. She's unsure how many minutes have passed, but the morning sun still can't breach the darkness of the cave behind. The longer they wait outside of the depths, the more tense the air feels.

Rustling in the forest brings everyone to attention. Aya holds her breath, eager and nervous to see how many will be arriving to join them on their journey to the cliff city.

Elder Mirrah appears, followed by many of the freed slaves and former arena workers. Including Dolus Otho, the former Voice of the Arena. They each carry additional packs of supplies and small weapons.

Mirrah smiles at those waiting, her eyes pausing on Jaxon. "I apologize for being late. The townsfolk wished to provide more supplies and those who have chosen to stay behind needed comforting."

Those who came with the Elder hand out the extra bags to

those waiting. The rest of the group gathers the remainder of the supplies and torches are pulled from one bag. Those who had been waiting happily welcome those who've decided to journey with them, bringing the number of the group to almost fifty.

Mirrah walks up to Aya, Jaxon, and Yme. "There is more food and a little medicine." She turns to Aya. "Use your magic wisely, Life Healer. Losing your strength in these caves can be dangerous."

"Thank you," Aya says, stepping forward and hugging her.

"Please, watch over Jaxon," Mirrah whispers in her ear. Aya nods her head and pulls away. Mirrah turns to Yme. "May the gods watch over your travels and bring you all good fortune. We will pray for you and protect your path as long as we are able."

"Thank you," Yme says.

"We should go before the day runs long," Jaxon states. He hesitates before hugging Mirrah, the woman's eyes widening as his arms squeeze her tightly. Jaxon whispers something to Mirrah and sadness fills the Elder's expression.

Pulling away, Jaxon walks to the front of the group and grabs a torch. He lights it with flint and walks into the cave. Aldur and Fleance follow quickly while the rest of the group waits for Aya and Yme.

Aya looks at Yme. He nods to her. Her eyes move to Daniil and Kylii, Tanith sitting next to them. They smile and she looks around at the rest of the group. Drawing a deep breath, she takes in the forest one last time. The similarity to the forest that surrounded her home village is unmistakable.

This time I'm choosing to leave, Aya thinks, staring into the overwhelming darkness of the cave. She walks towards it, her steps slowing as she crosses the threshold into the cool, moist darkness. She hears the sound of the others following her inside and Yme finds his way to her side.

The rising sun provides a little light for a few hundred yards before the torches are lit. Several who know a little fire magic assist in lighting the torches. They use Jaxon's already lit torch, since none other than Kylii know how to create fire without a source. Once the torches are lit, earth mages close the entrance of the cave, cutting off the last of the sunlight.

Jaxon leads the group, carrying the map, and followed by Aya, Yme, Daniil, Kylii, and Tanith. Aldur and Fleance have slowed and now bring up the rear, guarding from any attacks from behind. Those who carry torches circle those without, the group naturally moving close together. Fear of allowing too much space and wanting to prevent anyone from accidentally wandering off keeps those with torches close.

Aya glances behind, spotting Bern, Mava, and Rava carrying torches. They hold their weapons in their other hand, searching the darkness for signs of any movement.

The caves are quiet, the only sounds being distant echoes of water dripping and wind blowing through the caverns. It's larger than she expected. In her mind she imagined crawling through small openings or only being able to walk in a single file line. But the group is able to spread out pretty well even with the torches.

Insects scurry from the flames of the torches into any available shadow. Strange insects with long limbs hanging from the ceiling disappear into small holes burrowed into the stone.

Small, flying creatures crowd larger holes in the walls. They shriek at the disturbance caused by the group. One flies through the group, causing a small panic as it becomes entangled in a woman's hair, but Aldur cuts it free.

"Thank you," she says, but she can't hide the sadness in her voice that her hair had to be cut.

"Are you sure you know your way through these caves?" Kylii asks Jaxon as they turn into a narrow passageway.

"I used to sneak into these caves when I was a child. Never been this deep, though. The stories kept me from venturing too far from the entrance," Jaxon answers.

"What stories?" Aya asks.

A sly smile grows on Jaxon's lips. "The stories that tell of things that lurk in the dark. These caves are older than mankind, born from the very creation of this land. There are so many passages that it would require many lifetimes to explore them all. The creatures that call these catacombs home have existed long before mankind came into being. Most are insects or bats."

"Bats?"

"Those small, flying creatures we passed earlier. But the stories tell of strange, twisted creatures that never go into the light. Their eyes are said to have never grown and they rely on other senses to find food. Their skin is so pale you can see their insides. Their mouths are filled with razor sharp teeth and some say their hands and feet are great suction cups that allow them to climb the wall like insects. Once they grab hold of flesh, they never let go. Even when they are killed."

Jaxon's words echo through the darkness among the group. Several members make small whimpers of fear and move closer together. "We're well protected if we remain close together and in the light. The fires will keep them away. They're afraid of the heat. Stay away from the dark."

Daniil shares a look with Kylii. "Those are nice ghost stories. But you didn't answer Kylii's question. Do you know your way through these caves?"

Pulling out a small journal, Jaxon lowers his voice so only those close hear him. "There've been many who attempted to navigate their way through these caves. Of all who passed through our town, only one group returned." He opens the journal and shows the pages of handwritten notes. "They took great care in writing down details of their ventures through these walls."

Yme moves next to Jaxon. "And we're following their path?"

"One of the many they wrote down, yes. Elder Mirrah and I have read through this journal many times during the past two days and found the quickest route. If the directions are correct, it should take us no more than two days to reach the exit."

"How long did it take the ones who made this map to find the correct path?"

"They went into the caves when I was a small boy. Elder Mirrah told me they only emerged a few years ago. They were a much smaller group when they finally returned to the light."

"How much smaller?" Aya asks.

Putting the journal into his pack, Jaxon says, "When they entered the cave, they were a group of twelve. Only two came back."

The group continues the next few hours in silence following Jaxon as he leads them deeper into the caves. The passage narrows even more the farther they go, until they can only stand two across. The ceiling lowers until the group is forced to crouch for a good distance. When the passage opens up again, the group squeezes closer together back into a mob. Torches burn out and the circle of light shrinks. Members of the group who are at the center refuel the torches and hand them back relit.

Half a day of traveling brings them to a large open cavern. Numerous openings in the walls lead off in different directions. The wind creates strange sounds as it moves through the cavern.

"We'll rest here for two hours," Jaxon tells the group.

The torches are placed in a circle on the ground and a few are placed at the center. Food and water are handed out and most try to speak of light topics to pass the time in the dark.

Aldur and Fleance stand outside of the flames, one on each side of the group. They keep their hands on their weapons as their eyes search the darkness. Aya wonders if it's a left-over habit from their time in the Black Caravan. Or if Jaxon ordered them to be so vigilant.

Mava and Rava move close to Fleance. They offer him food and the young man's face is hard to read in the dark, but Aya could almost believe she sees a slight blush to his cheeks. He shakes his head, but Mava insists, holding the offered food closer. Fleance eventually takes the food and eats it.

Sitting on a rock separate from the group and outside the circle of light, Jaxon keeps his torch next to him, sticking it between two rocks to keep it upright. He pulls out the journal and studies it and the map in silence.

Aya wonders why he doesn't try talking with the others. He never seems to have trouble talking with her.

"How long do you think it'll be before we see any monsters?" Kylii asks no one in particular.

"Tanith hasn't sensed anything near us besides insects for a while. Maybe they *were* just stories," Daniil says, eyeing his brother. "Back home they told stories about monsters in the dark to keep children from wandering into caves and becoming lost."

"Getting lost is the greater danger in these caves," Yme says.

"Jaxon knows the way," Aya says. "If we stay with him and not let anyone lag behind, we'll be fine."

Kylii snorts. "If that map really does show the correct way out."

"The ones who made it managed to escape."

Scanning the rock walls around them, Yme shrugs his shoulders. "It took them years to make that map. Between then and now any number of things could have changed. There could've been rockslides, earthquakes, other people, or anything like that." Lifting a small rock with his earth magic,

Yme throws it into one of the many passages. "Caves are perfect places for earth mages to practice."

Aya spies Dolus sitting alone and walks over to him. "I'm glad you decided to come with us."

Jumping at her voice, Dolus grimaces. "I wasn't welcome to stay at that town."

"I don't think that's true."

"You shouldn't always believe what you see with your eyes. You are beloved by these people. My family is known for obeying the Blood King without question. I oversaw many deaths and encouraged slave traders to bring as many new fighters as they could find." He stares nervously at the former slaves. "As with any who find themselves in positions of power, the ones around the powerful will hide their true nature to appease whoever they need to appease."

"Are you saying those around me are all pretending to be someone else?"

"I'm saying... when you aren't around, I see the sides of those you trust that you will never see."

They rest for another hour, some preparing small meals while others try to catch extra sleep. Conversations remain whispers for fear of attracting the attention of whatever may lurk in the darkness of the cave.

Jaxon rejoins the group, holding his torch so it lights his face. "It's time to move."

Everyone gathers their belongings and Jaxon leads them into a large passageway. Rock formations from the ceiling and floor remind Aya of teeth. She hears others whisper about a similar feeling behind her.

The dampness of the cave makes the stone glisten in the torchlight. Dripping water echoes against the walls and the sound of falling rocks sends shivers through the spines of many. Several times the sound of rocks falling sounds similar to footsteps and fear shoots through the group. Jaxon assures them the noises are normal and nothing to be afraid of.

Hours pass in silence. A domed cavern opens in front of them. Jaxon stops the group as he walks to the center, moving his torch in front of him. There are small holes in the ground, barely wide enough for a child to fit into, leading deeper into the earth. Insects run from the torchlight, scurrying into the holes or beneath rocks.

"We've reached our first checkpoint," Jaxon announces. "We'll sleep here for the night. Tomorrow will be a long day in the dark. There'll be fewer rests so we can make it through quickly."

The group disperses, laying out blankets for comfort and building fires for cooking. Their shadows dance on the wall and soon the cavern is filled with jovial voices.

Aya sits next to Mava and Rava, enjoying a warm soup with the sisters. Fleance stands close-by, keeping watch, but his glances seem to fall on Mava more than once.

As members of the group fall asleep, Aya and the sisters stare into the fire, finding comfort in the dancing flames. Beside Aya, Mava softly hums. Rava, hearing her sister, soon begins singing.

Aya recognizes the song. She heard it her first night in the Arena. Daniil and Kylii told her the song was for the Fresh Flesh as a comfort before their first fight, but they didn't understand the language.

"What is that song?" Aya asks.

Mava shrugs her shoulders. "It's a lullaby."

"A lullaby in a different language?"

"There are three versions. One for children, one for adults, and the true lullaby." Mava scoots closer to Aya. "Have you never heard it?"

"I've heard the melody, but the words were different."

"We sing the one for children. It's simpler, but soothing. The lullaby for adults is calming but requires deep thought."

"And the true lullaby?" Aya asks.

"The true lullaby has magic in the words. It can put anyone and anything to sleep. But nobody remembers it." Mava places her hand on her heart. "When I heard the lullaby in the Arena, I felt safe. If only for a moment, I could close my eyes and pretend I was back home."

"But what is the language of the lullaby?"

Mava smiles. "It's not any language. It's complete gibberish."

"I feel like I'm going crazy! I swear that rock is the same one we passed an hour ago," Kylii whines.

Aya stares at the rock in question and shakes her head. "How can you possibly remember what rock we passed an hour ago?"

"Because I'm looking at it again right now."

The group has been walking for many hours. Waking up in the cave caused many to think they were still in the Arena. It took a few minutes to calm the group and prepare for the day's travels. Aya had trouble sleeping, even with others lying close-by.

"I think you're seeing double, Kylii," Daniil says, walking a few steps behind his brother. Tanith keeps a steady pace beside him.

A sour look crosses Kylii's face. "Don't need any input from you. Unless you agree with me."

"Are you and Daniil okay?" Aya asks, lowering her voice.

Kylii's golden eyes flash with anger, but he forces a smile on his lips. "We're fine. Just having a little *spat*." He spits the word and stomps ahead.

"What did you say to him?" Daniil asks, catching up to Aya.

"I asked if you two were okay."

"We had a little fight back at that town. But we'll be fine."

"What did you fight about?"

"The usual stuff. I treat him like a child, his temper will get him in trouble... he's jealous of Tanith," Daniil says.

"Jealous? How is he jealous?" Aya asks.

"Talking about me like I can't hear you two. We're in a cave, sound echoes." Kylii glares back at Aya and Daniil.

"Better than ignoring the problem," Daniil snaps back.

"I'm not the one ignoring the problem. You don't listen!" Kylii's voice rises with his emotions. The air warms, the flames on the torches growing larger.

Yme grabs Kylii's arm. "Calm down. If you lose control in here, we're all going to burn."

"What's going on? Do we need to stop?" Jaxon asks, appearing behind Yme.

The group stops and attention snaps to the disturbance. Aya sees worry in many of the faces around her. Adding that to the tension caused by the caves is likely doing more harm than good.

"No, we can keep going. We've got it under control." Aya locks eyes with Kylii. "Right?"

The air cools and Kylii pulls his arm free from Yme. "Yeah. It's under control."

Jaxon returns to the front of the group. Kylii glares at his brother before rushing to the front with him. Daniil and Tanith keep their distance.

"Somehow, I feel like you caused that little upset." Yme turns to Aya. "I told you to leave them alone."

"But what if you're wrong? What if this is more than a sibling spat?"

"Then we'll deal with it when we aren't buried deep beneath a mountain. Okay?"

"Fine."

The group continues forward, the ground angling downwards. It's cooler as they go deeper into the earth. Aya tastes moisture in the air and hears dripping water. A cool wind gently moves through the group, bringing chills with it. The deeper they go, the more rampant the rock formations grow.

Aya overhears Bern explaining the formations to Eka. "The ones on the roof are called stalactites. The ones on the floor are stalagmites."

"How do you know that?" Eka asks.

"I read about them in a book. Never thought I'd see them, though."

The sound of rocks falling in the distance stops Jaxon. He raises his hand and the group freezes. Aya watches Jaxon's blue eyes search the darkness. She strains her ears to listen to the strange sound. The rocks settle and a new silence fills the cave. The dripping of water has stopped, and no wind blows through the caverns, something Aya only notices now.

Jaxon remains still a moment longer, sending a wave of unease through the group. Fleance and Aldur ready to draw their weapons, keeping their attention on Jaxon's still frame.

Jaxon signals the group forward, but motions for them to remain quiet.

They enter a smaller cavern with pools of water on either side of their path. The pools reflect the light from the torches, but in the darkness it's impossible to tell how deep they are. Those with torches, and curiosity, wave the light over the water. The brief light shows the water is perfectly clear. They can see straight to the bottom, but they're still unable to tell how deep the pools are. Water drops fall from the stalactites on the ceiling, creating ripples in the water.

Aya stares into the water and sees fish. Strange fish, but fish. Their bodies are nearly see-through, and they have no eyes. There's a surprisingly large number of them, but they don't seem bothered by the group's presence.

Another sound of rocks falling stops Jaxon. It sounds much closer than before. He moves his torch in front of him, trying to find the cause. More rocks shift around the group and they search the cavern for the cause.

Aya stares at Jaxon, her heart pounding loudly. She sees the confusion and fear in his eyes, causing her breaths to quicken. Movement in front of Jaxon draws her gaze. It lasts for only a second, but she swears she saw something reflect the light of Jaxon's torch.

Something large and alive.

13

A shaky breath escapes Jaxon's lips and he presses on. His thoughts race. He fights the urge to slip back into the familiar cold façade of caravan leader, but he knows he shouldn't let his nerves show. The group behind him is placing a lot of trust in him to get them through.

But he saw it. He saw the pale body scurrying from the torchlight.

A memory crosses his mind. A memory from when he was a child. He'd ventured to the cave entrance in the middle of the night. He wanted to see the bats flying. But when he reached the cave, he saw something else. An animal carcass was in front of the entrance. Curious, Jaxon approached it and saw the claw marks, deep cuts in the flesh. He looked at the cave and saw shadows moving inside. He heard the inhuman shrieks and ran home. The next morning, the carcass was gone, but a trail of blood led into the darkness of the cave.

He never saw what killed the animal, but the older villagers whispered stories of creatures venturing out to kill animals and small children.

Was coming here a mistake?

The group follows cautiously, moving carefully along the path. Aya slips on a wet patch of stone, but Yme catches her before she falls into the water. As she opens her mouth to thank him, a scream from the back of the group startles everyone.

"Something grabbed me! Something grabbed my leg!" a woman's voice shrieks.

"Jayda, calm down!"

Eyes turn to the woman who had her hair cut by Aldur. One of the men tries to calm her down, but she only grows more hysterical. Others try to hush the frantic woman, but her screams only escalate. Jaxon signals to Aldur and the large man grabs the woman and drags her forward.

Jayda struggles against Aldur's hold as he moves her towards Jaxon, Yme, and Aya. Jaxon sees a dark spot growing on Jayda's skirt and quickly grabs the cloth, lifting it up. He moves his torch close to see her leg. Yme and Aya lean close to see a dark spot on the frightened woman's leg.

"What is that?" Kylii asks, spying over Jaxon's shoulder.

The light of Jaxon's torch reflects something wet on Jayda's leg. Jaxon reaches out and touches the liquid. Jayda winces and releases a small whine of pain. The group's voices rise as uneasiness rushes through them. Jaxon brings the liquid closer to the torchlight and his expression darkens.

Blood.

"Everyone be quiet!" he orders, allowing his caravan voice to fill the words with such force he knows all will hear it.

The group falls silent and their voices fade in the cavern, but another sound rises from the darkness. The group huddles closer together as the strange sounds seem to surround them.

"Jaxon?" Aya asks, searching the darkness.

Jaxon hears the unasked question in her voice. "Aldur! Fleance!"

The two men move to opposite ends of the group quickly, grabbing torches from nearby members of the group. Splashes in the water cause some in the group to scream, startled. Those still holding torches wave the light in front of them, trying to make the circle of light wider.

Jaxon grabs Aya and pulls her down to Jayda's leg. "She needs your magic."

Aya's eyes widen as she looks at Jayda's leg. Jaxon stares at the strange mark on the crying woman's flesh. A misshapen handprint is carved into Jayda's skin. It looks as though the skin was ripped away as whatever had hold of her leg lost its grip. The blood dripping to the ground has a milky substance mixed in.

Turning to Aya, Jaxon sees her mind racing. *She's trying to understand what did this.* He leans close to her. "Aya, you have to hurry."

His voice snaps Aya into action. She places a hand on Jayda's leg and quickly heals the wound.

Jaxon's attention is caught by movement in his peripheral vision. Dark shadows appear outside the circle of light, small flashes of light hit wet flesh. Strange shapes in the pools surrounding the group rise and a new sound is heard. A soft clicking followed by a wet suction sound.

"Is she healed?" Jaxon whispers in Aya's ear.

Nodding, Aya helps Jayda to her feet. Jaxon stands and signals to Aldur and Fleance. The two pull small jugs from their bags and take large sips of the contents.

"Those who can control fire! Get ready!" Jaxon yells.

Confused eyes meet him, but the few who can manipulate fire raise their hands. Aldur and Fleance raise their torches in front of them and spray the liquids from their mouths. The torch flames mix with the liquids creating large fireballs that fill the cave with sudden bright light. Screams fill the caverns as the group sees what is crawling in the darkness.

Hundreds of creatures fill the cavern, surrounding the group. They crawl across the walls, appear from the pools, or stand on the small stretches of stone. They're each no larger than an infant, but that doesn't matter with the sheer numbers. Their long bodies are pale, dark organs visible beneath the thin flesh. Tails move across the surfaces around the creatures, searching for anything to grab. Occasionally one grabs a fish, and the small animal is devoured instantly. Limbs are long, ending on webbed fingers and toes. Milky substances are left behind anywhere the creatures place their hands.

The heads are triangular, but where there should be eyes there are only rows of slits that open and close, creating the wet suction sounds. Below the slits, a line cuts across the entire length of the head. When it opens, rows of teeth are revealed as the mouth takes up most of the head.

Screams erupt through the group echoed by the high-pitched shrieks of the creatures. Those who manipulate fire frantically rush to send the flames out at the creatures. The heat from the fire balls chase creatures closest to the group away.

Two members of the group drop their torches in their panic, and the flames are immediately extinguished in the water. They shove others to the side, knocking Skara into a pool of water. Ripples increase as the small creatures move swiftly through the water towards her, but Tristan and Bern grab for her flailing arms. Dolus rushes to help and the three pull Skara from the water. Several creatures leap from the water after her but ice envelopes them and they drop to the ground, shattering.

Tristan, Bern, Dolus Otho, and Skara look at Daniil, his hand raised in front of him. "You okay?" he asks.

Skara nods her head. "Thank you." She stares at Dolus. "All of you."

Surprise fills Dolus's face and he nods his head at her.

The two men who knocked Skara into the water run back the way the group came, disappearing into the darkness. Creatures chase after them. Their screams fill the cave and the shrieking from the creatures escalate.

The screams stop and new sounds rise from the dark, tearing flesh and breaking bones. The group presses forward, trying to escape the terrifying sounds.

Jaxon grabs Aya's hand. "Run!"

14

Aya is pulled forward as Jaxon breaks into a run. The group follows. Aldur and Fleance draw their weapons and swing at the creatures moving too close.

The cavern ends and the group enters a large hallway. Jaxon waves his torch to chase away any creatures in their path. Yme cautiously uses his earth magic to clear their path while Kylii pulls fire from torches to send projectiles at the creatures. Tanith snaps her tail at the creatures and swipes her sharp claws to keep them back.

Those with magic try their best to fend the creatures off, but only succeed in slowing them down. The only ones who have any success are those who can fling fire from the torches at the creatures.

Jaxon releases Aya's hand and quickly pulls out the map. He looks from the map to the walls and makes a sudden right turn, announcing it so those behind don't miss the passage. Mava and Rava stand at the passage entrance to help ensure no one gets separated.

Light ahead sends a wave of relief through Aya and the group runs faster. The light grows larger and they emerge into an immense cavern thousands of feet high. The top is open to the outside and sunlight shines down, creating a large circle of light. The group runs into the circle, momentarily blinded.

The pursuing creatures explode from the passage behind the group, but most stop before entering the circle of sunlight. The slits on their heads open and close quickly and they shriek. The few that run into the sunlight leap at those lagging behind in the group. Large birds appear from above and grab the creatures in their sharp talons.

The creatures that stayed out of the light move back into the passage, their sounds fading away. The group stops and some collapse to the ground, gasping for air. Mixed sobs of fear and relief are heard.

Yme moves to Aya side. "Are you all right?"

"Yes. Are we safe here?" she asks, glancing up at the circling birds. She sees large nests built into the walls towards the opening where the birds bring their freshly caught prey. They don't seem interested or bothered by the group's presence, but Aya wonders for how long.

"It sounds like those things know not to come in here," Kylii states.

Daniil stares up at the opening. "Yeah, but what happens when the sun goes down?"

The sun is already moving away from the opening, beginning its descent into night. Aya searches the walls of the cavern. There are dozens of openings leading in all directions. She turns to Jaxon. "Do any of those passages lead outside?"

Jaxon searches the map, tracing the numerous lines on the paper. "None of them lead directly outside. The only way to reach the exit is to go farther down."

"Why can't we just climb up there?" Kylii whines.

"This way!" Jaxon yells. "We have to keep moving!" He heads for a smaller opening. The group hesitates, only wanting to rest.

"Come on! We can rest when it's safe!" Yme grabs Aya's hand and runs after Jaxon.

The group groans, but they know Yme is right. They follow, heading back into the darkness. The smaller passage stretches them into a longer line, but they push against one another to stay close together. The sounds of the creatures grow louder as they travel farther into the passage.

Aya and Yme try to keep up with Jaxon's figure, but the uneven earth slows them down. Suddenly, Jaxon stops. Aya and Yme almost crash into him. Looking past Jaxon, Aya sees the passage open onto a subterranean canyon. A drop stretches several yards across.

"Stop!" Jaxon screams back to the group before they crash into each other and send those in front over the edge.

Aya peers over the edge, but the darkness of the cave prevents her from seeing how far down the canyon goes. She looks at Jaxon. "What do we do now?"

"There should've been a bridge here." Jaxon traces his finger on the map, shaking his head. "I don't understand. We went the right way."

Aya squints in the darkness at the opposite wall. An outreach of earth stretches over the canyon opening, too far for the group to jump. The edge is uneven and cracked "It looks like something broke off there."

"Or someone purposefully destroyed it. Whatever happened we have to get across." Jaxon stares across the large drop and points to an opening across the gap. He faces Yme. "Can you make a bridge?"

Moving carefully to the edge, Yme leans down and places a hand on the earth. He closes his eyes and breathes. Opening them, he stands and slowly pushes his hands forward. Earth moves forward, smoothing into a bridge. Once it settles, the group hurries across.

Yme and Aya wait on the other side of the bridge, encouraging everyone to pick up the pace and follow Jaxon into the passage. Aldur and Fleance are the last to cross and Yme grabs Aldur's arm. "Hold the light high. I'm going to buy us some more time."

Aldur does as Yme says and Yme watches the darkness for movement. The creatures emerge from the passage and hesitate at the bridge. They touch the stone cautiously before racing across. Yme waits until a large number have reached the halfway point and then stomps his foot on the bridge. It collapses, sending most of the creatures down into the deep canyon.

Those that didn't cross the bridge shriek at Yme and climb the walls, searching for another way across. Knowing they'll eventually find a way across, Yme turns to Aldur and Aya. "Go!"

The large man hurries into the passage followed by Aya. Yme follows, slamming his fist into the side of the passage. The earth rises, blocking the entrance of the path and Yme increases his speed. Aya, Yme, and Aldur eventually catch up to the group.

The group slows and Jaxon allows them to stop as they enter a smaller cave with only one other entrance. Jaxon approaches the three, grabbing Yme. "Did you seal off that passage?"

"Yes. It should buy us more time. Unless there's another way for them to get in," Yme says as he closes the doorway they entered from.

The group listens intently, waiting for Jaxon's answer. Studying the map, Jaxon shakes his head. "No. We should be safe to rest here. Unless they can dig through the earth, we should be fine."

A great sigh of relief moves through the group and everyone falls to the ground. Torches are placed around the group to light the entire cave. Some prepare food while others fall asleep, exhausted by the chase.

Aya searches the group for Jayda. She passes Tristan, Skara, Bern and Dolus. The three former slaves are offering to share food with the former voice of the Arena. He reluctantly accepts and Aya catches the relief crossing his face.

Aya finds Jayda and asks to check her leg. It's fine, but Aya wants to be sure the young woman isn't scarred on the inside. After assuring herself that Jayda's fine, Aya joins the brothers, Yme, and Jaxon.

"What were those things?" Kylii asks.

"The creatures from your stories, Jaxon?" Daniil adds.

With a hesitant nod, Jaxon sits on the ground. He pulls out the map. "I never imagined there would be so many. But that explains this line in the notes on the map."

"What line?" Aya asks.

"'There are too many.' I thought it had meant too many passages, but now I think it meant those creatures."

"Is there a name for them in those notes? Or anything else useful?" Kylii asks, peering over Jaxon's shoulder.

Jaxon closes the map and glares at the inquisitive brother. "No. In the village, the older folk called them flesh carvers because of the strange marks we'd find on dead animals near the entrance of the cave, but it was only a joke name. We never truly believed they existed."

"Well, looks like they do," Kylii says, walking back to Daniil and Tanith.

"Glad you were wrong about that," Daniil sarcastically adds. He strokes Tanith's mane as she lays next to him.

A sneer from Jaxon silences the brothers. "Anyway, we should rest here. According to the map, we should be safe here if Yme closes that pathway up. We can open it in the morning and make a run for the exit."

"Do you think we'll need to run the rest of the way?" Aya asks.

Jaxon doesn't answer, giving her an expression she can only describe as unsure. Aya looks at Yme and he swallows before closing the only way in or out of the cave. He leaves a pattern in the rock so he can easily find the passageway again.

"How many did we lose?" Jaxon asks Aldur, Aya noting the tone of his voice. He had slipped into his caravan leader voice earlier, but now it's more relaxed.

"Only those two who ran off at first," Aldur reports, appearing from nowhere.

"Are we sure about that? Everyone, do a head count," Jaxon yells out suddenly. The group begins checking those who made it. They discover one other missing. "Well, that's lucky."

"Lucky?" Rava hisses. "We lost three people!"

Jaxon stares at her and shrugs. "We could have lost more. Our torches may not last much longer and I'm sure those of you who know even a little fire magic are tired from that chase. We still have many more hours in these caves before we reach the exit. How many of you think you'll last that long?"

Mava places a calming hand on her sister's shoulder. "More people could have died, Rava. Right now, we need to rest and gather our strength."

"Everyone should sleep and eat a good meal. We'll figure out what to do about the torches after," Aya speaks up.

The group mumbles a tired agreement and prepares food.

After everyone has eaten their fill they prepare to sleep. Not until Yme assures everyone they are safe does the last eyelid close and the cave grow silent.

Aya smiles to herself when she sees even Jaxon lie down and sleep at Yme's comforting words.

15

I stand in a field. Grass rises to my knees, moving like waves in the wind. In the distance, I see a solitary tree. My feet move on their own, heading for the tree, but no matter how long I walk it never grows closer.

I stop walking and lean down. I place my hand on the soft earth and I feel a heartbeat. The earth shifts allowing a thick root to rise. It lifts me into the air and the tree grows larger in the distance. It isn't moving closer, simply growing. Its roots rise from the earth looking like the backs of large creatures.

Other trees grow around the now enormous tree creating a lush forest. I rise higher and higher into the sky, towering over the forest. I watch the tree at the center continue to grow. Blue light shines from its canopy and a voice whispers in my thoughts.

Help me, Life Healer.

Aya sits up, her sudden movement startling those around her. She blinks, confusion filling her. Shadows dance on the cave walls from the torchlights, but she swears she sees the shape of the tree in the shadows.

I haven't had one of those in a while. She used to have recurring nightmares growing up and an occasional dream predicting injuries she'd be requested to heal. But this was the first time she had a dream that felt... calming.

Waking in the cave startles many in the group, but the main panic comes from the loss of comforting light from the torches. Only three remained lit as the group slept and the darkened cave fills many with fear.

Aya yawns. In the dark of the cave, it's hard to tell how long they slept. In the Arena, there was always a sense of morning even deep in its bowels. But here, Aya feels like she only slept for minutes.

"We have to figure out the torches," Yme says, climbing to his feet.

Groaning, Aya stands and they gather those awake together. They count the remaining torches and decide to use only a small number at a time. Hopefully, it will make the light last longer. Those who know fire magic are paired up with a torchbearer and told to only use their magic if they see the creatures. If a torch goes out, they aren't to use their magic to relight it. They must be relit using the already burning ones.

The last of the group awakens and eats prepared food. They're filled in on the new plan with the torches and soon, everyone begins gathering their supplies.

Ironically, the last awake is Jaxon. He's jerked from sleep when Aldur and Fleance bring him food and water. Aya sees a brief flash of embarrassment cross Jaxon's face, but it disappears quickly.

Another hour passes before the group is ready to continue

through the caves. Yme lowers the barrier blocking the entrance and darkness stretches before them yet again. Jaxon takes the lead, and they enter the narrow passage, continuing forward.

The sounds of the cave have returned to the normal dripping of water, rocks settling, and wind blowing through the rock walls. Still, at each sudden sound, members of the group jump or let out a scream.

The passageway remains narrow for a great distance much to everyone's relief. It's easier to keep an eye out for the creatures... the flesh carvers.

Hours pass, but no one can truthfully determine exactly how long they've been wandering in the darkness. Jaxon doesn't speak as he leads them down different passages. He slows only to double check the map and make small notes.

The passages start looking the same and many think they've only been going in circles. But Aya sees the differences. She understands how Jaxon seems to know the way so effortlessly. Small carvings in the stone walls, occasional symbols on the ground stand out to her.

They reach a passageway that narrows so much the only way to pass is for the group to crawl on their stomachs one by one. A number in the group grow nervous, afraid of getting stuck, but Jaxon assures them there's plenty of room. "I'll go first. When I reach the other side, I'll signal for the next person to follow. It should be a straight path to the other side."

"I'll go next." Aldur steps forward. "If I can make it through, none of you should have any problem." He locks eyes with Dolus. "Even you, big boy."

Jaxon takes his bag off and holds it out in front of him. "To make it easier, you can either push your bag in front of you or drag it behind. Whatever is most comfortable for you." He puts the map inside the bag and crawls into the small hole.

He holds his hand out for a torch and Aldur hands one to

him. It takes several minutes for the light of the torch to fade from the hole and the ensuing silence makes the sounds of the cave seem much louder than normal. Those at the back of the group keep glancing behind, straining to see if the shadows are just that or something alive.

Aya watches the hole for any sign of distress. Her chest tightens as questions swirl through her mind. What if as she crawls through the cave collapses on top of her? What if those flesh carvers follow them? They're small enough they could easily overwhelm them where they can't use their magic.

"All right! It's clear!" Jaxon's voice echoes from the hole. "Aldur, come on over."

Aldur takes his bag off and squeezes into the hole. The group collectively holds their breath. Grunts from the hole put images of Aldur being trapped in the tiny passage into Aya's mind. Would that be worse? Being trapped and dying of hunger? Minutes pass excruciatingly slowly.

"Made it! Whoever's next, come on through!" Aldur's voice echoes from the hole.

Many in the group relax and they line up to crawl through. Tanith easily makes it through, leading Daniil and Kylii. Mava, Rava, and Bern follow. When half the group has made it to the other side, Aya readies to enter.

She turns to Yme. "See you on the other side."

"Yeah."

Taking a deep breath, Aya leans down and stares into the hole. She sees those in front of her slowly crawling. She swallows a growing lump in her throat and takes off her bag. She places it in front of her and enters the hole.

Yme watches Aya's form disappear into the hole. He wants to follow her, but as he looks around at the last of the group, he sees the fear on their faces. He turns to Fleance, one of Jaxon's men. The young man is standing with his back to the hole, his eyes searching the darkness for danger.

Grabbing Fleance's shoulder, Yme motions to the last members of the group. "Help me get them through." Fleance nods and stands on the opposite side of the hole. He and Yme motion the last of the group into the hole.

Fleance motions Yme to go before him, but Yme shakes his head. "If anything follows us, I can collapse the passage. You go."

Hesitating, Fleance hands Yme his torch. "Make sure you collapse it, so it doesn't crush us, too."

Before Yme can respond, Fleance is already crawling in, his bag dragging behind him. Yme turns and waves the torch in front of him. He can't see anything moving, but it doesn't mean the flesh carvers aren't there.

Steeling his nerve, Yme crawls into the hole. He has a little trouble keeping the torch in front of him and dragging his bag behind him. He manages to find a comfortable crawling position and makes his way easily through the passage. As he crawls through, he's impressed Aldur was able to fit.

At the halfway point, Yme feels his bag catch on something and struggles to free it. Before it comes free, he feels something brush against his leg. He quickly turns, holding the torch in front of him, but sees nothing. He hesitates a moment longer, but then continues ahead at a faster speed, dirt rising and making his eyes water.

He approaches the end of the passage and hands reach in to help Yme out of the hole. He's helped to his feet and Yme hands the torch back to Fleance. Aya smiles at him, relief clear in her face. Yme returns the smile but can't shake the feeling something had been in the passage with him. He looks at the hole one last time before collapsing it, almost expecting to see an arm reaching out. But there's nothing.

They continue forward, but the darkness of the caves sends panic through the group. Yme wonders if limiting the number of torches lit was a premature decision. The less light, the more those in the group grow anxious. The fear they'll never escape the darkening abyss settles in and every sound sends someone into a terror-filled frenzy. Yme and Aya do their best to reassure the group, but the fear weighs the group down, dragging their feet and slowing their progress.

Yme quickens his pace to be next to Jaxon. "We should rest. It may help to calm everyone down."

"You may be right. Our pace is slowing every time someone sees their own shadow. We could probably spare a couple of hours," Jaxon agrees.

Daniil appears on the other side of Jaxon. "I wouldn't suggest that."

"Why not?" Jaxon asks.

"We're being followed," Daniil says, speaking so low Yme can barely hear him. Tanith and Kylii move close behind the three men. "Tanith has been hearing the creatures move closer for a while now. Most likely due to our slower pace. But they sound different."

"Sound different, how?" Yme lowers his voice to match Daniil's volume.

"Faster, for one."

"What else?"

Hesitating, Daniil licks his lips. "A bit bigger, I think."

"How much is a bit?" Jaxon asks.

"How tall are you?" Daniil answers the question with a warning.

Jaxon turns his eyes on Yme. "What do you suggest?"

"I suggest we start running."

"I agree."

A terrified scream echoes from behind and everyone turns. One of the torchbearers at the rear is thrown to the ground. His torch rolls behind him, revealing the flesh carver now on his back. It's the size of a man and its tail wraps tightly around the torchbearer's throat, stifling his screams. Its hands tears flesh from his arms and legs and the man struggles to throw the creature off. With a sudden movement, there is the sound of a loud crack as the flesh carver's tail snaps the man's neck. His body goes still.

Aldur rushes forward, waving his torch in front of him and slashing at the creature with his sword. The flesh carver hisses and leaps from the dead man's back, but its tail is still around the man's throat. The body disappears into the dark and the sound of ripping and tearing flesh fills the caves. Shrieks of more flesh carvers echo through the darkness and more emerge, unafraid of the torches.

Those who have fire magic throw fireballs at the

approaching creatures, but they dodge them or ignore them completely. Two are hit with the fire and fall to the ground shrieking in pain, but once the flames are out, they lurch forward.

"RUN!" Yme and Jaxon bellow.

The group explodes into a run, their exhaustion forgotten and their screams barely overpowering the shrieks of the monstrous creatures behind. The flesh carvers are more in number, larger, faster, and fiercer. The torches do nothing to keep them back and they venture far closer than their smaller counterparts. Aldur and Fleance hold off the beasts with their weapons and many in the group pull out the weapons given them by the villagers.

Yme uses wind to throw a few of the creatures back but, deep down, his fear is turning into anger. *I survived the Arena. I will not fall here!*

When a flesh carver falls dead, those around it immediately stop to feed on their fallen brethren, occasionally fighting each other for the fresh meat. There are only a few the size of a man, but these flesh carvers living deeper in the caves are more violent.

The passageway opens up, allowing the group to move closer together into a clump rather than a line. But the sounds of the flesh carvers crawling on the walls around them help their feet move faster. The creatures crawling on the walls and ceilings grab at the group with sharp claws. Several fall from the ceiling, trying to land on top of members of the group, but those with weapons attack the creatures, killing them.

A flesh carver grabs for Aya, almost reaching her arm before Kylii throws a torch at the creature and uses his magic to set the creature on fire. It shrieks in pain and tries to roll on the ground to put out the flames. Kylii keeps the flames burning and the flesh carver runs into a group of its own kind, setting a few more on fire.

Screams fill the cave and another member of the group is pulled into the darkness. They push through, emerging into another underground canyon. It's wider than the last, a ledge along the wall large enough for the group to run along without fear of falling. A naturally made bridge crosses the large gap leading into more passages.

Jaxon orders the group to cross, waving them across. "Go! Follow the passage on the other side! Don't stray! Keep going straight!" He stands at the edge of the canyon, ensuring no one misses their step.

There is no questioning or fear of the bridge collapsing. The group hurries across. Yme, Aya, and Fleance hold back to assist Jaxon.

Flesh carvers emerge from a passage at the foot of the bridge and Jaxon draws his sword. He kills the creatures easily, knocking others over the edge of the cliff. Fleance draws a second blade and attacks the creatures following on the heels of the group. Yme slams his fist into the cave wall. Blocks of earth shoot out of the wall, throwing flesh carvers into the canyon.

Aya waves the last members of the group across the bridge and follows. Yme yells for Fleance to cross the bridge and the young man quickly does. Yme turns to Jaxon, preparing to cover both directions so the other man can cross safely.

"We go together!" Jaxon yells, kicking another man-sized flesh carver into the canyon.

Yme doesn't argue and the two men slowly cross the bridge, fighting the flesh carvers as they go. Yme is able to knock most off with his wind magic. Jaxon takes care of those who manage to hang on with his torch and sword.

Halfway across the bridge, the flesh carvers have thinned

enough Yme turns and runs after the group, eager to get off the bridge.

"Jaxon!" Aya screams.

Yme turns and sees flesh carvers appear from the sides of the bridge. More crawl on the underside of the bridge to emerge in front of Jaxon, cutting him off from the rest of the group. The flesh carvers at the foot of the bridge rush forward and overpower Jaxon. They grab him and begin dragging him back off the bridge, into the darkness of the passage. Their teeth bite into the thick armor and their tales wrap around Jaxon's legs and arms. His torch falls from his hand down into the dark abyss below and he tries to use his sword to free himself.

Yme, Aldur, and Fleance rush the flesh carvers. Aldur and Fleance swing their blades at the creatures and Yme stomps the earth, knocking the flesh carvers into the chasm. As they clear bodies, more creatures crawl from under the bridge.

"Keep moving!" Jaxon's screams echo over the flesh carver's shrieks. "Follow the passage straight ahead! Don't stop!" He disappears into the passage. Waves of flesh carvers follow while others turn to run after the group.

Aya screams for Jaxon and tries to run after him. Daniil and Kylii grab her and drag her forward into the passage the rest of the group has already run into, but she breaks free. She runs for the bridge as Yme turns, stopping her. Aldur and Fleance keep the flesh carvers back. Yme sees their energy fading fast.

"Aya!" Yme yells at her. "We have to go! There's nothing we can do!" He whistles at Aldur and Fleance. The two men back off the bridge, Aldur throwing his torch at the creatures. Once all four are clear, Yme destroys the bridge, sending most of the flesh carvers to the bottom of the canyon, but others are ready and find another way across.

Yme, Aya, Aldur, and Fleance run into the passage and quickly catch up to the group. Without Jaxon leading, the group runs blindly through the dark passages. The only clues they have are Jaxon's final words. They continue straight, ignoring the branching passages. The sounds of the creatures giving chase grow louder.

Light appears ahead and the group cheers, believing they've finally reached the exit. Their excitement pumps new energy through them and they push their bodies faster. The sound of rushing water lifts their spirits higher and they emerge into the light.

Their hearts drop. They haven't made it outside.

A giant cavern rises around them with large crystals embedded in the walls, emitting light. The cavern is filled with the light from the crystals, but as the group looks around, there is no exit. The only way out of the cavern is back the way they came.

The group is forced to stop as the earth beneath them ends at a cliff. Waterfalls cascade from the walls down into a deep pool below. The members of the group stare down at the pool from the cliff edge, but the fall is too great for them to safely jump down.

They're trapped.

The flesh carvers emerge from the passageway and push the group closer to the edge. They shriek at the group, clawing the air and opening their razor teeth filled mouths.

There are only two options. Jump or fight.

17

"Well, at least we'll take a lot of them with us," Daniil says, raising his hands. Tanith growls next to him, hissing at any of the creatures that take tentative steps closer to the group.

"Just how I imagined we'd die. So far beneath the earth no one will even know we're gone," Kylii jokes.

"Shut up, Kylii," Yme grumbles. "Better here than in that damn Arena."

Words of agreement escape the lips of the group. Weapons that weren't already drawn appear and the group readies for the flesh carvers to attack.

Aya looks at Yme. He reaches out for her hand. She takes it and squeezes then pulls out the knife her parents left her. The black blade dully reflects the light of the surrounding crystals. She and Yme face the flesh carvers and prepare to fight. Prayers are spoken and those who don't have weapons move to the back of the group.

One of the creatures releases a deep roar and runs for the group. A few follow, while the rest stay back, waiting. The flesh carver in the lead leaps for its closest target, Daniil. He raises his hand, freezing the creature. He and Kylii kick the frozen flesh carver and it smashes into thousands of pieces.

Aldur and Bern cut another at the throat and tail, respectively. Fleance, Mava, and Rava dispose of a third and then a fourth.

Tanith fights with a fifth, rolling on the ground and clawing the creature, while avoiding its razor-sharp teeth. She roars as the flesh carver grabs the side of her front right leg and pulls a large chunk of flesh free. She digs her long fangs into the flesh carver's throat and holds the struggling thing until it dies. She throws it away, limping to Daniil's side. She bares her teeth at the rest of the flesh carvers, angrily.

The last of the charging flesh carvers leap for Aya. Taking a deep breath, she allows a little of her magic to fill her. She sees the creature's muscles and blood working and easily dodges the attack. Yme impales it with a stone pike, allowing Aya to stab her blade deep into the flesh carver's heart. Yme throws the stone pike and the dead flesh carver over the side of the cliff.

The rest of the creatures charge, and the group prepares for the onslaught. The air fills with different mixtures of magic and nervous gasps of air.

A strange light fills the tunnel behind the flesh carvers and the creatures closest to the passage stop. The creatures twitch their heads around, unable to see, but able to feel the strange light, smell something strange in the air.

Aya's eyes widen. She feels a large surge of magic rushing towards them and readies for whatever is the cause.

Blue flames explode from the passageway, engulfing the creatures still swarming into the cavern and by the opening. The flesh carvers caught in the fire are instantly burned to ash and those that manage to escape leap for the walls. The flames chase the creatures up the wall as though alive. None can escape and their screams fill the cavern.

After clearing the walls and passageway of the flesh carvers, the blue flames rush towards the group. Tension fills Aya's body as she prepares for the pain of death, but the flames split down the middles and circle the group, killing the flesh carvers crawling up behind them, under the cliff edge.

The flames cover the group in a circular tornado of blue fire, but there is no heat. Screams from the few flesh carvers still trying to escape the fire fade and several in the group sob with relief. Aya watches the flames and feels her magic longing to reach out and touch the magic within the fire. She feels it recognizing the magic. It knows who is in control of the blue flames. She places her hand on her chest, confused at this new sensation.

Words a healer from the Arena whispered to her echo in her mind. *Your magic feels alive. It sensed my magic and... mixed with it, explored it.*

The blue fire opens in front of the group, allowing them to see a figure emerging from the passageway. The flames die out and not a single flesh carver is left. Yme, Aldur, Fleance, Daniil, Kylii, and others at the front of the group prepare to face this new horror coming for them.

"Finally caught up to you. I wasn't sure you'd actually follow my directions. But thank the gods you did. I was able to make it in time, no thanks to Yme's destruction of the bridge."

Aya's heart jumps into her throat. Tears threaten to roll down her cheeks, but she forces them back. Instead, she steps forward to see the figure better.

They lower their weapons and stare at the familiar face in shock. Many are so shocked they have to rub their eyes to make sure they aren't seeing things and others fall to the ground.

Yme is the first to find his voice. "Jaxon?"

Jaxon holds his hands out to his sides and smiles. Blood covers half his face from scratches. The belt around his waist holds his gloves securely and his clothes are torn. Blood on his arms and legs can be seen through the holes in his clothes showing where flesh carvers managed to rip some skin away. But he is mostly unhurt. His blue eyes appear brighter in the crystal lit cavern, but those who know magic understand it is the magic inside of him making his irises glow.

He walks towards the group. A large number of flesh carvers flow from the passageway, running for Jaxon. He turns and throws his hand out in front of him and the blue flames erupt from his hand. The fire flows into the passageway, killing the creatures.

Aya's mouth drops open. This isn't the first time she's seen fire appear from nothing, Kylii does it frequently when he fights, but this is the first time she's seen the fire move so fluidly. Jaxon's control of the magic is breathtaking.

The flames fade and the cavern fills with the sound of the waterfalls. Jaxon faces the group and walks towards the dumbfounded faces.

Aya rushes forward to meet him, wrapping her arms around him. She feels his body tense under her touch, but it doesn't stop her magic from reaching out and touching the magic inside of him. She hears him gasp and reigns her magic back in.

"You're a magic user?" Yme asks, the shock making his voice come out as a whisper.

Gently moving Aya away, Jaxon nods.

"I saw blue flame," Kylii says.

"That's rare fire magic," Daniil adds.

Aya's awe changes to confusion. "Why did you hide you were a magic user?"

Jaxon's smile fades and his expression becomes somber.

"Magic users have a higher chance of being thrown into the Arena, especially rare kinds. I chose to hide my magic in order to survive." He looks at the entire group. "We should go. More will come."

"Can't you just, you know," Kylii motions with his hand, "burn 'em up?"

The smile returns to Jaxon's face, but his sight seems unfocused. "Unfortunately, I haven't used my magic in many years. If I use too much too fast, I may pass out."

"Well, that's inconvenient," Daniil says.

"Enough talk. We'll have plenty of time for that once we get out of here." Jaxon heads into the passageway, stopping at the entrance to grab the wall. He shakes his head and continues forward. The group follows, excited to hear the mention of escaping the caves.

Aya, Yme, Daniil, Kylii, Tanith, Aldur, and Fleance hesitate for a moment.

"Did *you* know he was a magic user?" Daniil asks Aldur and Fleance.

Fleance shakes his head as Aldur puts his weapons away. "We all carry secrets. Secrets do not define us. Our actions do." The two men follow the group.

Aya looks at Yme and the brothers before they follow, hurrying to catch up with the rest of the group.

18

Jaxon leads them back to the underground canyon. He takes them along the edge to a second natural bridge where they cross and enter a large passageway.

Hours pass and they reach a cave with a stream flowing through it. Jaxon stops the group. "We can rest here. It's safe." He walks to a large rock by the stream and sits.

Most of the group collapses to the ground and falls asleep. Those who choose to stay awake cook a large meal for those sleeping. They eat their portions and as one person awakens, another lies down to sleep.

Yme and the brothers eat quickly, then he and Kylii fall asleep, bodies drained from using their magic. Daniil sits with Tanith, stroking her head gently. Aya finishes her meal and looks at Jaxon. The rock he's sitting on is the closest to the entrance. If any flesh carvers followed them, he is in the best position to attack them. He grabs bandages from his pack and covers the worst wounds on his arms and legs.

Aya watches his shaking hands struggle to tie the bandages and she walks over to him. She squats. "Let me heal you.

You've lost a lot of blood." She reaches her hands towards his arms.

Dropping the loose bandages, he grabs her wrists, shaking his head. "Not now. You need to keep your strength up. I'll be fine."

"You say that, but you're ready to pass out."

Meeting her gaze, Jaxon's eyes glow with his magic. "Rest, Aya. I've been worse and *in* worse situations than this."

Reluctantly, Aya nods and moves back to the sleeping forms of Yme and Kylii. Tanith whines, catching Aya's attention. She licks her wounded leg and stares at Aya with her white eyes. Aya carefully approaches and looks at Daniil.

"Looks like she wants some help."

"I think she would appreciate it," Daniil says, placing a hand on Tanith's back. The Khorgoi looks up at Daniil, nipping his fingers with her mouth. He laughs. "She would *really* appreciate it."

Tanith stands and limps to Aya, turning her wounded leg closest to her. Aya smiles and strokes Tanith's brown mane. The Khorgoi chirps and nudges Aya's hand with her snout. Aya touches the wound, expecting Tanith to growl at the pressure, but the Khorgoi stays still and looks ahead. Her tail thumps on the ground and Aya closes her eyes.

She wasn't sure she could heal Tanith as easily as a human, but as she feels her magic flow into the animal's leg the knowledge of what to do fills her mind. Her magic allows her to understand the differences between human and Khorgoi, though much beneath the skin is the same. She sees the skin reform and scales grow. The work is done quickly, and as Aya pulls her magic out of Tanith, she hears a soft, female voice.

"Thank you, Life Healer."

Aya's eyes open and she stares at the Khorgoi. Tanith coos and rubs her snout against Aya's chest. Aya strokes the cool scales of Tanith's back and smiles, knowing it was the Khorgoi's thoughts she heard. She feels honored.

Small flesh carvers venture close as the group rests, smelling the food and feeling the warmth of the burning fires. Jaxon easily dispatches them with a flick of his finger. Small balls of blue flames keep the creatures from attacking and even chase a large number away.

The stream allows the group to clean wounds and dirt from their skin. Farther upstream, where the water is fresh and clean, they refill their jugs, and a small sense of normalcy returns.

Jaxon soon announces the time to move has come. As though hearing his words, the shrieks of distant flesh carvers echo around them. Quickly gathering their belongings, the group follows Jaxon out. He navigates the passages easily, changing directions often. After the third hour of turning down different passages, the group's fears return as the darkness surrounds them once more.

The screams of the flesh carvers can be heard, but as time goes on the screams grow more distant. Beyond all odds they are actually moving farther away from the creatures or, at the very least, the creatures' territories.

Two hours pass before Aya realizes she can no longer hear the flesh carvers. Relief fills her at having escaped one threat, but Jaxon doesn't slow his pace. He hasn't allowed the group to rest again since the cave with the stream and exhaustion is returning to many in the group.

Watching him, Aya sees him waver as waves of light-headedness hit him, but he manages to regain control and continue. A few times she catches Aldur and Fleance ready to grab for their leader but deciding against it, knowing Jaxon won't accept their help.

A hand on her shoulder surprises Aya. She turns her head

to Yme and releases a sigh of relief. "Even when you're standing next to me, you startle me. These caves are using up the last of my nerves."

Yme smiles. "I don't know if I should be insulted or concerned. But you know he'll be fine. He's very stubborn and stubborn men survive."

"Or they die because they're too foolish to let anyone help them," Aya says, moving his hand. "And I seem to remember another stubborn man who almost got himself killed when he tried to fight Klaeon alone."

"But he *did* survive."

"Not without help."

The torches start going out and soon the group is left with only a third of the original number lighting the way. Food is running out as it is passed around though they have plenty of water left, especially after filling at the stream.

The air grows cooler and Jaxon's speed increases again, making it difficult for the group to keep up. Making it even more difficult is the floor naturally angling upwards. The uphill climb sends a few in the group into exhausted gasps.

As the caves continue to stretch ahead, realization dawns on them. As time passes and the torches die out, the group understands why Jaxon has picked up his pace.

The darkness of the cave has been lessening. The group turns a corner and bright light is seen far ahead, across a mighty cavern. Green plants grow on the walls and floors, providing color to the browns and blacks of the earth.

This light cannot be confused with glowing crystals. It's sunlight. They've finally reached the end of the caves.

II

FOREST OF SPIRITS

19

Sunlight.

After being trapped in the darkness for so long, it hurts Aya's eyes. She moves slowly out of the darkness; as the light becomes bearable and her vision clears, Aya gasps at the sight before her.

The cave exits from the side of a mountain, but a short climb down leads to a small field of tall, green grass. At the opposite end of the field from the cave, a wall of trees leads into an immense forest stretching beyond the horizon.

The trees are different from anything Aya has ever seen. Even from a distance the trees appear incredibly tall, taller than any tree Aya can remember from her village—and she can feel it. This forest is old, and the magic hidden within it vibrates through her bones.

"The Forest of Spirits," Jaxon announces, staring at the amazing sight with wide eyes.

Aya wonders if he can feel the magic, too. She glances around the group and notices similar expressions even on the faces of those without magic.

The group carefully begins their descent, taking extra care on the rocky terrain. The tall grass of the field feels strange against their skin, but it's a pleasant feeling. Excitement flows through the group like a powerful river. They celebrate their escape from the dark caves by walking quickly towards the trees, eventually breaking into a gleeful run. The warmth of the sun and the feel of wind on their skin fill their spirits. Their cheers and whoops of joy tear across the field.

Aya and Yme look at each other. She sees the relief in his eyes, and it brings a smile to her lips. They join in the excitement, running for the trees. Aya spies Tanith leaping through the grass, chasing small animals startled by the sudden rush of people. The Khorgoi falls to the ground and rolls in the grass, cooing happily. Daniil and Kylii laugh and race each other to the forest, leaping over any obstacle in their way. Tanith springs to her feet and chases after them.

Slowing her pace, Aya turns to stare at the mountain they spent the last two days inside. She hopes to never step foot inside another cave again. Though she knows if Klaeon chose to follow them, it would take longer to go over the mountain or around. As dangerous as the caves were, Aya knows going through them was the best option.

She watches Jaxon follow the group. He finally allows his exhaustion and the pain of his wounds to show. Aldur and Fleance move to either side and help him towards the forest. He looks from one man to the other, but neither speak. A wave of emotion flows across Jaxon's face. Aldur and Fleance don't need to speak. Their loyalties are clear.

The forest trees rise high above the ground, creating a stunning natural wall cutting across the field, clearly marking the forest's beginning. As soon as the group enters, passing through the line of trees, new sensations wash over them. The feeling of ancient magic fills them, but it's a calm feeling, a welcoming feeling.

Giant birds fly through the air and their songs are beautiful to the ears of the group moving across the forest floor. The trees are spread apart enough to allow sunlight to reach the earth below, allowing flowers and other plants to grow around their mighty trunks, as big around at their bases as the giant pillars that held up Bloodfall Arena. No hands of man have made their marks in this great forest.

The group runs through the trees until they reach a large clearing with a stream cutting through the trees. Gathering together, the group collapses, one by one, onto the grassy forest bed. Tears of joy and panting breaths mix with laughter.

Aldur and Fleance set Jaxon down on the soft earth before joining him. Jaxon's breath is short, and his eyes go in and out of focus. "We'll rest here. Tomorrow, we continue farther into the forest. The canyon we seek is beyond these trees. Though I'm not sure how many days it will take to pass through."

Even before he finishes speaking, many in the group have fallen asleep. Others follow suit, the sounds of the forest a perfect lullaby. Aldur and Fleance alternate between resting and staying awake to ensure no one or nothing sneaks up on the group, leaving Jaxon alone.

As Fleance begins his first round keeping watch, Mava joins him. She brings him water and stands with him. Aya watches the two as she lays between Yme and Tanith. Mava gently touches Fleance's arm as they speak. They sit on the ground as their conversations grow more intense.

Aya wakes from a short nap, startled at not remembering falling asleep. She sits up and sees Jaxon has moved away from the group and propped himself against a tree. His head hangs low and his hands lay limp at his sides. If she couldn't see his chest moving, Aya would've thought he was dead.

The sun is moving behind the mountains, casting shadows. Aya carefully moves away from Yme's still figure and walks to Jaxon. She kneels and takes a look at his injuries.

"Is it all right for me to heal you now?"

Jaxon laughs and rolls his head to the side to look at her, dark bags under his eyes. His skin is pale making the dried blood on his head more noticeable. "If I say no you won't leave me alone, will you?"

"I'll wake Aldur and have him hold you down."

"He would, too. All right, heal me."

Aya touches Jaxon's leg with her hands. The wounds on his arms and legs aren't too severe, but she sees infection threatening to spread. "Why didn't you want me to heal you sooner? It wasn't just to keep my energy from draining."

Jaxon sighs as his injuries heal. "That was part of it. But it was also because I was afraid."

"Afraid of what?"

"When you embraced me, I felt your magic. It... explored me, as though alive. I was afraid it would find things I didn't want you to know."

Aya finishes with one leg and moves to the other. "I learned about that when I arrived at the Arena. One of the healers told me the same thing, but I don't know what that means."

"If there were any Life Healers still alive, I'm sure they would be able to explain it. It's probably part of the rarity of your magic," Jaxon says.

Aya bites her bottom lip. Questions dance through her mind. Questions she's been asking herself since she first learned her magic was rare. *Can she ever find someone to answer them? Or will she be forced to continue finding her own answers?*

"You should sleep," she says, without looking up, longing to change the subject.

Jaxon winces. "I have been."

She snaps her attention to the dark circles under his eyes. "You're lying." Though she knows the dark circles are from more than exhaustion.

He shrugs, his gaze focusing ahead of him on a distant memory. "Old habits are hard to break. And these wounds don't quite lull me into a peaceful sleep."

Aya finishes his leg wounds and moves to the wounds on his arms. "You don't have to be the watchful protector. There's no one here who wants to attack us. We're safe."

"This forest is full of old magic. These trees are older than most of those mountains." He nods his head in the direction they came from. "There are things in this forest no man has ever seen."

"But none of it is going to hurt us. You need to sleep. Especially, to regain your strength from your magic. You've been ready to pass out for hours." She places her hands on either side of Jaxon's face and closes her eyes. "Why didn't you at least let me heal your head wounds?"

The surprise on Jaxon's face quickly fades. "I guess I shouldn't be that shocked you noticed."

"I didn't need my magic to tell me. Any traditional healer would see the blood and know what kind of injury you sustained." She furrows her brows. "Though it frightens me to know you would hide these from me. There's internal bleeding. If you waited any longer..."

"I could have died. In fact, you're thinking I should already be dead."

She finishes healing Jaxon's wounds and leans back on her heels, opening her eyes. "You knew? How did the bleeding not spread?"

"An interesting side effect to my blue flame magic is an ability to slow a bleeding wound for a short time. It's not as powerful as other healing magic, but it's saved my life more than once."

Anger rushes blood to Aya's face and she glares at him. "It wouldn't have saved your life this time if I wasn't here."

A smile spreads slowly on his face, one Aya hasn't seen on Jaxon's face before and it cools her anger. "I knew you would be able to save me."

The blush on Aya's face brings tears to her eyes. "I don't want to see you almost die in front of me again. Promise you won't keep anything else from me."

"I promise."

Aya wipes the tears from her face and takes a deep breath. "Can I see your fire? If you aren't too exhausted?"

Jaxon raises his hand and a small blue flame dances on his palm. He watches it with half-lidded eyes. "I haven't used my magic in front of others in so long. Even when I thought I was alone and out of sight, I wouldn't use it. I knew if anyone in my caravan discovered it, they wouldn't hesitate to throw me into the Arena."

Aya stares at the flames in awe. She sees the fire on his skin, but it doesn't burn him. She wants to touch it, touch his palm to discover how the magic works. "I have a confession to make. When I healed you at the Arena, I think I felt your magic. I wasn't sure then since I was still learning my own magic, but I felt it."

"I almost lost control that day. I wanted to burn Seera for what she did, but instead I stormed out without speaking to anyone. Aldur and Fleance were too afraid to speak to me until a day passed."

Aya looks at Fleance and Aldur. Both are sleeping against two different trees with their weapons on their laps, ready to be taken up quickly, but the peaceful looks on their faces prove they are in a deep sleep. Mava is still next to Fleance, her head resting on his armored shoulder.

"Aldur and Fleance don't seem to be treating you any differently now that they know you're a magic user."

Jaxon casts an eye over his men, the flame dying out on his palm. "If they'd been given the chance, they would've given me up. I wouldn't have blamed them either. We do what we must to survive."

"Or they would've kept it a secret. They respect you for the man, not the magic user. Sometimes, survival means fighting for the ones you care about instead of taking the easy route."

"Maybe..." Jaxon stares at Aya, curiously. "Do you know why I chose Fleance to watch over you in the caravan?"

"You had a reason?"

"I have reasons for everything I do. I chose Fleance because I knew he would never hurt you. He's a good man. He joined my caravan shortly after Aldur became my second in command. He never tried to impress me or take over. He would do as I asked without complaint or questioning." Jaxon held up one finger. "Except one time. I ordered him to punish a slave who continuously gave us trouble. Biting my men, kicking rocks at our riding beasts, once even pissing in the water supply. But Fleance refused."

"Did you punish him?"

"No. I asked him why he refused. He told me he didn't find enjoyment in being cruel. He told me the slave was only doing what any man would do. I asked him if he believed I found enjoyment in being cruel." Pausing, Jaxon eyes Fleance. "He responded, 'You do what's necessary to keep the others from viewing you as weak. But I can see in your eyes you hate this life as much as I do.' I accepted his refusal but warned him that if the slave in question did anything to put the caravan at risk, he would be responsible for the man."

"And something happened," Aya asks, enthralled in the story.

"The slave killed another slave in a fit of rage. Choked him with the chains on his wrist. He threatened to kill more slaves unless we released him. Of course, I wasn't going to risk my entire load on a crazy man. We released him and I sent Fleance after the slave in secret. He came back with the man's head and I asked if he regretted killing him. He told me the slave had become one of the men he abhorred. From then on, Fleance stayed with my caravan, returning to the one who followed orders without question or complaint. Though I made sure it fell within his belief system."

"But why didn't you have Aldur watch over me?"

"Well, Aldur didn't want anything to do with you, at first. He thought you were turning me soft," Jaxon says, smiling. "He thought you'd change me."

Aya stares into Jaxon's blue eyes. Her mind flashes back to her village when she first met Jaxon. He'd only been the man in black armor, he'd been the cause of Elder Mircien's death. "Have I changed you?"

"Aldur's always been the only man who could ever read me. Elder Mirrah used to be the only woman who could ever read me. But I think that's changed, too."

Aya stands, ready to walk back to where Yme is sleeping. She hesitates, biting her bottom lip. "Promise me you'll sleep."

Jaxon doesn't answer her, but she doesn't wait. She knows by his droopy eyelids that he will. With the pain from his injuries gone, nothing is keeping the exhaustion at bay.

She walks back to Yme and lies down next to him. She presses her back against his and takes a deep breath, happy for the warmth.

"I'm sorry I didn't trust him before," Yme's voice whispers behind her. "I trust him now."

A knowing smile lights up Aya's face. "I knew you would eventually." She hears his soft laughter as her eyes close. She falls into a deep, peaceful sleep, free of the nightmares from the dark.

20

Birds sing loudly, their voices filling the forest with music. It's a familiar sound to Aya and yet new; different birds than those who used to wake her back in Foula Valley, but the same kind of warmth fills her.

Opening her eyes, Aya is greeted with the sight of Yme's peaceful, sleeping face. She carefully sits up, realizing quickly a blanket has been placed on her and Yme. She slips out from under it without disturbing Yme and stands. She glances across the clearing and sees a gentle mist flowing through the trees.

Dew shines on the grass and she sees most in the group have pulled out blankets to fight back the cool morning air. It's the first true calm the group has had in days and they're taking full advantage, sleeping without fear of a sudden attack.

Aya spies Jaxon asleep, lying under a thick blanket, a few feet from the tree he'd been propped against the night before. His armor is next to him, as well as his weapons. His face is calm and relaxed with a small smile at the corner of his lips.

Standing close to Jaxon, Aldur keeps his eyes to the trees. Aya wonders if he was the one who placed the blanket on Jaxon and helped him out of his armor. She sees Fleance and Mava asleep with their arms around one another and Aya laughs to herself. She wonders if Rava is aware of her sister's company.

Walking in the opposite direction of Jaxon and Aldur, Aya is surprised to see Dolus sleeping close to Skara and Tristan. She notices the two healers are sharing a blanket while Dolus sleeps beneath two.

Aya walks to the stream and splashes water on her face. The cold water shocks her body, but also refreshes. She looks deep into the forest at the morning sun shining through the trees. The early morning mist, slowly dissipating as the temperature rises, creates an ethereal vision of the forest.

Strange animals with antlers the color of ash move slowly through the trees. Their long necks lower to the ground as they feed on the grass. Occasionally, they dig into the dirt with their antlers, pulling up roots and seeds. Smaller animals follow, grabbing anything left by the larger beasts. The largest buck spots Aya staring at them and freezes, like a statue. The other animals continue moving forward and after realizing Aya poses no threat, the buck follows.

Aya waits until the animals disappear among the trees before slowly standing. Sounds travel along the gently blowing breeze and she hears low voices. She wades across the shallow water and into the forest.

"What's your problem, Kylii? You've been pissed at me for days, but you haven't explained to me why. You said we needed to talk, so let's talk." Daniil's voice sounds unusually heated.

"I said you needed to listen," Kylii grumbles.

Aya moves behind a thick tree closer to where the brothers are talking. She carefully peeks around the trunk. Kylii is sitting on the ground, leaning against a tree. Daniil is standing in front of him, Tanith lying at his side like a guard.

"Fine. I'm listening. Talk."

Kylii crosses his arms across his chest, reminding Aya of a pouting child. "Ick im na *falla* batter, Daniil-li?"

Daniil stares at his brother in surprise. "Really? You want to speak like that?"

"Ick im na *falla* batter, Daniil-li?"

Sighing, Daniil shrugs, his hands hitting the sides of his legs. "I'm the older brother. Why?"

"Iks im na falla batter's bo?"

"To protect the younger brother. What's the matter with you, Kylii-li?"

Kylii suddenly stands. Tanith jumps at his movement, her ears lowering against her head. "We are brothers. We're twins. We share everything. We even share our own language."

"Jei."

"Then why can't I *hear* her?" Kylii points to Tanith.

Tanith's ears perk up. Daniil looks down at her then up at his brother. "That's why you're so upset with me?"

Kylii looks hurt. "And you wonder why? We share *everything*, Daniil-li. Daniil-li o Kylii-li pomised to faways garet achinee. Everything! Now you share something with that beast that I can't understand. And it scares me."

"Isk?"

"What if you start having other things we can't share?"

Daniil laughs. "There are going to be things we can't share. That's life, Kylii-li."

"I don't want there to be anything we can't share! We promised!"

"I already told you, Tanith is sorry you can't hear her voice. She can only link with one person at a time."

"We are the same person!"

Daniil raises a finger at Kylii, anger filling his face. "No! No, we're not. You know that."

Kylii sits back down against the tree, glaring at Daniil. The air steadily grows warmer. "I still don't understand why she can't speak to me, too."

Daniil walks to his brother. Tanith stands to follow, but Daniil stops her. She freezes and watches the two curiously. Daniil sits down next to Kylii. "It's the limit of her magic. You know what that means. You know it can't be broken. If it is, the consequences can be high." As he speaks, the air fills with a cool breeze, calming the heat.

"It's still not fair."

"Magic isn't that great at being fair."

Tanith cautiously walks closer. She keeps her head low and her ears against her head, submissive. She nudges Kylii's foot, softly. Kylii stares into her white eyes.

"She says, she understands your concern. She knows what it's like to have someone you love and trust completely. She doesn't want to come between us and wishes you to know once we've reached land close to her home, she'll leave. She only wishes for you to trust her as you trust your brother," Daniil says. Tanith huffs at Daniil. "Okay, I added the part about trusting your brother."

Kylii reaches his hand out to Tanith and she carefully moves forward. She presses her snout into his hand. He strokes her red scales and sighs loudly. "Fine. But no secrets! I want to know everything she says. Especially about me."

Smiling, Daniil grabs his brother roughly around the neck. He wrestles him to the ground, and both laugh.

Aya smiles, happy to see her worries, like Yme said, were unfounded. She carefully stands to leave, but steps on a stick. The sound draws the brothers' attention to her, and they quickly separate.

"Aya!" Kylii's cheek flush red. "How long have you been there?"

Aya timidly steps out from behind the tree and walks up to the two. "Sorry, I heard everything."

"Were we being too loud?" Daniil asks.

"No. Everyone else is still asleep. I only heard you because I was by the stream," Aya says. Tanith approaches her and rubs her nose against Aya's hand. Aya leans down to pet her behind the ear. "What language were you speaking just now? Is it your home language?"

The two brothers eye each other, a conversation happening with only a look. Aya feels embarrassment rising inside her. "What? Did I say something wrong?"

Daniil's face flushes, matching his brother. "We were speaking in our own language. When we were little, we created it in secret. Because of our magic we were always treated like outsiders."

Kylii's brows furrow and a frown forms on his lips. "Because we were twins, we were treated like outsiders."

"What? Why?" Aya asks. "In Oula Village, twins were a sign of good luck."

"In our village, twins were a sign of troubled times to come," Kylii says, his voice shaking with anger. "Something which proved true when our home was destroyed and our mother among those killed."

Daniil rests a calming hand on his brother's shoulder. "After we were taken to the Arena, it became the only way for us to feel safe. We refused to talk to anyone and only communicated in our language."

"Until Yme came along. He encouraged us to be more...outspoken."

A horn blast tears through the forest silencing the three. Their eyes immediately move to the trees and search for the source. Daniil and Kylii ready for an attack, raising their hands in front of them while Aya grips the handle of her knife. Tanith sniffs the air and looks at Daniil.

"Tanith doesn't sense anyone nearby. We should head back to the group, just in case."

Quickly, the four move through the trees as a second horn blast shakes the surrounding air. They splash loudly across the stream, seeing members of the group, woken by the horn, searching the area in confusion. Jaxon is already standing, his sword drawn, and scanning the forest.

Yme is on his feet, searching the group. When he sees Aya and the brothers, he rushes towards them. "Are you all right?"

"We're fine. But where is that horn coming from?" Kylii asks.

A third bellowing horn blast fills the forest, and the group moves closer together in fear. Jaxon quickly dons his armor, his eyes searching the canopies. The deafening silence following the third horn blast creates an uneasy feeling in the group. Weapons are drawn and magic is gathered.

The horn cuts through the air so suddenly, many in the group jump or scream. They ready for an attack, but there's no movement in the forest. Jaxon slowly lowers his weapon and listens. The horn rings out again.

"It isn't moving," Jaxon says under his breath. "It doesn't sound any closer than the other blasts."

"What does that mean?" Aya asks.

Another horn sounds and Jaxon signals for Aldur and Fleance to put their weapons away. "It's a signal. Someone wants us to follow it."

"Someone? Who?" Yme asks.

"We won't know until we find them."

"What if it's a trap? Maybe Klaeon beat us here and is trying to lure us out?" Kylii asks.

Jaxon shakes his head. "There's no possible way he could have beaten us here. Going through the caves is the fastest path. Whoever is sending that signal is from this side of the mountains."

"Even if it isn't Klaeon, is it still safe to follow it?" Yme asks.

Eyes turn to Aya and she frowns with uncertainty. She looks to Jaxon and he gently nods. "We don't really have a choice," she says. "If they're sending us a signal, let's answer it and see what we're up against."

21

The group gathers their belongings and follows the sound of the horn. As they move deeper into the forest the surrounding trees grow larger and thicker, towering above the group. The enormity of the tree trunks makes them feel as though they're shrinking.

Aya stares at the massive trunks in awe. She remembers an old tree by her village she used to climb as a child. It had been too wide for her to wrap her arms around and Elder Mircien used to tell her the tree was over one hundred ages old. These trees are far thicker and reach higher than the Arena's walls.

How old is this forest?

Jaxon stops the group after walking several hours. Progressively, the horn had been growing louder as they moved through the forest, but the past thirty minutes had been silent. The horn had stopped, having completed its task in leading the group.

A thick collection of trees blocks the path forward. These trees grow so close together the trunks intertwine as they grow.

The largest tree has a tunnel carved into its thick trunk. Bright sunlight is seen at the end of the tunnel.

Approaching slowly, Jaxon searches the walls of the tunnel, touching the inside with his hands. "It's smooth. Man made."

"Amazing," Aya gasps.

"There's no other way around and only one path through," Jaxon speaks, turning to the group. "If it's a trap, we won't be able to escape."

The group shifts nervously, gazing upwards at the dark wood of the trees. The wall created by the thick trunks hides any view of what lies beyond.

"We've come this far, might as well keep going," Yme says.

The group cautiously enters the tunnel, hands hovering over weapons. The darkness of the tunnel and the closeness of the walls remind many of the caves. Nerves rise and the group moves closer together.

They emerge from the other side of the long tunnel to see a depression of land, making a bowl shape. Surrounding the bowl are tall, white trees. They create a protective wall, keeping the city at the center safe.

The city is made of white stone and fills the bowl-shaped valley. The size of it is awe-inspiring, especially in the midst of such an ancient forest. There are no trees in the city, only stone and buildings. Three levels divide it, but there is no evidence of what each level houses. The buildings all look the same, made from the same white stone.

A tall tower takes up the center of the city. It's the largest building in the city in height as well as overall size. Balconies and windows cover the tower, representing different floors, but it is the top of the tower that is the most intriguing. The top of the tower is made entirely of a bright blue stone glowing with the light of the sun.

Two triumphant horn blasts from the tower send more

chills through the group, as they stand awe-struck at the sight before them. The city glows with the sunlight and the movement of people amongst the white stone seems unreal.

Jaxon tears his eyes from the city and smiles at Aya, Yme, and the rest of the group. "Shall we go?"

Without responding, the group walks forward. They tread carefully down the hillside leading into the valley and another sight appears before them. A wide river crosses between them and the city, disappearing into odd-shaped caves in the hillsides to the left and right. A bridge crossing the river, made of the same stone as the city, provides them passage.

Many in the group stare around at the tall white trees towering above the city like walls. The tree with the tunnel they came through stands out with its darker bark but is reminiscent of a great door.

The bridge is wide and allows the group to spread out and take in the approaching city. The stone is unlike anything Aya has ever seen. She walks close to the edge of the bridge, her fingers tracing the carved railings. The stone is smooth to the touch and, though it is white, reflects light without blinding the observer.

The river flowing beneath the bridge is alive with fish and other small aquatic creatures. Aya even sees plant life waving beneath the water. Along the banks, men and women are throwing nets into the rushing water. The nets are tied to poles, some located on the banks while others are placed in the water. Several of the fishermen wade into the water to secure the nets and take in others that are full of fish. Others wait on the banks with hooked poles, ready to grab the heavy nets and help pull them to shore. When their eyes catch sight of the group crossing the bridge, they stop to watch. Some wave, friendly smiles on their faces. A few in the group wave back, eagerly.

The horn sounds again, giving two quick, triumphant

blasts. Aya jumps at the noise and turns to see a large group of people gathering at the far end of the bridge. Most are curious spectators, having ventured from their homes to see the new arrivals. They wear clothes that are light, in color and material, and several carry baskets of food or other things. Children cling to their mothers in a childlike mix of fear and excitement.

Standing in front of the gathering gawkers is a line of men and women wearing plain, gray hooded cloaks. Blue brooches at their necks are the only splashes of color on their clothes. A couple wear the hoods up, but most keep them down, showing their long hair.

A solitary figure standing in front of the cloaked men and women wears a cloak of white and gold with intricate blue embroidery. He is the oldest among the cloaked group, white hair resting at his shoulders and beard cut cleanly just below the chin. His piercing green eyes are full of youth, though the lines around them reflect the wisdom gained by many years of life. His hands are crossed in front of him as the group approaches and rings on his middle fingers echo the green of his eyes.

A smile grows on his thin lips as the group comes to a stop before him, and he looks at each member of the group as he speaks. "We welcome you, travelers, to our home, Eraunel. We have been expecting you." His voice is strong, but kind. A slight rasp is the only tinge of age to reach it.

His green eyes come to rest on Aya. "Especially you, Life Healer."

Aya meets his gaze with a surprised look, but before she can respond he continues, moving his eyes through the group. "I am Wynsil, the overseer of this city. We have prepared rooms for you as well as supplies you may need to complete your journey."

Wynsil turns to the cloaked men and women. He nods his head, and they bow before heading into the city. Most of the people who came to see the newcomers open the path for the cloaked ones before wandering away to continue their day's chores.

Aya steps forward before Wynsil has a chance to follow the cloaked ones. "How do you know about our journey? About us?"

Turning back to her, Wynsil motions his hand towards the tower at the center of the city. "We'll talk soon. Come." He walks on without looking back to see if the group follows.

The remaining crowd bows their heads at Wynsil and leaves. The group focuses on Aya and she looks to Jaxon. He shrugs his shoulders.

Yme steps close to Aya. "Seems odd, but I don't think they intend to harm us."

"I don't think so either." Aya hesitates before following Wynsil. The group follows, hesitant at first, but afraid to be left behind.

They enter the city, passing homes and workshops, feeling the eyes of the people on them as they walk, but it is curiosity, not a desire to do them harm. Curiosity for what Aya thinks must be the first group of outsiders the city has seen in many ages. The people stand at their windows, doors, or out on the streets to see the group pass. Children, possibly too young to remember ever seeing outsiders, pull at their parents' clothing to ask questions.

The first level of the city is mainly made of homes and workshops. Smoke from the workshops blows away from the city, but there is no noticeable difference in quality of living as compared to the other levels. Wynsil leads the group to a large tunnel with stairs leading up to the second level. Climbing the stairs, the group marvels at the blue stones lighting the tunnel.

The second level is also made of homes, but instead of workshops there are outdoor and indoor shops. The houses, however, are the same as the first level homes. Other buildings become apparent as the group walks through the streets of the second level. Multiple buildings have older children inside reading and writing, others have tables made of stone where people sit to talk or eat meals together, and wells are spread out through the streets. Some have spouts with continuously flowing water falling into grates that people walking by stop to drink.

Wynsil leads them through the second level of the city to another large tunnel with stairs. When they reach the top and enter the third level of the city, the difference is striking. There are fewer homes and more open areas with fountains or standing pools of water. Most who walk around wear the gray cloaks and look at the group with blank stares.

The tower fills a majority of the level. As with the city the tower is clearly divided into multiple levels, the lower being the largest. Stairs surround the entirety of the tower base, leading up to a balcony like entrance. Doors are spread around the tower, some open while others remain closed.

"You will be staying here in the main building. We have reserved rooms for your group. How you divide up is for you to decide," Wynsil explains as the group climbs the set of stairs and enters one of the open doors.

"This is quite a large building. What exactly goes on inside?" Jaxon asks.

Wynsil glances at Jaxon and a strange light fills his eyes, but it's gone as quickly as it appears. "I would humbly suggest you all eat, rest, and wash. Our talk can wait until after you have settled in."

Gasps of amazement escape the lips of the group as they enter the main hall of the tower. It's an immense room with a grand staircase leading up to the next floor. Tapestries hang on the walls, gently moving as a breeze moves through the tower. Aya stares at the symbols on the large cloth pieces with shock. She's seen the symbols before in her nightmares. She also saw them at the Blood Fall Arena. Blood King Klaeon enjoyed the odd symbols. Jaxon had told her they were from a dead language. Is it possible the ones here know it?

Doorways under the staircase lead into a library. The doors are open wide, and men and women are seen reading. Even from the main hall, Aya can see the library is multiple stories high and a large window allows sunlight to fill the room.

The floor of the main hall is a mosaic of a large tree with

roots reaching towards the many doorways. At the top center of the tree, blue stones create a circle with lighter blue streaks snaking away from it.

Aya feels magic emanating from the blue stones, the same magic she's felt ever since they set eyes on the forest. Aya spies a woman staring at her from under the stairs. The woman is in shadow, but Aya can still see the blue light in her eyes and the shockingly white of her hair.

Stopping on top of the blue circle at the center of the main hall, Wynsil turns to the group as two cloaked men approach him. "Please take this time to rest and acquaint yourselves with our tower. Tomorrow, we will speak."

The cloaked figure to Wynsil's right lowers his hood. His violet eyes take in the group with an odd clarity for such a young face. His sandy brown hair falls over his brow messily, being shifted by the movement of his hood. An odd, circular scar sits above his right brow. He bows his head at Aya and Yme, his stare seemingly piercing through them.

"Until then, please follow Lyrrel and the other Seers to your lodgings," Wynsil says, quickly making his way into the library.

Jaxon's breath catches in his throat. "Seers?"

Lyrrel and the two other cloaked men move forward. "If you will follow us, we have quite a few floors to ascend before we reach your rooms," Lyrrel says, his voice soothing to the ear.

The group follows, but Aya notices Jaxon staring after Wynsil with suspicion in his eyes. She nudges his arm with her elbow, and he quickly looks at her.

"Are you all right?" she asks.

"Fine," Jaxon responds, his tone strained. "Eager to speak with Wynsil."

"I'm eager to get some warm food in my stomach," Kylii

says. He, Daniil, and Tanith walk past Aya and Jaxon to follow the cloaked men.

"I'm eager for Kylii to wash up. He stinks," Daniil fake whispers to Aya.

Kylii grabs his brother's head with his arm. "Shut your mouth. You smell just as badly as me."

Daniil begins fake coughing and struggles against Kylii's arm. "Oh gods! The smell!"

"You both smell horrible," Yme interrupts. "Now come on, we're falling behind."

Aya, Jaxon, and the brothers follow Yme. The stairs clear for the group as cloaked men and women move to the side or wait before descending or ascending the white stone steps. Aya glances over the railing to the mosaic floor below. She spies the same woman staring up at her from the circle of blue stones. Something about the blue light in her eyes sends a wave of uneasiness through Aya.

After climbing for several stories, Lyrrel and the other cloaked men finally lead the group down a hallway. A pair of double doors stands open and the smell of warm food drifts down the hall. The group whispers excitedly and picks up their pace.

The room is bright and filled with tables of food. Before the group can run to the delicious spread, Lyrrel blocks them.

"For your comfort this entire floor has been prepared for you. Bedrooms are located down the hall. Feel free to pick for yourself. Baths are located through those doors." Lyrrel points to two doors at the opposite end of the room. "I will be seeing to your group's needs. If you have any questions, we are here to help." He moves out of the path of the group and they run for the food.

"Are we permitted to leave this floor?" Jaxon asks.

Nodding his head, Lyrrel stares from Jaxon to Aya and then

to Yme. "You are not prisoners here. You may come and go from this tower as you like. Though we do kindly ask that you not disturb those who are studying." With that Lyrrel heads away from the three to speak with the cloaked men.

"Guess all we can do is eat," Aya says, her stomach rumbling its agreement.

23

After filling their stomachs with food, the group splits between the baths and their rooms. Yme, Aya, Jaxon, Kylii, and Daniil are among those who choose to bathe first.

Once clean, they split off. Jaxon wanders down to the library. Daniil, Kylii, and Tanith leave to explore the floor.

Aya finds a room with a small balcony overlooking the southern half of the city. There are two beds and Aya turns to Yme. "Willing to share a room with me?"

Glancing around the room, Yme shrugs his shoulders. "We seem to keep being placed together."

"You're not being placed here. I'm asking if you want to sleep here." Aya realizes what she's said and turns away before Yme can see the rush of blood on her cheeks.

She walks to the balcony and looks down at the city. She sees many of the people of Eraunel milling about, but her heart hammers in her chest as she stands against the railing. *The top of Bloodfall Arena wasn't this high. How can anyone build things so tall?*

Yme walks to stand beside her. He leans on the railing,

unafraid of the height. "I'm more comfortable with someone in the room. I don't think I could get any sleep if I was alone."

"If I had spent as many ages with Daniil and Kylii as you did, I think I'd prefer the silence," Aya jokes.

A smile grows on Yme's lips but fades quickly. "Without them, I wouldn't have survived Klaeon's Arena."

"You're the only one who never calls him Blood King."

Yme spits. "He's no king. There hadn't been kings in these lands for centuries before him. He's a man who wants power. All men who know forbidden magic want power."

"In my village, we didn't even know there was a king. I can't imagine what it must have been like living under his rule."

Gripping the railing, Yme glares at the ground below. "He's been self-proclaimed king since before I was born. No one ever questioned his rule. Even when his men occasionally terrorized us."

Sensing his growing anger, Aya thinks of a way to change the conversation. "What was your home like? Was it like the city around the Arena?"

"No," Yme turns to her, his eyes lightening. "It had trees like those in Jaxon's village, but they bore the sweetest fruit. We lived next to the sea beneath a sleeping volcano. Plants grew quickly because of the rich soil. My grandfather used to tell me our ancestors were from an island in the middle of the sea. But one day they saw smoke along the horizon. They chose to follow it and discovered a beach of black sand. When they reached the volcano, it fell asleep and they tended the earth until plants grew. The ocean provided fish and plentiful rains gave drinking water until wells were dug. Then the first magic user of the village was born. An earth elemental mage. Then more were born. Water mages, air mages, and once in a genera-tion a fire mage. For generations we lived beneath the volcano and became a town well known in the region for our fish and our mages."

Yme's expression grows dark and he clenches his fists. "Then Klaeon came into power. At first, he sent his men out to villages, towns, and cities in his proclaimed domain to terrorize the people into submission. Once they pledged their loyalty, the terror stopped. He provided protection and encouraged trade. As long as we obeyed his decrees, our town flourished. But it didn't stop his men from mistreating us. They routinely stole our food, water, and money. Naysayers would be forced to eat rotten fish as the soldiers laughed. If anyone used their magic against them, their family would be executed as traitors to the king."

His expression relaxes, but his fists remain clenched. "I was the first in my family to be born with magic. I say born with magic, but it didn't appear until I was around nine years old. There were others in the village, but my magic was unique. Many can use one element, but to control them all is extremely rare. I used to help around the town and keep an eye on my younger sister. My parents were proud, but they warned me never to use my magic when the soldiers were in the village."

"One day, five of Klaeon's men attacked my sister while she was out picking berries. They beat her until she couldn't fight back or scream for help. Then they..."

"Villagers found her body in the bushes, left for the animals. When I found out, I became inconsolable. I went after the men, against my family's wishes. I promised myself I wouldn't use my magic, to protect my family. But when I found them, I couldn't beat them with physical strength alone. Something snapped inside of me."

Voices from a balcony below surprise Yme. He backs into the room and hits one of the beds, sitting on it. Aya walks inside the room and closes the balcony doors before sitting beside him.

"What happened?" Aya asks, softly.

Yme's eyes grow distant and he shakes his head. "They taunted me with details of how they violated my sister. I killed all but one of them with my magic. I burned one alive, crushed another in the earth, tore one apart with wind, and drowned another by forcing water down his throat. I told the lone survivor to return to Klaeon and tell him to leave our town alone. If he didn't, I would kill every soldier that came even within the farthest border. The survivor hurried back to Klaeon and several days later more men appeared in our town. I kept my promise and killed each one. Klaeon arrived soon after. He asked the town who was the one killing his men. I naively thought they wouldn't give him my name. They gave him my family claiming all of us were traitors. He offered my parents a deal, hand me over or suffer my punishment.

"I was still a stupid, young boy then and without thinking attacked Klaeon. He easily defeated me and, to make an example of me, took away my fire magic, then ordered me to be taken to the Arena to die in the games. He thought taking my magic would destroy my spirit, but it made me stronger. I vowed to survive every fight. I vowed to someday kill Klaeon as revenge for my sister and return to my family."

Swallowing the growing lump in her throat, Aya allows the tears to roll down her cheeks. "And that's when you met Daniil and Kylii."

Yme takes a deep, shaky breath. "They took a liking to me and helped me with my first few fights. But eventually I didn't need their help. I could kill any man placed before me."

"Do you... enjoy killing?" Aya asks.

Yme's breath catches in his throat and he shakes his head. "I do what I have to in order to survive."

Wiping the tears from her eyes, Aya sniffs. "I understand."

"The only ones who know about my past are Daniil and Kylii. It's nice to tell someone else who can understand."

"What was your sister's name?"

"Niya."

She's heard the name before. During the tournament in Bloodfall Arena. When she and Yme were forced to fight against two of Klaeon's soldiers. One used magic to create illusions. While Yme was trapped in an illusion, he'd said Niya. And after the soldier died, Yme had been filled with intense rage. Now Aya knew what the soldier had shown Yme.

"Niya means night sky in the language of my ancestors. Her hair and eyes were the deepest black, like the night," Yme says.

"What does Yme mean?" Aya asks. Yme's face goes blank and then an embarrassed smile forms on his lips. Aya sees his cheeks flush and laughs. "What?"

"Sweet fruit."

"Sweet fruit?"

Yme nods. They stare at each other for a moment before laughter explodes from Aya's lips. The flush on Yme's cheeks fills his entire face making Aya laugh harder. She falls off the bed, forcing a small scream from her that brings a fit of laughter to Yme. After what feels like ages of laughing, both calm down and Yme helps Aya back onto the bed.

"I'm sorry. Sweet fruit just doesn't seem to fit with Bloodfall Arena's champion fighter," Aya explains, emphasizing each word with her hands.

"It was my grandfather's name. Most don't even know the meaning behind our names anymore, but he loved the old stories." He turns to her. "Did you ever ask your parents if your name meant anything?"

Aya's smile falters. She shakes her head. "They didn't talk much about their pasts. Though my mother told me my name meant something precious to them." She sees the realization in Yme's face. He'd forgotten her parents were dead.

"I'm sorry."

"It's fine. A lot has happened, and I don't expect you to remember everything I've said to you."

"I remember the name of your village. Oula. But you didn't really talk about the people," Yme says.

"The people in my village were wonderful people. Iria taught me about traditional healing long before my magic appeared. Elder Mircien treated me like family after my parents died. She was the only one who saw me for more than my magic."

"You still have them to go back to."

"Mircien was killed when Jaxon's men attacked my village. I don't think Iria will ever recover from losing her."

Yme turns away. "I should stop talking. I'm making things worse."

24

Yme clears his throat. "So, when you heal someone, what does it feel like?"

Aya stares at him in surprise. "You really want to know?"

"As someone who has been healed by you multiple times, yes. I would like to know."

"I don't know if I can explain it properly," Aya says.

"Try."

"It gathers here." She touches her chest, over her heart. "And when I'm healing someone, I send it into them. I feel warmth flow from my chest, down my arms, and into whoever it is. I direct the warmth where it needs to go, and it heals them. I see the wound and if I know how to fix it, I fix it."

"If you don't know how to fix it?" Yme asks.

Hesitating, Aya remembers how she knew to heal Rava's illness, Paki's broken leg, and the many other injuries she had never healed before doing so the first time. "I think my magic guides me. If I let it explore the injury or whatever needs healing, it shows me what to do."

"And what about when someone is close to death?"

Aya furrows her brow. "I feel their warmth disappearing. I send my warmth, my magic to bring it back, but if they're too far gone it takes away my own warmth. I think it could kill me. If I could find someone to teach me, maybe someday I could bring someone back from the farther reaches of death, but I don't know what the cost would be to me."

"All magic has a cost," Yme says. "When I first used my magic, the toll it took on my body was intense. I passed out for three days. If I overuse my magic, sometimes it feels like something else takes over and by the end, all the strength in my body is gone."

"The illness that took my parents, Iria believed it had to do with their magic. He believed if I used too much of my magic over my lifetime, the illness would attack me, too." Aya plays with the silk bracelet on her wrist. "Every time I heal, I wonder if I'll feel the illness coming on."

Yme places a hesitant, comforting hand on her leg. "Your parents survived whatever happened to Life Healers. I'm sure others did, too. If we can find them, I'm sure they'll know how to stop the illness."

Smiling, Aya touches Yme's hand. "What does your magic feel like?"

Yme holds up his free hand, staring at it as though the answer is written on it. "Each one feels different." He reaches his hand out in front of him. "When I use my air magic, it sort of feels like an extension from my body, like the air reaches out and moves everything around me."

He places his hand on his thigh, rubbing it. "Earth feels like it comes from my legs. I feel it below me, even better if I'm not wearing shoes. When I open the earth it's like I can shift all of it. If I wanted, maybe I could make mountains or split the earth into new lands." He places his hand on his stomach. "Water... water is my favorite to use, but not for fighting. It feels like my whole body is controlling it. I feel the water in my body telling the water around me what to do."

He pauses.

"What about fire?" Aya asks.

Yme's eyes dart back and forth as his mind searches for the words. He sighs and lowers his hand. "I remember the first time I used my fire magic. It scared the hell out of me. My sister and I were walking through the forest by our town and a wild lurgen attacked us."

"Lurgen?"

"They're little, four-legged animals that our villagers some-times kept as pets. But this one was mad, feral. It tried to bite my sister. When I tried to stop it, fire erupted from my hand. I didn't know exactly what happened, but the lurgen was gone. Niya had to tell me over and over that fire shot out of my hand before I believed her. I tried to do it again but couldn't. As I practiced more and more, I realized the secret. The difference between fire magic and the others was I didn't need a physical source nearby. I could create it myself. I don't know exactly how, but it's similar to your healing magic."

Yme takes Aya's hand in his and places it on his chest. "I feel the fire here, in my heart. I need to use my other magic to bring it out. It's like they all work together somehow to bring the fire in my heart into the real world."

Aya stares at her hand on Yme's chest. She feels his heart beating beneath her palm. Her own heart flutters and she pulls her hand away slowly. "What... what did it feel like when the Blood King took your fire away?"

Anger flashes across Yme's face and he leans forward. "It's a horrible feeling. His power rips your magic from inside of you. I could feel my other magic trying to keep my fire from being taken, but nothing could stop it."

"When we defeat him, we'll get your fire back."

"If we beat him."

"Of course, we will. We're going to find that city in the cliffs, we'll get an army larger and more powerful than his, and we'll win."

Yme laughs. "You sound very sure."

She nudges him with her elbow. "I know it will happen. We rare kinds have to stick together." She smiles.

Yme returns the smile. "We should sleep. We don't know what tomorrow is going to be like."

"I have a feeling, there's going to be a lot of talking," Aya says, falling back on the bed. "You were very calm about us just walking into this unknown city."

Yme leans over to look in her eyes. "Any city this hidden doesn't have anything to do with Klaeon. He's a bit of a showoff."

"I hadn't noticed," Aya says, sarcastically.

25

"**A**re you ready to meet with Wynsil?" Lyrrel asks.

The group sitting at the table, eating breakfast, stares at the soft-spoken man in surprise. None heard him approach.

Aya swallows her mouthful of food and stands. "I'm ready."

Jaxon stands next. "We were ready yesterday. We have many questions for him."

Lyrrel bows his head, ignoring Jaxon. "Then follow me."

"Tanith, do you want to go back to our room?" Daniil asks the Khorgoi sitting on the floor next to him. She looks at him and chirps. "Fine. Outside then. But don't bring me another dead animal."

Lyrrel watches Tanith saunter out of the dining room. "Who will be accompanying the Life Healer and Elemental Mage?"

"Just these three. That's all." Aya motions to Jaxon and the brothers.

Lyrrel's left eyebrow twitches before he nods his head and leaves the room. The group of five follows quickly. Lyrrel leads them up two flights of stairs before heading down long hallways past many rooms. In one, Aya sees a group of men and women in cloaks meditating in silence. In another, a group of children study thick books and speak with the cloaked woman at the front of the room.

Aya quickens her pace to walk next to Lyrrel. "Is this a school for magic users?"

"Yes. More specifically, this is a school for Seers. However, on the lower floors we do offer educational classes for those without magic. And we have a few teachers who venture out into the city. Education is important, even for those who choose to work with their hands." Lyrrel turns his head slightly to glance at Jaxon. "Or those who choose more...physical paths."

Aya sees Jaxon tense, but he stays silent.

They go up more stairs, reaching the top of the final set of stairs after nearly five minutes of climbing. The only room located on the final floor is behind a set of large, silver double doors. Lyrrel opens the large doors with ease and ushers the group into the circular room.

The room is two stories. Stairs lead up to the second story where cloaked men and women stand as though guarding. The ceiling is made entirely of glass, allowing sunlight to fill the room. But it's the large blue stone that grabs Aya's attention. It hangs in the air, casting blue light as the sun's rays shine through it. Chains are wrapped around the immense stone and Aya sees pulleys hanging from the walls.

Can they raise and lower that thing?

Opposite the double doors is a large balcony overlooking the city. There aren't any doors, allowing a breeze to always pass through the room.

At the center of the room is a clear stone standing almost two men high, glowing with the light shining from the blue stone above. Around the clear stone is a U-shaped table with a number of chairs. The opening of the U is facing an elegant chair where Wynsil is sitting.

The group walks slowly forward. Aya glances at the clear stone at the center of the room and a strange vibration moves through her body. She shudders and moves closer to Yme.

Lyrrel stands beside Wynsil, his hands resting at his sides. Wynsil motions the group forward. "You all look well-fed and rested. Come closer so we may talk normally."

As the five move closer, cloaked men and women appear seemingly from nowhere and place chairs before Wynsil for them to sit. They do and the men and women disappear.

"Thank you for showing us such generosity. But how did you know we would be coming?" Yme asks.

"And how do you know about us?" Aya leans forward curiously.

Wynsil smiles. "We foresaw your arrival many weeks ago." He motions his hand to Lyrrel. "Our Seers are very skilled."

Jaxon moves to the edge of his seat, his expression darkening. "Seers. You mean those who can see into the future."

"Yes and no. Our Seers can foresee the future, but not in the way you think. They see the different branches, or paths, the future may take and the probability of said path occurring. They have also seen your pasts and the choices you have all made on your journeys to reach Eraunel."

Aya sees the reactions around her. Daniil and Kylii share a nervous look, fear filling their expressions. Yme and Jaxon tense at Wynsil's words, their breaths catching in their throats.

"You say you've seen our futures," Aya asks, meeting Wynsil's eyes without fear. "Does that mean you know whether or not we will be successful in defeating Blood King Klaeon?"

Wynsil looks at Lyrrel, who avoids his ruler's gaze. "Our

Seers have struggled to see what your actions may lead to. Some things even magic likes to keep a surprise."

"So, you are not a Seer?" Jaxon asks.

"No, the overseer of Eraunel shall never be a Seer," Lyrrel says, a hint of anger in his voice.

Wynsil raises his hand and Lyrrel regains his composure. "It's normal that as a Seer ages his or her mind deteriorates with each vision until they succumb to complete madness."

Surprise fills Aya. It sounds so similar to the illness that took her parents' life. That could one day take her own.

"We have yet been unable to figure out a way to stop it from happening. Until then, only one of no magic may rule to prevent chaos," Wynsil continues.

"What do you do when a Seer shows signs of the madness?" Daniil asks.

"That is private business between Seers," Lyrrel answers. "And that is all that will be spoken of the matter."

A somber expression overcomes Wynsil's face. "There are few things we won't share with you if asked, but that is one thing we kindly ask you do not inquire about. It's a painful subject."

"Are all magic users of this city Seers?" Jaxon asks, steering the conversation towards something lighter.

"That is correct. Our ancestors fled into this forest for protection many centuries ago. A ruthless ruler went on a rampage, killing many in the north. Our ancestors learned to live off the forest's many resources while being careful not to disrupt the beasts and plant life. Several generations passed before the first Seer was born and learned the truth of his magic."

Aya places a hand on her silk bracelet. "The truth of his magic?"

"The forest gives us our magic and in return we protect it

from the threat of others. Those who enter the forest with intent to harm it are quickly taken care of."

"How?"

Pointing to the clear stone at the center of the room, Wynsil smiles. "That is a spirit stone taken from the most sacred of grounds in the forest. It boosts our Seers' magic, allowing them to inhabit the spirits of the forest and chase away any who would do it harm. It also allows us to watch those who enter the forest without their awareness."

"That's how you knew to blow those horns of yours," Kylii says.

"We knew about your group arriving in our forest for many days, but when we finally saw you, we imagined you needed rest from your ordeal in the caves before making your way to Eraunel. I also determined following the sounds of horns would be a little less threatening than men suddenly appearing around you or voices in the trees urging you through the forest."

"Why are you helping us?" Kylii demands. Daniil hits him. "Ow! I'm just curious! You said you've seen our pasts. How do you know you can trust us?"

"Because we are meant to help you. Because you are the only ones who can stop the great evil growing in this land."

Yme shifts uncomfortably in his seat. "Great evil?"

"The one you call Blood King."

"He may be a ruthless dictator, but great evil seems like a stretch," Daniil says.

Wynsil's green eyes lock onto Aya and her breath catches in her throat. "What else would you call a man who eliminates entire branches of magic?"

"Eliminates entire branches of magic?" Aya asks. "What do you mean?"

"It's as I say," Wynsil answers. "Klaeon is responsible for many branches of magic disappearing."

"That doesn't make sense. No branches have been completely erased," Yme interjects. "At least, I haven't heard of any."

"We have," Daniil says, bluntly.

Kylii clenches his fists and glares at the floor. "Our hometown was burned to the ground. Every man, woman, and child were taken prisoner and never heard from again."

"They weren't taken to Bloodfall Arena. They simply disappeared... because of their magic," Daniil adds.

"But your magic wasn't wiped out," Yme argues.

"Our magic wasn't what our hometown was known for." Daniil looks at Wynsil, discomfort clear on his face. "The people of our town were gem mages."

"Gem mages? I've never heard of that magic."

"You wouldn't have. It's not found south of the Great Mountains," Wynsil says.

You'd have to ask those singing. Kylii and I aren't from these lands. When Daniil said those words to Aya that first night in the Arena, she didn't even notice. Or maybe she assumed he meant they weren't from Bloodfall.

"It was one of the last towns the Blood King sent soldiers to before the other lands threatened retaliation." Lyrrel shrugs his shoulders. "Though he didn't stop wiping out branches south of the mountains."

A dark thought crosses Aya's mind. The way Wynsil and Lyrrel's eyes constantly flash to her as they speak makes a knot form in her stomach. "I've got a bad feeling you're going to say something horrible."

"I don't believe we need to say anything. You understand the implication, I'm sure," Wynsil says.

"Life Healers. Klaeon is the one who wiped them out."

"They were the first branch of magic to truly be eliminated." Wynsil stands and walks towards her. "Or, so many thought. You survived. Or to be more precise, your parents survived."

"But why eliminate entire branches of magic?" Daniil asks.

"I can't speak for many, but the Life Healers were a threat."

"He felt threatened by healers?" Aya asks. "How?"

"Life Healers were rare before the Blood King sought them out. Old stories claimed they could turn the very tides of war. An army whose soldiers never stayed dead? That power was feared by many. In response, Life Healers chose isolation," Wynsil says, stopping in front of Aya.

"Didn't work very well," Kylii says. Daniil elbows him in the side.

"Even if there are no more Life Healers, Aya could potentially give birth to more."

A blush fills Aya's cheeks. "Why would Klaeon care about that?"

"It is ingrained in his blood. To understand why, you must first understand where he came from."

Jaxon crosses his arms across his chest and shakes his head. "No one knows where he came from. Most stories claim he came from a tiny village in the Karrion Desert. When his magic revealed itself, he destroyed the village and disappeared deep into the desert. He reappeared much later with an army and took over the land."

Wynsil stares at Jaxon with a disinterested expression. "A nice story to keep the truth away."

Lyrrel pulls a parchment from his pocket and crosses to Aya. She takes it from his hand, confused. "What's this?"

"The true story of the Blood King is hard to find, unless one knows where to look." A smile fills Wynsil's face and he winks at Jaxon.

Jaxon quickly turns away. "What's on it, Aya?"

Aya unravels the paper and scans the contents curiously. A drawing of a strange village fills the page. The buildings are windowless and constructed oddly, as though purposefully built at a slant. At the center of the village is a dark spot, a large hole. No buildings are built too close to the hole and even though it's only a drawing, Aya gets an unnerving feeling as she looks at the hole.

Lowering the parchment, Aya returns her gaze to Wynsil. "I don't understand."

"The Blood King is not from your lands. He is from lands much farther to the north. His village, depicted in that drawing by one of our Seers is located in a vastly different forest, one of dark spirits." Wynsil pauses and takes a deep breath. "Do you know why Blood Magic is forbidden?"

They shake their heads.

"It is an unnatural magic. One is not born with it inside them. You must earn it through a dark ritual. Those who dwell in that village choose one child each generation to perform the ritual. Normally, the child would then become ruler of the village. But Klaeon left."

Aya remembers the feeling of Klaeon's magic. How it felt unnatural and how it felt alive. "The magic told him to leave," she says softly. "It wanted to become stronger."

"Become stronger?" Yme asks.

"That's why he took your fire." Aya fights the fear growing inside of her. "The magic he steals from others, the magic of those who die in the Arena... he feeds it to the living magic inside of him."

Nodding his head, Wynsil returns to his seat. "He travelled to your lands because he heard of the many different kinds of magic found there, but mainly for the *rare kinds*, as he calls them. His magic wanted to feast on the powerful magic. That's also when he found the Life Healers."

"But why exterminate Life Healers? Why not enslave them or keep them alive for his own uses?" Daniil asks.

"I was getting to that. As Aya mentioned, Blood Magic is alive. When Klaeon killed his first Life Healer and fed the magic to his own, he learned something that terrified him. Life Healers are the only ones who can return him to a normal human. You, Aya, are the only one who can take his magic away. Permanently."

27

Aya stares down at the city from her room's balcony. Watching those below go about their day without worry reminds her of her village. She'd been like these people once. It feels so long ago she walked through her village and spoke with Elder Mircien for the final time. It had all been a false sense of safety, quickly and easily broken.

"Are you all right?" Yme asks from his bed. "You've been very quiet since the meeting with Wynsil."

Turning to him, Aya frowns. "If I take away his magic, like he took away yours, do I become like him?"

"What?"

"If I take Klaeon's magic away, what will it do to me? Will it only encourage others to fear Life Healers if they believe we... I can take magic from others."

Sitting up, Yme shakes his head. "You're nothing like him. He steals magic. You heal. His magic is something that shouldn't be in anyone's control. Wynsil didn't suggest you would keep it and use it. You would remove it from him and from this world."

"You don't know that. Even if you're right, others might not see it that way. In the Arena, I used my power to injure as well as heal. Once I crossed that line, however good the reason, others saw the potential for evil in me."

"Others don't matter. Klaeon needs to be stopped. You know that."

Aya walks to her bed and sits, facing away from Yme. "But what happens after we stop him? Do I take his place? Do we? Does someone even more terrifying rise up? Or…"

"Or what?"

"Will fighting Klaeon continue the cycle of fear?"

Aya hears Yme shift on his bed. "What cycle of fear?"

"I've been thinking about it. With so many magic users, how could Klaeon possibly come into power without any form of resistance?" Aya asks.

"There was resistance," Yme starts, spitting the words out angrily.

"After he came into power. But how did he amass enough support to easily take over?" Aya waits for Yme's answer, but he remains silent. "Klaeon preyed on people's most basic emotion. Fear. He built up fear of what magic users could potentially do to those without it."

"People aren't afraid of magic users. They're afraid of Klaeon, who, if you don't remember, is a magic user."

Aya remembers the expressions of those from her village. She remembers the borderline idolatry and fear they showed her after she healed a young boy's broken leg. She also remembers the audience in the arena rooting for the magic users to be killed and Yme's own story about the people in his village turning on him.

"He's presented himself as a magic user who protects those who follow him from dangerous mages, like us. He's holding them hostage to a lie, but what if our actions make that lie appear true?"

"Which is why we have to stop him and show those people he's a monster," Yme says.

Aya slowly turns to him. "But if we just fight back, we'll only be proving his words correct in their eyes. It's like Elder Mirrah said. The people will only see us as the monsters. How do we gain their trust at the same time we remove the threat Klaeon poses?"

"Are you saying it's hopeless? You?" Yme asks in disbelief. "After all your talk of fighting together and putting trust in others?"

Aya takes a slow breath in. "No. But we have to think not just what needs to be done, but how we do it. I'm saying, things are a lot more complicated than I thought."

"Yes. They are." Yme stands, anger clear on his face. "But it's too late to stop now. More lives are at stake than yours or mine."

Aya stands. "I know that."

"Those people who followed us here, they didn't do it for me. They didn't do it for freedom. They did it for you. They did it because they believe you will stop Klaeon."

"I didn't ask them to believe in me."

"No one does!" Yme's yell fills the room with a heavy air. "Do you think I chose to be the star fighter of the arena? I was given that title and for some, my will to survive inspired them. I didn't choose to inspire them. I didn't *ask* for them to be inspired. But knowing it helped them survive a little while longer, I accepted it."

Anger rises in Aya. "You accepted it? Where was that acceptance when I arrived at the Arena? You, Daniil, and Kylii didn't care about anyone else. You let so many innocent fresh flesh die! Then you spouted bullshit about how *rare kinds stick together*, but truthfully, you didn't care about us either!"

Yme storms up to her, holding his finger up. "Don't you dare say I didn't care! You saw a few dozen die. I've witnessed hundreds! But what was I supposed to do? Save them all? How? Did you save everyone?"

"I tried!"

"You *tried*, but you didn't save everyone! And now, a handful of us have escaped. What about those who stayed behind? Lili? Géroux? Do you think Klaeon will make the Arena easier with his prize fighters gone?"

"We couldn't get to them—" Aya starts to say.

Not letting her finish, Yme moves close to her. "We didn't even try."

The words feel like a slap. Aya stares at Yme in shock. *He's right. We abandoned them all.*

The door to their room opens. Aya and Yme turn to see Daniil and Kylii walking in. Tanith follows, her ears lowered against her head.

"The entire floor can hear you two. What's going on?" Kylii asks.

"A discussion that got out of hand," Yme says, stepping away from Aya.

Aya looks from the brothers to Yme. Her breathing grows shallow and she hears pounding in her head. *The room is shrinking around me.* Panic fills her and she quickly walks towards the brothers. Confusion clear on their expressions, they separate to allow her to leave.

Clear of the room, Aya quickens her pace to a run. She passes the open doors of other rooms, seeing faces staring into the hallway. Concern and even a little fear are on many and Aya knows the words she and Yme spoke were overheard.

Running, Aya reaches stairs and runs down them, skipping

steps when the momentum overpowers her. She passes Seers and others in the halls, but to Aya they all appear as blurs. She reaches the bottom floor and runs outside. She runs around the tall tower, hoping anyone chasing after her would run straight out into the city.

Finally slowing her pace, Aya finds herself in a garden with flowers on stalks taller than her. She gasps for air and collapses to the ground. She quickly searches for anyone nearby, but upon seeing no one, she lets out a muffled cry.

A dark thought fills her mind as tears roll down her cheeks. *It's all my fault. Elder Mircien's death was my fault. Those lives I couldn't save in the Arena were my fault. Those we left behind... my fault!*

Aya cries, her hands holding her head. She watches the tears drip onto the dirt and leans forward. She rests her forehead on the ground and wraps her arms around herself. *I wish I could wake up back home. I wish this was all my nightmare. I'd never wish to leave the village again. Just please, make this all a nightmare.*

"Your wishes can never come to pass, Life Healer," a voice says.

Aya sits up quickly, staring at the figure in front of her. When she meets the woman's glowing blue eyes, the world around Aya spins and goes dark.

28

"So instead of comforting her about the life changing information we all heard, you yelled at her," Daniil says.

Yme glares Daniil, being careful not to lose his balance on the stairs. "There was more to it than that. We both said things the other didn't want to hear." Yme grabs the banister of the stairs before he nearly falls.

"Sounded to us like you said most of the things," Kylii says.

"We *both* said things."

Reaching the bottom floor, Yme searches the crowd for Aya. Seers stare at the three in confusion but continue to their destinations without slowing. Yme storms towards the library, nearly colliding with a group of young Seers. They move out of his way and watch the two brothers following with wide eyes.

Yme gazes around the large room. There are many in cloaks, but no Aya. Where else could she have gone? Outside? Turning around, Daniil and Kylii block his way. "We have to find her."

Daniil shrugs his shoulders. "Why? We're safe here. It's not like she's in trouble."

"She probably needs to let off some steam. Why chase after her? She'll come back." Kylii leans close to Yme, narrowing his eyes. "You're unusually caring."

Yme shoves his way past the brothers. "We may be safe here, but it's still a new place." He stops when he hears a small snicker behind him. He turns back to Kylii.

"Sounds more like... you don't want her to be upset with you."

"What?"

"Sounds like," Kylii smiles to his brother, "you *really* care about her."

"Of course, I—" Yme stops. *I care about her.* He turns away from Kylii and walks out of the library. He hears the brothers follow after him, laughing at his reaction. Yme spies a familiar face standing in the doorway leading outside.

"Lyrrel!"

The Seer turns his head at his name. When he sees Yme, he leans his head to the side. "I see you three are up and about. Is Aya not with you?"

"Yme here got into an argument with her and now she's run off. We wondered if you've seen her?" Daniil asks, patting Yme on the back.

Shaking his head, Lyrrel moves his hands behind his back. "I haven't seen her since your meeting with Wynsil. I'm sure she's fine. Eraunel is a safe city."

"That's what *we* said," Kylii mumbles.

"If you are truly worried about her, I could see where she is," Lyrrel says.

Yme steps closer to him. "It's that easy?"

"It's that easy."

"Kylii and I will do a quick look around outside," Daniil says, grabbing his brother and heading for the door. "Don't want to be a distraction." Kylii struggles against

Daniil's hold, but ultimately allows his brother to drag him away.

"It may take me a moment," Lyrrel says, bringing his hands in front of him. He draws a symbol in the air with his right hand. He clasps his hands together and closes his eyes.

Yme waits patiently. A few minutes pass and his nerves grow. *Should it be taking this long if this city is so safe?*

He notes those around him and realizes everyone is frozen. Every Seer is standing still, their arms hanging limp at their sides. Their eyes glow with an odd, blue light. Turning back to Lyrrel, Yme sees he is still in the same position. Though his clasped hands are now shaking slightly, his knuckles turning white as he grips tighter and tighter.

"Lyrrel?" Yme reaches his hand out to touch the Seer's shoulder.

"The Life Healer is safe." The seers standing around Yme and Lyrrel speak together, their voices echoing in the hall. They all turn to face Yme. "The Life Healer will be fine."

"Will be? Where is she?" Yme asks, looking at the dozens of faces staring at him.

"The Life Healer is safe."

"You say that, but forgive me if I don't believe you, mysterious voices."

"Yme!" Daniil's voice catches his attention.

"Whoa, what's with the creepy faces?" Kylii asks, the two brothers rushing to Yme's side. Daniil holds Aya's knife in his hand sending a chill through Yme.

"Did you find Aya?" Yme asks.

"No, but we found this on the ground outside." Daniil hands the knife to Yme. "There wasn't any sign of a struggle, but she wouldn't just leave this behind."

"Should we be worried about him?" Kylii motions towards Lyrrel.

The young seer's hands are still shaking and sweat rolls down his forehead. Yme cautiously approaches him. "Lyrrel?"

Blood rolls down Lyrrel's chin from him biting his lip too hard.

Yme grabs the seer's arms and shakes him. "Lyrrel! You can stop."

"I... can't," Lyrrel gasps. "It won't... let me."

"Uh, Yme. The creepy faces are getting creepier," Kylii says, he and Daniil moving closer to Yme.

The Seers circle the four, their eyes glowing brighter. "The Life Healer is safe. We will return her to you soon."

"Who is the 'we' in this conversation?" Daniil asks.

Shaking his head, Yme glares at the group closing in. "I don't know, but we have to find Aya." He tries to shove past two of the Seers. The circling group links arms, keeping Yme from passing.

Daniil and Kylii try to force their way through, but the Seers won't budge. "This is ridiculous," Daniil says. "Get outta the way!"

"You... need to separate... my hands," Lyrrel exclaims through gritted teeth.

"How is that helpful?" Kylii asks.

Lyrrel struggles to open one eye. The same blue glow as the other Seers can be seen. "It's... using me... to channel to the... others. If you... break... the connection... they'll be free."

Yme grabs Lyrrel's hands and strains to pull them apart. The strength keeping them together is astounding. Daniil and Kylii each grab one arm and pull. After several seconds of seemingly no effect, Lyrrel's hands separate. Lyrrel collapses to the floor, gasping for air. The Seers surrounding them collapse, unconscious.

"Gods, what is going on?" Daniil asks.

"I know where Aya is," Lyrrel says, slowly sitting up. He

wipes the blood from his cut lip and stares at Yme, his eyes back to their violet color. "I can take you there."

Helping Lyrrel to his feet, Yme nods his head at those on the floor. "Daniil, Kylii. Get them all somewhere safe."

"Us? What about you?"

"It'll be harder for four of us to get there without drawing unwanted attention," Lyrrel explains. "She's in a very sacred area of the tower. Only a few Seers are permitted entrance."

"And you're one?" Yme asks.

Lyrrel nods his head, the motion causing him to almost fall over. Yme grabs the Seer's arm and places it over his shoulders. "All right. Take me to Aya."

29

L *ife Healer.*

The dark veil lifts from Aya's eyes and she winces at the bright blue light. Blinking the spots from her vision, she searches the strange room she's in.

Tree roots fill the large room, some thicker than a man. Growing from the wood are blue crystals, the light emanating from deep within each. The walls of the room are made of earth, allowing the roots to easily pass through without damage.

"Where am I?" Aya asks aloud.

"You are in the most sacred room in Eraunel," a voice answers. A woman walks from behind the largest root, her fingers gliding along the wood. Her eyes glow with the same blue light as the crystals. "This is where Seers may commune with the Forest Spirit."

"You don't look like you're communing. You look like you're being controlled."

"Life Healer, please." The woman holds her hand out to Aya. "It wishes to speak with you."

Scrutinizing the root, Aya raises a brow, confused. "The Forest Spirit wants to talk to me. Why?"

"It will explain."

Hesitating, Aya carefully walks towards the woman, tripping on a small root. She catches herself, placing one hand on the large root. Magic fills the air. Aya's skin tingles, as though thousands of insects are crawling all over her. She quickly pulls her hand away and the magic fades.

"I've felt this before," Aya whispers.

A voice echoes through her head, a remnant from the brief connection to the root. *Help me, Life Healer.*

"Aya!" Yme's voice echoes across the room.

Turning, Aya spots Yme climbing over the roots to reach her. The woman grabs Aya's hands and places both on the large root. Magic shoots up her arms and into her chest. The magic in the air around her writhes across her skin, squeezing her whole body tighter and tighter until she can't breathe. The last thing she sees before complete darkness is Yme's worried expression.

Life Healer. The voice is a breeze through Aya's mind. The sounds of the forest surround her, and her vision reveals an enormous tree before her. It's the largest tree she's ever seen, easily towering over even the mountains.

Life Healer. The air hums with power and the root Aya is standing on rises from the earth, bringing her closer to the tree. Blue crystals cover the tree's bark. Some grow from deep within the wood, reminding Aya of a disease.

"Are you the Forest Spirit?" Aya asks.

That is what those gifted with the Sight call me. The power they inherited is a side effect of these crystals feeding on the magic stored within my roots. But as the crystals continue to grow, their hunger exceeds what I can provide.

Aya glances up at the tree's canopy. She notices several branches bare of leaves and blackened. "You're dying."

All things eventually die.

"But if you die, what will happen to the Seers?"

As the crystals cease their feeding, the power of Sight will fade. But there is still need of Seers in this world and I must ask a great burden of you. Please, heal me, Life Healer.

"I don't think I can. I've never healed a tree before."

I will guide you as well as I can. Please, try.

The root brings Aya right up to the heavy, thick bark. A nearby crystal glows brightly and Aya feels drawn to touch it. Reaching her hand towards the blue crystal, the root beneath her pulls her back.

Don't touch the stones on my bark. They will try to pull the healing power from you.

"The Seers carry these stones. Why aren't their powers drained?"

The stones growing beneath the Seers city are too weak to drain but carry enough of my life force for Seers to channel their own power. But these crystals are overgrown and seek to feed on any power they sense.

"If these crystals are draining your life force, why let them grow to such a number?"

The Forest Spirit is silent for a moment. *I enjoy the company of the Seers. I feared they would leave if they didn't have the Sight. They also keep others from attacking this forest which will be needed even more when I do leave this world.*

"All right. I'll try to heal you. But I can't promise anything." Aya takes a deep breath and gently touches the rough bark of the tree's trunk. She closes her eyes, reaching inside where her magic lies.

Answering her call, her magic unwinds and moves through her arms. When it reaches the wood, it repels back. With a gentle nudge, Aya encourages her magic into the tree. A guiding light appears in her mind, meeting and mixing with her magic.

I will do my best to guide you.

The light expands and strange pathways fill Aya's thoughts. They remind her of arteries and veins, but instead of blood, green energy is moving through the tree. Mixed within the green are flecks of blue and as her magic journeys lower in the tree, the blue grows more frequent.

I'll lead you to my roots. That is where you will need to heal.

The paths of light spread out into many branches and Aya sees where crystals have buried themselves deep into the Forest Spirit's roots. The usual flow of energy that would feed the rest of the tree are blocked, moving into the crystals instead.

Don't worry about the crystals. I will show you where to focus your magic.

Aya's magic is pulled deep into the roots. A chill fills Aya and she recognizes the feeling. It's the same as those close to death and fear fills her. The deeper her magic reaches the colder it becomes. At the center of the cold is a faint orb of energy. The energy bleeds from the orb, being drawn towards the crystals infecting the large tree.

"I don't know what to do," Aya admits. "This is nothing like a human or beast."

Please, try. Let your power find the way.

Aya pushes her magic towards the orb, feeling slight resistance. "No, not resistance. It's pulling away," Aya whispers to herself. It's as though her magic wants to explore without her. She slowly releases her magic, allowing it to explore on its own. Dancing around, her magic reaches out and touches the orb. Images flash across Aya's vision. An egg hatches into a baby bird, a field of grass waves in the wind, small four-legged beasts fight over a fresh kill. The visions are numerous and vivid.

Aya pulls her magic back before the quickly flashing visions overwhelm her. Fighting against her, her magic clings to a strand of energy, following it back towards the roots and the crystals. Unlike the rest of the life force being drained, the strand leading to the orb is actively feeding the crystals. Numerous other strands appear to be feeding the rest of the tree, but even more go straight to the crystals.

Her magic bounces from strand to strand before stopping on a particularly thick one. Investigating, Aya feels a familiar magic emanating from it and realizes it is the source of the Seers of Eraunel's magic. Unlike the other strands, this one splits, half going to the rest of the Forest Spirit and the other half going into a crystal. Her magic swims around before moving to the next closest strand feeding another crystal. With a sudden burst of energy, Aya's magic severs the connection. The strand fades, but Aya feels the life force it held returning to the orb. A new strand rises and feeds back into the flow of the tree's energy.

Understanding what she now must do, Aya focuses on the links between the orb and crystals, moving slowly from one to the next. The short bursts of energy from her magic easily sever the bonds, returning energy to the Forest Spirit. She's unsure how many strands connect to the crystals, but as she cuts one, she discovers at least a dozen more. They vary in size and she tries to focus on thicker ones, hoping they were transferring larger amounts of life force energy. She tries to cut two strands at the same time, but one only reconnects to the crystal, solidifying that she has to work on one strand at a time.

"This will take forever," Aya says, frustrated. "There has to be something else I can do." Turning her attention back to the orb, Aya feels her magic pulling against her again, longing to touch the orb.

Let your power find the way. The Forest Spirit's words echo in her mind. Leaning forward, Aya places her forehead against the wood of the tree. With a slow breath, she releases her magic, allowing it to roam freely.

Her magic latches onto the orb, spreading over it like a cloth. The images of the forest rapidly flash across Aya's vision and she struggles against pulling away again. She fights to focus on her magic, feeling something slowly rip from it. Her hands and feet grow cold. Rushing up her arms and legs, the coldness of death threatens to fill her.

More visions flash through her mind , but one keeps reoccurring. A strange field of white grass with a figure made of light sitting in front of her. As though sensing her, the figure's head turns to glance towards Aya. In the distance a similar figure of darkness sits amidst a field of black grass. It mirrors the figure of light, turning its head to glance behind.

A force slams into Aya, knocking her away from the tree, breaking her connection to the Forest Spirit. Her magic circles through her body, chasing the cold away and returning to its home deep within Aya.

Her legs give out beneath her and Aya sits on the large root beneath her. She gasps for air, but quickly crawls to the bark of the tree and places her tingling hands on the wood. She concentrates, gently urging her magic to show her what happened. The orb of energy is now covered in a layer of Aya's magic. It blocks strands from connecting to the crystals, protecting them as they feed the flow of energy into the roots and rest of the tree. The largest strand is the only one still connected to the crystals, slowing the drain of life energy, but allowing the Seers to retain their Sight.

The giant tree shudders, leaves falling from the towering canopy onto Aya. She moves away from the trunk and sits back.

Thank you, Life Healer.

"Why are you thanking me? I couldn't save you. I only delayed the inevitable. I don't even know for how long."

You risked your life to slow the process. Something that will not be forgotten in these woods. And whatever you did achieve, my strength is returning and shall be given to the Seers to aid you in your coming fight.

The root beneath Aya's feet rises to one of the many crystals burrowed into the tree's bark. A blue light emanates from deep within the crystal, a moderate vibration filling the air.

To thank you, I must show you something. The truth of your inheritance.

"What do you mean?"

Look into the crystal.

Aya moves closer to the crystal. She peers into it, the light swirling like smoke. Images form inside, two familiar figures.

"What is this?" Aya's voice chokes with emotion. "Why are you showing me this?"

The figures are her parents. Her mother and father walking through a forest. Their expressions are of terror and she sees blood on their clothes. The images swirl around, creating a village before her parents. Her home, Oula village. Mircien, then not so old, welcomes the two.

Your parents escaped the Blood King's attack on Life Healers. But they didn't survive it.

The images swirl again, showing her parents surrounded by burning buildings. A dark shadow overtakes them. Dark magic hits them, but they manage to escape.

They escaped with their lives, but they were infected with a deadly magic. It slowly fed on their magic each time they used it. Once their magic was depleted the darkness began to feed on their life energy. You've witnessed the outcome.

"Why are you showing me this?" Aya asks, tears rolling down her cheeks.

You were born with this magic inside of you as well. But it doesn't feed on your magic, it created a new magic. A new living magic. That is why you are the only one who can end the forbidden magic from simply being passed on to a new host. You can end the cycle.

The root shakes violently and Aya nearly falls off. Falling to her knees, she holds onto the root tightly.

Our time is up. I must send you back. Please apologize to the Seer with violet eyes. I did not mean to cause him harm.

Before Aya can respond, she's thrown back to the larger room with roots. She collapses to the floor, her body tingling with remnants of the Forest Spirit's magic.

30

"Aya!" Yme appears above her. "Are you okay?"

Aya tries to nod her head but can't find the strength. "I'll feel better once I'm back on a comfy bed instead of a damp floor."

Lifting her into his arms, Yme carefully maneuvers through the roots towards the door. Lyrrel waits for the two, leaning on the wall. A cut on his lip catches Aya's attention.

"Did you hit him?" Aya asks Yme.

"No!" Yme's eyes widen in shock and embarrassment.

"Did Daniil or Kylii hit him?"

"No!"

"I resisted the Spirit's influence," Lyrrel explains. "I don't enjoy being controlled. Even by the one who gave me this gift."

"Who is this Spirit?" Yme asks.

"It's the one who gives all Seers their sight. It rarely calls for outsiders to meet it"

"It's dying. The spirit stones are killing it, sucking the life from it," Aya says, motioning to one of the closest roots with numerous crystals embedded in it. "I tried to heal it, but all I've done is postpone the inevitable."

Lyrrel's eyebrows lower and a sad frown forms on his lips. "I'm sure you did exactly what the Spirit wished. That's all any can do when called."

A short scream makes the three jump in surprise. The woman who brought Aya stands, fear on her face. She glances around the room in shock. "How did I get here?"

"Kat, you're all right," Lyrrel calls, slowly making his way towards the woman. "You two should head back up. Do you remember the way?"

Yme nods his head. "Do you need help with her?"

"It's fine. It can be disorienting after being controlled by the Spirit. I'll see her to her room for rest. As you should do for the Life Healer. She used a lot of magic and will need to recover."

Yme climbs the stairs, holding Aya tightly in his arms. The room disappears behind them as they move higher. The stairs and wall change from earth to stone and they emerge in a dark hallway.

"You can put me down. I think I can walk," Aya says.

Pausing, Yme slowly lowers her to the floor. "Sorry."

Aya feels her legs shake a little, but there's no fear of falling. "Sorry for what? Assuming I wanted to be carried like a child? I'm still not sure I won't fall after a few steps." Yme doesn't answer and she faces him. "What?"

"I'm sorry for what I said. I didn't mean to upset you."

"You don't have to apologize for that. We both said upsetting things." She tries taking a few steps, the muscles in her legs tightening, painfully. She places a steadying hand on the wall. "How do we get out of here?"

Yme takes her other arm and drapes it over his shoulder, wrapping his left arm around her waist. "This way."

They move down the hallways towards a dead end, but Aya

notices several of the stones of the wall are a different color than the rest. Yme touches a crack in one of the stones and the wall opens in front of them. Walking through the new opening, they emerge beneath the stairs of the main hall.

The sound of multiple voices echoes in the hall. As they walk out from beneath the stairs, Aya spies numerous Seers sitting on the floor or leaning against the walls. Daniil and Kylii freeze when they see Aya and Yme.

Aya raises her hand and smiles sheepishly. Kylii waves back at her, but Daniil elbows him in the rib. He nods at Aya and Yme. The brothers continue checking on the Seers as Yme helps her up the stairs.

The long climb feels extra tedious, but they manage to make it back to their room without bumping into anyone else, much to Aya's relief. Yme sits her on the closest bed before reaching into his pocket and holding her knife out.

"Here. You dropped this when you were taken."

"Thank you." She takes her knife and lays it on the bed. She glances up at him, her breath catching in her throat. The expression on his face is one she hasn't seen before. "Are you okay?"

Kneeling down so he's eye-level with her, Yme leans forward, his arms wrapping around her. He pulls her into a hug and Aya fears her eyes may pop from her head.

He doesn't speak. His arms tighten slightly as a shudder shakes his body. Aya gingerly raises her arms, returning the hug. Another shudder shakes Yme's body and Aya feels dampness on her shoulder.

He's crying?

"You're scaring me a little with the silent treatment here," she says, softly. "Did I do something wrong?" She feels his head move back and forth.

"Don't tell Daniil and Kylii about this," Yme whispers. "I'll never hear the end of it."

"Why would I tell them about this?"

"Because they become unbearable when they find out they're right." Yme gently pulls away, his eyes red and tears staining his cheeks. He wipes them away, a flush rising in his cheeks of embarrassment.

"What were those two right about?"

"That I really care about you."

Aya's heart pounds loudly, heat filling her cheeks. Without thinking, she covers her face with her hands and lowers her gaze to her lap. She's had admirers in Oula, but she never felt like this when they confessed their feelings. She always believed they only had feelings because she was the rarity in the village. She was the only magic user and chose to live separate from the rest. But she hears in Yme's voice the true emotion behind it and thinking on it... she realizes she feels the same.

Yme sits beside her on the bed. "I hope that reaction means what I think it means."

Peeking through her hands, Aya sees Yme's hand resting on his leg. Swallowing the lump in her throat, she cautiously lowers her hands to the bed, gripping the blanket. Then she raises her hand and places it on top of his hand. He slowly turns it over and intertwines his fingers with hers. The feeling of his hand in hers brings a smile to her face and she finds the strength to look at Yme. He watches her carefully, but she sees the question in his face.

"I really care about you, too."

31

The bright morning sun streams through the window. Daniil rolls away from the light and squeezes his eyes tighter, trying in vain to block out the sun. The heavy, warm body lying close to his feet moves and a low chirp greets him. He groans and pulls his pillow over his head. He feels movement and then warmth against his back.

"Tanith, it's too early to cuddle," he remarks, his voice muffled.

"It's never too early to cuddle, Daniil-li," Kylii whispers close to Daniil's pillow-covered ear.

Daniil sits up, his pillow falling onto his lap. Kylii smiles at his brother, already dressed for the day.

"Why are you in my bed?" Daniil demands.

"Why are you still asleep? It's morning and there's an entire tower to explore."

"So, go explore it. I'm still tired." Daniil grabs his pillow and returns to his face covered position. The excitement of the previous day was draining. The meeting with Wynsil, Aya's kidnapping and reappearance. Not to mention the fact he and

Kylii had to drag almost thirty bodies around. "Take Tanith if you're too afraid to go alone."

Loud chirping argues against this suggestion as Tanith stretches her back. Kylii grabs the pillow from Daniil's head and throws it to the floor. "Come on. We haven't been outside of a cell for... well, forever."

"Not quite forever, Kylii-li. We also haven't been allowed to sleep through an entire day and I would like to experience that once before I die."

"You'll have plenty of time to sleep when you're dead. Come on," Kylii whines as he pulls on Daniil's arm. "Or do you *really* trust me on my own?"

A moment of silence passes before Daniil sits up and glares at Kylii. "Fine. Let's explore the tower."

Smiling victoriously, Kylii leaps from the bed and grabs fresh clothes from a chest. He throws the light clothing at Daniil. "Hurry and change. I know where we'll start."

Reluctantly standing, Daniil changes as Kylii hurries out the door. Tanith moves to the warm spot on the bed and curls up, but she doesn't get to rest long before Daniil taps her snout gently. "Oh no, if I have to go, so do you."

Tanith lifts her head defiantly and huffs out a short breath.

"Sorry but dealing with Kylii is part of the deal with me."

Grunting as she stands, Tanith rolls her eyes, an odd motion that involves her entire head moving. She hops to the floor and walks out the door.

Daniil finishes dressing and follows the two out. Kylii's smile is so wide on his face Daniil is afraid it will split his brother's entire head, but he recognizes the smile all the same. Kylii is excited about something and he won't share it until the last possible moment so he can enjoy Daniil's full reaction. That smile has led to many instances of Daniil nearly being killed or worse... nearly killing Kylii himself.

"This way!" The childlike tone to Kylii's voice sends a shudder through Daniil.

The three venture to the stairwell and Kylii leads them down three floors before he takes them down a long hallway with many doors. Voices come from each room and Daniil catches the voices of children answering in unison.

Confusion fills him and he grabs his brother's arm. "Where are we going, Kylii-li?"

"We're almost there. Be patient."

"I don't think I've ever heard you say that word before. I didn't think you knew what it meant."

Kylii pulls his arm free and fake laughs. "Funny." He stops outside of a door and knocks. The voices speaking on the other side stop and footsteps approach.

The door opens and a man wearing the robes of a Seer appears. He meets Kylii with his dark eyes. "Kylii, back so soon?"

"I promised I would be back with a surprise for the children, Oswen."

"Yes, I know, but I assumed you meant later. It hasn't even been half an hour."

Daniil pulls his brother away from the door. "Surprise for the children?"

The Seer, Oswen turns his attention to Daniil. "You must be Kylii's brother."

"Unfortunately, yes," Daniil says. He leans close to Kylii. "Why did you drag me down here?"

"The kids wanted to meet the other half of the Lakiin brothers. I couldn't say no. Plus, I thought they'd enjoy seeing Tanith, too."

Oswen stares at Tanith, who sits patiently next to Daniil. Her white eyes watch the two brothers curiously and her tail sweeps across the floor. "Since you came down here, you might as well see the children. They haven't been able to focus since you left, anyway," Oswen comments, reentering the room.

Daniil shoots his brother an icy look and Kylii taps him on the cheek. "Come on, Daniil-li. Smiles for the children." He follows Oswen into the room and excited voices echo out into the hallway.

After taking a calming breath and pushing the thought of walking away out of his mind, Daniil enters the classroom. Tanith follows behind slowly. The room is filled with separate desks lined up in rows. Some children are still seated while the rest crowd around Kylii, who scruffs the hair of a boy with freckles covering his nose.

A small girl, standing back from the gathered group, turns and looks up at Daniil with dark, chocolate brown eyes. Her black hair is braided and hangs over her shoulder. She plays with the end of the braid with her small hands, squeezing it tightly.

"Is she friendly?" She points to Tanith.

Daniil remains silent, unsure of what to say. He gazes at Kylii who is lifting some of the children up on his arm. They laugh, completely oblivious to anything else. Those sitting at their desks watch Daniil and the little girl curiously.

Kneeling to the floor, Daniil places a hand on Tanith's back. "What's your name?"

"Asha."

Tanith steps forward, closer to the girl. Asha hesitantly takes a step back, but Daniil holds his other hand up. "Don't be afraid, Asha." He turns his head to Tanith. "Tanith, this is Asha. She wants to know if you're friendly."

Tanith lowers her head and cautiously steps closer to the girl. She lies down at Asha's feet and chirps. She nudges the girl's leg softly. Asha takes a shaky breath. One of her hands releases the braid of hair and hovers down to Tanith's scaled head. She gently runs her hand through the brown mane and a small smile breaks on her face.

"She's warm and her hair is soft," Asha says. Tanith lifts her head and licks Asha's hand, releasing a short squeal of laughter. "That tickles!"

"Hey, hey. What's going on over here?" Kylii asks. He walks with children hanging from his arms and eyes fill with wonder at the sight of Daniil and Tanith.

Daniil stands and smirks at his brother. "I could ask the same of you. What are those growths on your arms?"

Kylii looks at each child hanging from his arms and beams. "These? I don't know. They just kind of appeared, but I think I'll keep them." He swings the children, and they erupt into laughter.

Oswen claps his hand and the children fall silent, facing their teacher. "All right, back to your seats. We'll do introductions and be a *little* more civilized before complete chaos takes over."

The children reluctantly return to their desks, but Asha stays next to Tanith, stroking the Khorgoi's mane. Oswen doesn't seem to mind and walks to a stool in the corner of the room.

"Well, you all know me already," Kylii begins. The children nod excitedly. "This is my other half, my brother Daniil Lakiin the ice mage. And that adorable animal there is Tanith, a legendary beast known as a Khorgoi."

A nudge from Kylii shoves Daniil closer to the children. He waves his hands, encouraging Daniil to speak. "Right, I'm Daniil. Kylii's twin brother. *Older* twin brother."

"By two minutes."

"Still older."

Kylii makes a face at Daniil, causing many in the room to laugh.

"As Kylii said, I'm an ice mage. I'm guessing he's already explained that he's a fire mage."

A hand waving vigorously in the back catches his attention and Daniil nods at the girl. She stands and crosses her arms in front of her. "If you're twins, why are your eyes different colors?"

The brothers look at each other and back to the girl. "Magic," they answer together.

The children mumble at this answer, confused. Oswen claps his hands for silence. "As you will learn in your further studies, children, there are still many things we as humans do not yet understand about magic. Especially in our fair city where the only magic we are exposed to regularly is our Seer magic, there is still much to learn. Some magic does affect the body in unexplainable ways."

"Basically, what Ossie is saying, kids, is my eyes reflect my fire magic and Daniil's reflect his ice magic. For some their magic can be reflected in their eyes or through other means," Kylii says.

"Ossie?" Oswen's voice sounds slightly irritated, but Kylii ignores him.

"Sometimes magic affects people, sometimes it doesn't. But a common place is the eyes," Daniil explains, elbowing his brother in the stomach. "Though in his case, I think it's also affected his brain."

"Um," Asha's soft voice catches everyone's attention. "Do Khorgoi know magic? I've heard some animals are capable of using magic."

Kylii nudges Daniil with his elbow. "Yeah, Daniil. Do Khorgoi know magic?"

Shooting his brother an angry look, Daniil answers, "Khorgoi can use bonding magic. They make a bond or pact with another living being. These bonds are determined between the Khorgoi and the one bonding and can't be broken until a specific condition is met. With a bond comes communication and a connection."

"So, you can talk to her?"

"Well, anyone can talk to her. She understands human language, but I can hear her voice in my head."

Sounds of amazement fill the room and hands shoot into the air. Most ask if they can pet Tanith and soon the children crowd around her. After each one has a chance to pet her, they return to their seats and ask questions about the Arena. Kylii tells of their time in the Arena and even acts out some of their favorite fights, being sure to keep graphic details to a minimum.

Daniil sits with Tanith, ready to jump in when Kylii's retellings go beyond truth. But he mostly remains quiet, watching his brother. It's been a long time since he's seen his brother so excited to share anything with anyone. But the energy in Kylii spurs a strange feeling inside Daniil. A small thought at the back of his mind steadily grows louder.

Someday he's not going to need you.

32

"Anyone know where Daniil and Kylii were off to this morning?" Rava asks, adjusting the heavy bag hanging from her shoulder.

Mava sits on a wall, placing the bags of freshly collected supplies she's carrying next to her. "Probably went to cause trouble." She rubs her sore shoulders.

"I saw Kylii wandering around on his own before breakfast. He looked really excited about something," Bern says, digging through one of Rava's bags. "Which bag has the metal files in it?"

Eka reaches into a bag, pulling a large file out. "Here. Why do you need it right now?"

"I want to grab ours before I forget. We couldn't afford enough for everyone to have their own."

"You can't wait until we get back to the tower? What if you lose it?"

"I won't lose it. I'll put it in your bag." Bern hands the file to her and smiles. "You're the responsible one, right?" He leans close and kisses her on the cheek. Eka blushes and a soft giggle rises from her.

"And with that, I'm ready to head back," Rava grumbles. She heads off.

Mava picks up her bags and hurries after her sister. "Rava! Wait up!" She waves back at Bern and Eka. "We'll see you later!"

Catching up to her sister, Mava senses a strange air about Rava. Though, knowing her sister, she doesn't want to be the first to talk. If something is bothering Rava, it's better for her to bring it up.

They walk past worn-down buildings, old farmhouses. Builders work to expand the old farmhouses though Mava isn't sure what their new purpose will be. However, remnants of pens for animals are now used as training grounds for guards.

In one of the pens, Mava spies Jaxon, Aldur, and Fleance training a few of the former slaves. Truthfully, Aldur is the one training. Jaxon and Fleance watch, only participating when Aldur drags them into it.

Sitting on the ground outside of the pen are Tristan, Skara, and Dolus. The three have become inseparable since the caves, something Mava doesn't understand. Tristan and Skara are healers, but Dolus used to work in the Arena. *Maybe he thinks healers are less likely to hurt him... or hopes.*

"Do you want to watch?" Rava asks, already walking towards the pen. She finds a spot close to Tristan and Skara and sits.

Mava joins her sister, finding a little relief not having to hold the heavy bags. She watches Aldur teach a few how to escape a grab from behind with varying results. He's patient with those who struggle, easily falling into a teaching role. Jaxon sits on the fence of the pen with his usual guarded expression.

Fleance stands beside Jaxon, the only one fully dressed in his caravan attire. Black leather and minimal armor cover his vital areas. His left arm has thicker leather on his forearm for when he uses his bow.

"I don't like him," Rava says, leaning close to Mava.

Shock hits Mava and she glares at her sister. "What? Why don't you like him?"

"I don't trust him. Do you really think he's changed?" Rava pulls her knees to her chest, wrapping her arms around her legs. "I think he's hiding something."

"You're just saying that because he's quiet. If you give him a chance, he's really very sweet."

Anger rushes to Rava's face, her cheeks turning red. "I'm not talking about Fleance! I'm talking about Dolus."

"Oh." Mava's face burns hot and she looks away. She should've known Rava was talking about Dolus. "That makes more sense."

"I don't understand how Aya can let him stay with us. What if he's a spy?"

Mava stares at the former Voice of the Arena. He's watching those training with a grim expression on his face. He picks at the grass with his hands, creating small piles beside him. She still wonders why he didn't remain behind. He claims Klaeon was going to kill him, but he was a major figure in Bloodfall. His family was one of the most well-known. Would Klaeon kill someone with such renown?

Dolus seems to think so.

"I don't think he's a spy, Rava. He won't even leave his room unless he's with those two or Aya."

A frown darkens Rava's face. "I still don't like him."

"You don't have to like him. Stop obsessing."

"I'm not obsessing!"

"Fine, you're not obsessing. You're overly invested in his

business." Mava stares at Dolus. He's moved on from picking at the grass to digging a hole with a small knife. "He's harmless."

"Skara says the same thing. But I think that's a lie," Rava explains, lowering her voice. "I've seen him sneak off on his own at night. I think he's sending messages or leaving clues behind for the Blood King."

Scoffing, Mava taps her sister's forehead with a finger. "I think you're letting your imagination get the better of you."

"What could he possibly be doing alone at night?"

"I can think of a number of things someone could be doing alone at night."

Groaning, Rava lies down in the grass, glaring up at the sky. "Why do you have to try to rationalize everything? You're not even listening to me."

"I *am* listening, but you have to agree there's a possibility you're wrong."

"Or *you're* wrong."

"If you won't listen to me, talk to Skara." Mava stands and walks to the pen, not really interested in continuing the argument. Or letting Rava know she agrees with her. She's seen Dolus sneak off on his own on multiple occasions, but she doesn't want to accuse him of anything until the facts are known.

She walks along the fence, heading for the spot where Jaxon and Fleance are. When he sees her, Jaxon jumps down from the fence. "I think I've helped enough. I'm going back to the library." He pats Fleance on the shoulder and nods his head at Mava. "Don't overexert yourself."

Fleance swats Jaxon's hand away, sending the former caravan leader away laughing. "Hello."

"Hi." Mava leans against the fence, crossing her arms in front of her. "Do you think Aldur would mind if I steal you away to help take these supplies back to the tower?"

"Maybe." Fleance grabs the fence post and hops over to get out of the pen. "But that's only if he notices."

They walk to Rava and grab the bags. "You ready to head back or are you going to stay a little longer?" Mava asks.

Rava looks from Mava to Fleance before standing. She wipes the dirt from her backside and sighs. "I think I'm going to hop in and get some practice."

Fleance and Mava head off to the tower. The main hall is abuzz with energy. Groups of Seers gather and practice their magic in circles. A class of youths venture into the library and Mava sees Jaxon perusing the shelves.

The upper levels thin out as the Seers head off to their destinations. Reaching the floor designated for the group, Fleance and Mava pass through the dining hall. The smell of cooking food wafts through the air, making Mava's mouth water. The weight of the bags on her shoulders overpowers her hunger and she leads Fleance to an extra room being used to hold gathered supplies.

Placing the bags inside, Mava turns to Fleance with a relieved smile. "Thank you for the help."

"Of course. Is there anything else you need?" Fleance steps closer to Mava, his brown eyes locked on her face.

"One more thing," she answers, closing the distance between them. She takes his head in her hands and pulls his lips to hers, all thoughts of her sister's worries gone.

33

"When did Fleance and Mava get so close?" Yme asks, watching the two in question head towards the tower.

Aya shrugs her shoulders. "I think it was while we were in the caves... or maybe at Jaxon's town? You know, I'm not actually sure."

They sit on the wall of the third level, overlooking the pens where Aldur is training. A fountain bubbles behind them and birds land in the water. Water lilies float in lazy circles around the center of the fountain and small fish eat away at growing algae.

"Do you think Rava's noticed?" Yme asks, swinging one leg over the edge. "Or, I guess, do you think she approves?"

"I don't think she's unaware. But I'm sure she'd approve if it's what Mava wants." Aya watches Aldur spar with Rava, a distant look in her eyes. "How much longer do you think we can stay here?"

"I don't know. But the longer we stay here, the higher chance whoever Klaeon sent after us may catch up."

"Do you really think he'd send someone after us this far?"

Yme looks at her, confused. "You sound like you want to stay here."

Aya's breath catches in her throat and she shakes her head. "No. Even if I wanted to, if anyone is following us then we put this city in danger by staying."

She plays with the silk bracelet on her wrist, drawing Yme's eyes to it. He wants to take her hand in his, stop the nervous habit, but resists the urge. Since confessing his feelings, he's felt weird attempting any act of comfort. He can't explain why, but the weight he expected to be lifted from his shoulders when he admitted his true feelings to Aya is still present.

He can't pinpoint the exact moment his feelings began to grow. He could argue it was during the tournament he and Aya were forced to participate in. Or maybe it was during the fight against the volacerta or the Brüdel. Or when Aya saved him from Klaeon. But he knows when he woke up in Jaxon's village and she was there beside him... that was the moment he knew he cared for her. That caring has only grown stronger.

Why do I still feel like I haven't told her?

"Why is Tanith staring at us like that?" Aya asks, staring across the fountain.

Turning, Yme spots the Khorgoi sitting on the opposite side of the fountain. Her white eyes are clearly locked onto them, but she's still as a statue.

"I have no idea." He searches the surrounding area for Daniil, but there's no sign of the brother. "Maybe we should see if she's okay."

Before either one can stand, Tanith turns and walks away. After a few steps, she turns and stares at them expectantly. Her tail twitches, reminding Yme of someone beckoning to them with their hand.

"I think she wants us to follow her," Aya says, standing.

"If this is a prank by those two, I'm going to drown them in this fountain," Yme grumbles.

They catch up to Tanith and the Khorgoi heads inside the tower. Climbing the stairs, Tanith leads them down a long hallway with many doors. Standing outside one door are Daniil and Kylii. They wave to Aya and Yme.

Yme is familiar with the expression on their faces. It's the kind of excitement that used to get Yme into trouble in the Arena. He remembers one of his first years in Bloodfall, the brothers wore these exact expressions when they convinced him to sneak up to the animal training floor. He was caught by one of the animal wranglers and nearly fed to a large urso. He doesn't even remember how he managed to escape back to his cell, but he'll never forget the mocking.

"We're leaving," Yme states, bluntly. He takes Aya's hand in his and tries to take her back the way they came.

Daniil and Kylii move in front of them quickly, stopping their escape. "Wait, wait, wait!" Kylii says.

"We promise this isn't a trick," Daniil adds.

Aya pulls away from Yme, a move that sends a painful jab to his chest. She crosses her arms, leaning her head to the side. "What is this about? What did you two do?"

"Why do you assume we did something?" Kylii asks.

Placing a hand on Yme and Aya's shoulders, Daniil gently moves them towards a door. "We actually have a request."

Kylii's eyes glow with eager excitement. "The children keep asking about the both of you and we don't want to presume anything."

Forcing the hand from his shoulder, Yme steps back from the brothers. "Say that again?"

"Did you say children?" Aya sputters.

Daniil motions to the door. "Come hang out with the little darlings for a while."

"Yeah. They're not *that* terrifying." Kylii leans on his brother's shoulder.

Yme shakes his head, but Aya grabs his arm. Her green eyes shine up at him and she gives him a comforting squeeze. "We've come this far. Let's do it."

"I don't think I can," Yme argues. "I don't know how to act around children. I mean, why do they want to meet us?"

"We won't know unless we go in."

Unsure, Yme peeks at Daniil and Kylii. The excitement in their expressions sends a shock of fear through him but feeling Aya's hand on his arm calms him. He reluctantly nods his head, preparing himself for whatever is on the other side of the door.

Daniil and Kylii knock on the door before opening it wide. Tanith eagerly trots inside, followed by the brothers. Taking a deep breath, Yme and Aya follow. The children stare at Yme and Aya with wide eyes and gaping mouths as they enter. A low, wondrous excitement fills the room.

Yme tenses as he looks at each young face. The fear growing inside is stronger than any fear he ever felt in the Arena. *Can they sense my fear? What should I do?*

"Look who we found wandering the halls!" Kylii announces proudly. "Yme, the elemental mage of legend and Aya, the Life Healer more powerful than any king!"

Yme snaps a glare at Kylii, but the sudden explosion of shouting voices wipes it from his face. It takes several minutes for the teacher to regain control of the room and an aura of order returns.

"I'm thrilled you're all eager to ask our guests questions, but we will do it like the young Seers we are. One at a time, please," the older Seer speaks using an authoritative tone.

"That's right. Listen to Ossie," Daniil says.

"*Oswen.*" The teacher points to a child waving his hand furiously above his head. "Yes, Lowe."

"Can we see your magic?" the boy asks quickly. The children around him loudly voice their agreement and repeat the request.

Aya nudges Yme forward. "I think they're asking you, elemental mage of legend."

Yme looks to Oswen. "Is it all right?"

"That's for you to decide. If you feel you can control it safely then it's fine."

"Okay. Maybe we should make some room."

The children quickly move the desks and chairs to the sides of the room. Daniil, Kylii, and Tanith sit at the back of the classroom, watching with large smiles. Aya finds a spot next to Oswen as Yme moves to the center of the room.

"Um, I'll need three volunteers." It takes a little corralling and discussion before three children are selected. They stand around Yme and he takes a deep breath. "Don't move."

He raises his hands slowly in front of him, the hair on his arms standing up. The air presses against his skin and he imagines it traveling down his arms to the tips of his fingers. Releasing a calming breath, he spreads his arms apart and then swings them up. He feels the air vibrate as it makes the image in his mind come true.

The three children are encircled by a gentle wind and rise from the floor. They squeal with delight and Yme turns, moving the three around him in the opposite direction. The other children, sitting around, ooh and aah. Some even clap their hands.

Raising his arms above his head, Yme raises the three children higher off the floor before gently setting them down on top of the closest desks. Lowering his hands, Yme kneels down so his fingers touch the floor. He feels the stone react to his touch and he knows it's safe to move the floor if he's careful.

Standing, Yme takes his shoes off, confusion filling the faces of the children. Wiggling his toes on the stone floor, he bends his knees. He bends over and slaps the floor with his hands. The floor beneath the children rises a few inches. Yme carefully stands up straight, the children slowly rising up with him until the floor is as high as their chairs. Excited yells fill the room and the children cheer.

"Don't know how to act around children, my ass," Kylii comments from the back of the room. "He outdid our performances."

Daniil nods his head in agreement. "Yeah, how are we supposed to top that?"

Yme returns the floor to normal and uses his wind magic to move the desks and chairs back to their positions. The children crowd around him when he finishes, talking over one another.

Clapping his hands, Oswen regains the attention of the students. "All right! All right! Thank you, Yme. Children, take your seats."

With moans of displeasure, the children walk back to their seats as Yme puts his shoes back on. He sits next to Aya, breathing a sigh of relief.

"Well, well. I guess the legend wasn't far off," Aya says, joking. "Who knew all it took to get you to show off was a room full of children?"

"There's a reason it's only a legend." Yme looks at her. "You're lucky your magic isn't as visual."

"Yeah, I'm not as flashy."

"Asha, do you have a question?" Oswen asks, pointing to the young girl with her hand in the air.

"I was wondering if Aya and Yme are husband and wife?"

Yme's eyes almost pop out of his head and his face burns red hot. He sees a similar reaction on Aya's face, but she's able to keep the red to a pink on her cheeks.

Riotous laughter from the back of the room draws a death glare from Yme.

34

"I don't think I've ever seen your face turn that shade of red before," Kylii tells Yme.

"Luckily for us, your insane laughing was a big enough distraction for us to escape," Yme says, throwing a piece of bread at Kylii. It misses and falls to the floor, bouncing off Tanith's head. She lifts her head up and growls at Yme. "Sorry, Tanith. Could you hit Kylii for me?"

"Don't listen to him. He's still embarrassed," Daniil says.

Tanith's tail slaps Kylii on the arm and he overreacts, grabbing his arm and falling onto the table. Daniil rolls his eyes and pours his cup of water over his brother's head. Kylii jerks up, shouting in shock.

Others in the dining hall jump at the sudden shout but ignore it once they see the source is Kylii. Aldur, Rava, Tristan, Skara, and Dolus walk into the dining hall, taking seats close by.

"You were out there for a long time. Aren't your muscles sore?" Aya asks.

"A little, but we didn't push ourselves too much," Rava says. "Just enough to work out some frustrations."

"We lost track of time." Aldur grabs food and glances around the hall. "Anyone seen Fleance? He snuck away when I wasn't looking."

"Saw him helping Mava with some things. I'm sure he lost track of time, too," Yme says. Aya snorts beside him and kicks him under the table. Jumping, he turns to her, but she's already stuffing her mouth with food.

"Aldur was telling us about his family," Rava says, changing the subject. "Did you know this mountain man is a proud father of two girls?"

"What?" Daniil and Kylii spit food on to the table.

Aldur puffs his chest up, his eyes sparkling with pride. "My youngest will be turning two in a few months and she's already the most beautiful girl the world will ever see! Next to her mother and older sister, of course. My oldest is six and has my strong jaw and my wife's fiery will."

"Is that a good mix?" Aya whispers to Yme. He smiles, but fears laughing may sour Aldur's mood.

The large man continues without hearing Aya's question. "She wants to be a hunter and go to unexplored territories to see beasts no living man has ever seen. My girls are my pride and joy. I hope to see them again once this is all over. If the gods will it so."

"The gods would never separate a good man from his family for too long," Jaxon says sitting down next to Aldur "You'll see them again, Aldur."

Suspicion hovers in Yme's mind at Jaxon's sudden appearance, a reoccurring habit. He didn't see him walk in and judging by the reactions of others, no one else did either.

"You've been spending a lot of time in the library. What've you been doing in there?" Kylii asks, grabbing more food.

"Looking for information on the lands here in the north. The more we know, the easier it'll be to talk to them and convince them to help stop the Blood King."

"Are you thinking the cliff city won't be enough?" Daniil asks.

"I'm thinking, it's better to be prepared."

"Do you think they'll want to help? I sort of got the impression from your mom they don't really care about the south," Kylii comments.

Jaxon's eyebrows rise slightly, and his jaw tightens. Yme wonders if it's because he doesn't know the answer... or if it's because Kylii said the word mom. "It's not that they don't care about the south. They don't care as long as it *stays* in the south. The city we're looking for is a kind of gateway to the north. You could think of them like the first barrier anyone with intentions to invade would need to break through."

"Does that mean they have an army?" Yme asks.

"It means they know how to fight. I couldn't find any current information about their military capabilities, but I did find the city's name. Kellahn."

Lyrrel walks into the dining hall, spotting Yme and approaching the group. "Wynsil has requested an audience with Yme and Aya."

"Right now?" Aya asks.

Nodding, Lyrrel glances around the table. "Unless this is an inopportune time?"

"Why does he want to see us?"

"He didn't provide a reason." Lyrrel's violet eyes flash blue for a split second and he shifts his weight, unease surfacing on his face.

"What does he want to discuss, I wonder," Jaxon says, carefully observing Lyrrel.

"We'll know when we know," Yme grumbles, standing from the table. "It can't be that important if he waited all day."

"Maybe he knows something we don't," Kylii suggests, leaning in as though to keep Lyrrel from overhearing. The Seer glares at the brother, clearly hearing him.

"Not hard since they're Seers." Daniil crosses his arms on the table and leans his head to the side. "But why only you two?"

"Insulted you weren't invited?" Jaxon asks.

"No. But there wasn't a problem talking to all of us before."

"When we get back, we'll let all of you know," Aya says, standing. "But putting it off and guessing won't do us any good."

"Ready?" Lyrrel asks, an annoyed breath preceding it.

"Let's go."

35

Aya's nervousness increases as they approach the large room at the top of the tower. What could Wynsil want to see them about? Why only her and Yme? If it had to do with what happened the day before... why did he wait until now?

"How are you feeling?" Yme asks Lyrrel.

"I'm well. The other Seers are doing well, too. They don't remember what happened, but ironically, that's a common occurrence with Seers." Lyrrel knocks on the large, silver doors before opening them.

The large, blue crystal has been lowered from the ceiling, hanging a foot off the floor. Cloaked men and women are seated around the U-shaped table, one chair empty. Lyrrel moves to the chair and sits.

The doors slam shut behind Aya and Yme, causing both to jump. The sound of chains moving draws Aya's eyes to the ceiling. More cloaked men and women use the pulleys, covering the glass ceiling with cloth and blocking the sunlight. The room fills with blue light and Aya feels the familiar magic of the Forest Spirit fill the air.

The Seers seated at the tables place their hands in front of them, drawing strange symbols in the air with their fingers. They close their eyes and bow their heads and one of the men begins a low, guttural hum. The others join in one by one.

Wynsil waves Yme and Aya over to him and they quickly cross the room, careful not to disturb the Seers. Laughing at their discretion, Wynsil doesn't even try to speak softly as they move to his side. "You don't need to worry. Once they begin the ritual, nothing can disturb them until they've finished."

"Why did you call for us? Is something wrong?" Yme asks, his voice still softer than normal even with Wynsil's assurance.

"Nothing's wrong. Lyrrel and Kat told me all about your experience with the Forest Spirit. I both apologize and thank you. I apologize for the worry we caused you and I thank you for healing our Spirit."

"I couldn't heal it fully, but I did what I could," Aya says. "Though I'm not sure how much longer I delayed its death."

"Whatever you did, I'm sure was enough. The Forest Spirit is a kind soul and could see in your heart how much you wished to help."

"How could you know that?" Yme asks.

"It told me through Lyrrel. In fact, it's the one that truly requested your presence. I believe it wishes for you to hear what our Seers will see during today's ritual."

"What is this ritual?" Aya asks.

"Every three days, our top Seers commune with the Forest Spirit and give it voice. Most times, it's how the Spirit informs us of trespassers in the forest, but on rare occasions it informs us of major deviations in the branches of what will come to be." Wynsil holds his hands out to Aya. "Such as your arrival and your goal to overthrow the Blood King."

The humming changes tone and Wynsil's attention returns to the Seers. They've finished making symbols in the air and their hands are now held in front of their chests. The crystal becomes cloudy and the blue light emanates brighter from within. Wynsil leans forward, expectantly and the intense look draws Yme and Aya's gazes to the crystal.

The volume of the humming grows in volume and dissonance. When the hypnotic barrage of sound ceases, the reverberating echo remains behind for several long seconds. The cloudiness of the crystal expands, the blue light growing brighter. When silence returns to the room, the blue light changes to white.

Wynsil sits back in his chair and raises his chin slightly, the aura of a ruler filling him. "Forest Spirit, we welcome you and are ready to bear witness to your sight."

"Hello again, Life Healer." The oldest of the cloaked Seers opens his eyes, the blue light filling his iris. The other Seers keep their heads bowed, but when he speaks the others speak with him. "And greetings, Elemental Mage."

"Hello?" Yme's voice is unsure and he looks at Aya.

"You asked for us. Is there something you wanted to tell us?" Aya asks.

"A warning. Whether you defeat the Blood King or fail to stop the destruction will be determined by a single choice."

"What choice?" Aya asks.

"The choice is unknown."

"Who will have to make the choice?"

"That is unknown."

"Then why tell us?" Yme demands. "What's the point of telling us about the choice if we don't know the choice or who will make it?"

"When the choice is made, the future will be set. The key to your victory or the beginning of destruction will be decided at that point." The oldest Seer focuses on Aya and the weight of his gaze bears down on her. "But I cannot see what that entails for either branch."

"There are only two options? There isn't a third branch?" Aya asks. "I refuse to believe the future is so black and white."

"The branches are set in stone. But what they actually mean are truly unknown. All that is known is there is a choice that will determine whether you are successful or not."

"What does that mean?"

Wynsil places a calming hand on Aya's arm. "Sometimes the sight is vague, but you must listen to what is *not* said. The vision does not specify the Blood King's success, only that you may fail."

"That seems pretty clear to me that if we fail, Klaeon succeeds," Yme says angrily.

"What does it mean... beginning of destruction? What destruction are you talking about if not whatever Klaeon will do to the world if we fail?" Aya takes a step towards the crystal.

The oldest Seer closes his eyes and Lyrrel stands. Opening his eyes, the usual violet irises are now glowing blue. "A great loss of what has always been. Slowly it fades from the world. Slowly it dies out, leaving behind only the chosen few to carry out the gods' work."

Wynsil jerks out of his seat, fear plain on his face. "What dies out?"

"Mixed blood of red and black. Children of two brothers gifted with their combined strength."

Aya knows what the Spirit is referencing. The story of the brother gods who created man and mages. How the Forest Spirit knows of the stories, she has no clue, but hearing the familiar tale makes her nervous to hear what else it has to say.

"Are you speaking of magic fading away from this world?" Wynsil asks, his expression darkening.

"Yes." Lyrrel says, the other voices staying silent.

"When?"

"In times yet come to pass."

"Why will magic fade away?"

"Unknown. *It* has not yet come to pass."

"What do you mean *it*?" Wynsil asks.

Lyrrel looks from Yme to Aya. "The choice that must be made." The blue light disappears from Lyrrel's eyes, returning them to violet. A gasp of air escapes his mouth, and he collapses into his chair. The other Seers gasp and collapse in their seats, a couple falling forward onto the table.

Wynsil curses under his breath and turns to Aya and Yme. "Time's up."

The crystal at the center of the room flashes blue for a moment. Aya sees the Forest Spirit's tree flash for a second before the crystal returns to its usual blue. Groans fill the room as the Seers slowly recover.

"Are they going to be all right?" Aya asks, motioning to the Seers.

Waving his hand to those standing above, Wynsil sits back down in his seat. "They'll be fine." The cloths covering the ceiling are pulled away and everyone winces at the sunlight pouring in. "The ritual lasted a little longer than usual. They're tired, but they'll recover quickly."

"I wish there was more information about this so-called choice," Yme says. "Knowing about it but *not* knowing seems counterproductive."

Wynsil slowly nods his head. "I wish I could tell you why the Forest Spirit decided to share this information with you. The only reason I can think of is to prepare you for when it occurs. Or perhaps to help you recognize when it happens."

"How is that helpful?" Aya asks. "If we can't affect the choice, why know about it?"

"I could not tell you."

Lyrrel approaches the three, his steps slow and careful. "Would you like for me to escort them back?"

"We're fine. You should rest," Aya says.

Nodding his head, Lyrrel winces and places a hand on his forehead. "I think you're right. I'm still a little drained from yesterday's unplanned ritual." He grabs Yme's wrist and pulls him close. "Agree to the sparring."

Yme stares at the Seer, confused. But Lyrrel is already walking back to his seat. He looks at Aya, but all she can do is shrug.

Jaxon and the Lakiin brothers are waiting for Yme and Aya outside of their room when they return from their meeting with Wynsil. They meet them halfway down the hallway, Tanith walking at Daniil's side.

"That was quite a long meeting. Anything interesting to report from Eraunel's great leader?" Jaxon asks.

"Not really," Aya lies. Without knowing the details of the mysterious choice, she doesn't think it's important enough to convey to the others. She hopes Yme feels the same.

"He wanted to express his thanks for Aya's healing of the Forest Spirit. Then we got caught up in some Seer magic, but there wasn't anything new from the last meeting."

"All that for a thank you?" Kylii asks. "He couldn't do it in the dining hall?"

"Apparently, not." Aya heads for her room, hearing Yme's footsteps behind her.

"Yme," Jaxon calls. Both Aya and Yme turn, curious as to what Jaxon could want. "I was wondering if you'd be interested in a little sparring match tomorrow. I'm curious to see if you've lost any of the fighting spirit you were so well known for in the

Arena. Plus, I wouldn't mind having a chance to fight you myself out of pure curiosity of my own abilities."

The surprise in Yme's face is reflected in Aya's own. Lyrrel's parting words make sense now. "Tomorrow at the training grounds?" Yme asks.

Jaxon nods. "If that is acceptable."

"Sure, why not."

36

The next day, everyone eats their morning meal quickly, eager to head down to the training grounds. Word spreads through the tower about the sparring match and many Seers venture down to watch. Daniil and Kylii even convince Oswen to allow the children to see the match, claiming it would be good for them to see magic being used for combat.

The spectators gather around the largest of the training grounds, a fenced-in circle. There are a few barrels of water, used for catching rainwater, placed around the circle. There are a few large logs available for seating, but earth mages from the group raise small sections of the ground to provide more.

Anticipation grows as the crowd increases in size.

Aya leans against the wooden fence, her uneasiness growing. Standing beside her are Rava, Mava, and Fleance. All three wear concerned expressions, reflecting Aya's own feelings. She plays with the bracelet on her wrist, rubbing the silk against her skin. *Why am I so nervous? Is it because I want both to win?*

A short distance away, Dolus watches with confusion. "Why are they doing this?"

"For fun, I think," Skara says.

"Fun? Why would anyone want to do this for fun?"

"They want to know one another better," Tristan comments.

Dolus snorts, crossing his arms over his chest. "Conversations aren't good enough?"

"Not for some men."

Tristan's words send another wave of unease through Aya. She's seen both men fight. She's seen both take on overwhelming numbers on their own. But she can't predict who, if they chose to fight seriously, would win.

"Feels like the Arena," Yme comments, making Aya jump. He and Jaxon walk to the fence. Aya notices Yme is no longer wearing shoes and Jaxon has a few weapons. He carries his sword, but there are two knives attached to his belt.

Yme climbs over the fence, giving Aya one last comforting look. "Except for the lack of death."

Jaxon easily swings himself over the fence. "Don't worry. No fighting to the death here. Just a friendly sparring match. Though I can't promise I'll go easy on you."

"You sound confident."

Walking a good distance from Yme, Jaxon raises his sword. A smirk takes the place of his amused smile and he points his blade at Yme. "You win if I have to use my magic."

Raising his fists and bending his knees, Yme returns the smirk. "Fine. You win when I can't use my magic anymore."

"Fine."

Aya bounces her attention from Jaxon to Yme. Both may say this is a friendly fight, but the tension in their muscles tells her another story.

The air thickens with excitement and the growing crowd rumbles. Aldur walks between the two men with his arm raised. He looks at Yme, who nods. He looks at Jaxon, who also nods. He stares straight ahead and inhales sharply before bringing his arm down.

"Begin!" As soon as his arm is down, Aldur dashes for the fence, leaping over it so quickly those on the other side barely have time to clear a path.

Yme raises the ground beneath Jaxon up, but Jaxon is already on the move. He dodges to the left, clearing the earth easily. Yme stomps his foot, shattering the raised earth into smaller sections. He pulls his fists towards his body and the earth flies through the air towards Jaxon.

Jaxon swerves to avoid being hit, managing to close the distance between him and Yme. His sword trails behind him, but the tension in his arm prepares a thrusting strike. Yme throws one fist up, raising another section of earth directly in front of Jaxon. The former caravan leader uses his trajectory to run up the side of the newly made wall. Grabbing the edge of the top of the wall, Jaxon pulls himself up and over, landing on the opposite side directly in front of Yme.

Jaxon uses the momentum of his fall to swing his sword down on Yme. Yme releases a powerful breath, using wind to not only move him away from the downward sword strike, but also slamming Jaxon into the wall. Before Jaxon can recover, Yme slams the palms of his hands onto the ground and the earth shifts, dropping beneath Jaxon like falling leaves.

Feeling the ground disappear beneath him, Jaxon buries his sword into the wall of earth behind him, keeping him from falling into the pit beneath him. He places both feet on the wall and kicks, freeing his sword, and landing on solid ground.

"Don't you have any other tricks?" Jaxon asks, not a shaky breath or drop of sweat to be found. "You use that earth magic a little too much." To emphasize his point, he brushes dust from his shoulders.

Annoyed, Yme holds his left arm out to the side. Raising his hands, he pulls water from the closest barrel into the air. Those standing near it, back away. Yme moves his arm forward and the water floats in front of him. Lifting his other arm, Yme splits the water into smaller orbs and creates a fan above his head.

"I wanted to end the fight quickly. But I guess we'll do it your way."

"My way?"

"No escape."

Yme spreads his fingers wide and softly blows on them. The fan of water stretches and freezes, turning the orbs into ice spears.

Jaxon raises his sword, but movements in the corner of his eyes distract him. Water from the other barrels float around the training ground. A quick nod from Yme and the water surrounds Jaxon on three sides. It freezes into thick ice, the only escape through Yme and his spears.

Aya strains to see what's happening, but the wall of ice blocks her view of Jaxon. Yme rears his arms back, the ice spears mimicking the movement. With a deep breath, he throws the spears forward. Two knives stab through the ice wall and carve downward, making a V shape. Jaxon kicks the wall and opens a way out. He quickly swings out and presses his back against the outer wall of ice.

The ice spears shatter against the thicker ice, but a few shoot through the newly created opening towards the audience.

Realizing Jaxon's trick, Yme releases his magic and all the ice melts instantly. The water hits the crowd harmlessly and the wall drops to the earth. Jaxon runs through the collapsing wall at Yme, his sword raised above his head for a downward slice.

Yme dodges to his left, but Jaxon easily changes the diagonal slice into a horizontal cut, preparing to bury the blade into

Yme's side. Yme throws his hand forward to meet the blade and uses wind to blow the blade back.

Using the force of the wind, Jaxon spins, taking steps back, and prepares to thrust his blade straight at Yme's stomach. The earth rises between them, absorbing most of the thrust of Jaxon's blade. Jaxon pulls the dagger from his belt and swings it around the earth at Yme, forcing Yme to leap backwards onto the muddy earth from his failed water attack.

Jaxon pulls his sword free and attacks Yme with both sword and dagger. Yme stumbles on the slippery ground, throwing the blades aimed for him away with his wind and blocking with his earth magic when he can. Jaxon tries to bring both of his blades together, attacking Yme from both sides, but Yme raises two pillars of earth to block.

Using the small opening, Jaxon kicks Yme in the stomach, throwing him back several steps. Yme tries to keep his footing, but only manages to fall to his knees and not his back. He grabs his stomach, gasping for air.

The blade of Jaxon's sword appears at his throat. "Concede?"

"I accept your surrender," Yme says, his gasps making the humor sound weak. He keeps his eyes on the muddy ground beneath him, placing a hand on the soft earth.

Realizing what Yme is doing, Jaxon throws himself to the side as the ground rises like a great mouth to swallow him. It closes over the spot where Jaxon had been, missing him, but tearing the sword from his hand.

The earth shifts until the sword reappears beneath Yme's hand. He takes it and stands. He sends the mouth after Jaxon, never giving Jaxon enough time to rest. All he can do is run and dodge, his attention focused wholly on the never tiring chaser.

Yme regains his breath and holds Jaxon's sword in front of him, the tip of the blade aimed at Jaxon. His wind magic lifts the blade off of his palm and Yme pulls his free hand back. He gathers more wind magic and punches the hilt of the sword with his fist, shooting the sword towards Jaxon at a terrifying speed.

Jaxon spies the blade and tries to dodge, but the muddy mouth blocks him, pushing him farther into the path of the sword. Cursing, Jaxon places a hand on the earthy appendage. Blue flames surround it, hardening the earth and shattering it.

To avoid the blade, Jaxon leans back onto his hands and kicks the center of the blade, sending it straight up into the air.

Yme smiles and lowers his hands to his side. "Looks like I win."

Jaxon stands and stares at Yme sourly. He takes a single step to the left as his sword penetrates the ground next to him. "Looks like you do."

37

The captivated spectators come to life as they realize the fight has ended. Cheers and applause ring out over the training ground, celebrating both men's abilities. Aya releases a long-held breath, happy the fighting is over.

Yme walks up to Jaxon and holds his hand out to him. Jaxon takes the outstretched hand in his and his sour expression melts into a smile.

People hop over the fence, entering the mini arena to swarm the two men. The children from Oswen's class are allowed to move to the front of the crowd. Their eager faces bring bashful smiles out of Yme and Jaxon. Others pat the two on the back, new fires of resolve burning in their eyes.

Aya stays at the fence, watching with a relieved smile. Those around her talk amongst themselves about the fight. But their words are muffled and Aya can't make out what they're saying. As she watches the crowd surrounding Yme and Jaxon, she realizes everyone is moving unnaturally slowly. The air vibrates with magic and Aya feels her own magic uncurling, reacting to something.

A sound from behind tears Aya from the celebration and she stares at the white tower. A bright, blue light flashes from the top of the tower, blinding Aya for a moment. Blinking the spots from her vision, she feels a throbbing in her heart.

The sky around the tower is now a fiery orange, black smoke circling around the tower. Turning to the city, Aya gasps at the sight before her. Fires burn in the lower levels, slowed as though time itself is fighting the blaze. The pristine white of the city turns gray as soot covers the beautiful stone.

Walking towards the pens, towards Aya, are men wearing blood red armor. At the head is Klaeon's second in command, Teron. The red sash around his waist discolored with blood and ash. In his hand is something wrapped in wet cloth. She looks away, afraid of what is inside the cloth, but a dark shadow covered in bloody chains takes the place of Teron.

Aya feels the heat of the flames growing stronger as the shadow slowly moves closer. The air burns around her, and she can feel the heat entering her lungs, tightening them.

She tries to scream, but there isn't enough air. The shadow moves ever closer, reaching for her. The chains move as though alive, snaking their way towards Aya. The blood dripping from the metal catches fire, the flames a dark red.

"Aya!" Wynsil grabs her shoulders and tears her from the vision.

The fire is gone. The shadow is gone. But her lungs still tighten against the nonexistent heat. She looks at Yme and Jaxon, both still in the middle of the large crowd. They're smiling and talking, unaware of anything wrong.

Mava and Rava appear next to Wynsil, their eyes filled with worry. "What happened?" they ask.

"Something's coming," Aya says, looking at Wynsil.

Surprise filling his face, Wynsil nods his head. He hands her a slip of paper. "One of our own returned from a venture into the woods. He saw men with flags bearing this symbol heading for the city."

Opening the slip, Aya feels a shot of panic race through her. She covers her mouth with her hand, fear tightening her throat. It's the Blood King's insignia.

Mava and Rava curse then call to Yme and Jaxon. But the crowd surrounding them is too loud. The sisters climb over the fence and force their way through the crowd. Daniil and Kylii, noticing the sisters, make their way towards Aya and Wynsil. Yme and Jaxon soon follow, all arriving at the same time.

"What's going on?" Yme asks, noticing Aya's hands shaking.

Wynsil motions his head to the paper. "An army bearing that symbol is headed for the city."

Taking the slip from Aya, Jaxon holds it so Yme can see the familiar symbol drawn upon it. "It would appear our time here is finished. It must be Klaeon's right hand, Teron."

"What?" Yme demands.

The slip burns with blue fire in Jaxon's hands and he stares at Yme. "You didn't think the Blood King would chase after us himself, did you? If Teron is coming that means he'll have a large number of men with him. We need to leave before they reach the city and find us. We aren't prepared to fight trained soldiers."

"What about Eraunel? We can't leave them like this," Aya says, calming the growing fear in her gut.

Ignoring Aya's question, Jaxon places a hand on Yme's shoulder. "Daniil, Kylii, and I will tell everyone to gather their belongings. We'll meet back here in an hour."

"Do we even have an hour?" Daniil asks. "How far is the army from the city?"

"You have enough time if you don't waste it. Our Seers are stalling the army with their magic."

"And how are they doing that?" Kylii asks.

"Their illusions will have the men walking in circles for hours. Though how long it will hold them can't be determined."

"How did they get so close without the Seers knowing?" Daniil asks.

"The forbidden magic has made it difficult for our Seers to easily foresee anything the Blood King does. So, I suggest you follow Jaxon's advice and spread the word quickly."

"Let's go," Jaxon tells Daniil and Kylii. The three run to the still excited group gathered at the center of the training ground. It doesn't take them long to gain the group's attention, and smiles turn to looks of horror.

Yme squeezes Aya's shoulder. "I'll get our things. Stay here." He runs towards the tower, followed by most of the group.

"Wait! We can't just leave without helping Eraunel," Aya yells after him, even though she knows he can't hear her over the screams and cries of the crowd.

Most are panicked and run for the tower. Others hug those staying before running to get their belongings. Oswen gathers the children and leads them away from the training grounds as Daniil and Kylii say their goodbyes. Tanith seemingly appears from nowhere in time to hear a goodbye from Asha.

Wynsil takes Aya by the hand and pulls her away from the panicked mob running past. "You mustn't be here when they arrive, Life Healer. Jaxon has spoken with me about guides for your group and I'll be giving you some of our best. They'll show you the quickest way through the forest. We'll try our best to mislead the men and buy your group more time."

"What about those who're choosing to stay behind? If they're found the Blood King's men may kill all of you or burn the city to the ground!" Tears roll down Aya's face and she speaks rapidly, barely having time to breathe.

Wynsil places a calming finger on her lips and brushes the tears from her face. "You must reach Kellahn, the city in the canyon. For those of your group who wish to stay, we will protect them."

"But I still have many questions!"

"There will always be questions. But there won't always be someone to answer them. You must find your own answers." He turns to leave, but a thought occurs to him and he looks back to Aya. "How did you know about the men coming?"

Aya hesitates before answering. "I saw them."

"You *saw* them?" Wynsil looks to the ground. "So, you had a vision. Do you have visions often?"

"I wouldn't call them visions. I have dreams and they sometimes spill into when I'm awake."

"You continue to surprise me, Aya. I will go to meet the men. My people going with you will take great care of you."

Aya stands in silence, playing with her bracelet as Wynsil walks away.

III

RACE TO THE CLIFFS

L ess than an hour passes before the group is ready to leave. Meeting back at the pen where Yme and Jaxon fought, those who are staying behind say their final goodbyes and head back to the tower to hide from the approaching army. Aya is only slightly surprised that over twenty choose to stay.

Among the five men Wynsil has given the group, Lyrrel takes the lead. He isn't wearing his Seer robes, wearing brown and green foraging clothes like those of the other men from Eraunel. Across their backs are dual blades and crossbows. Hoods cover their heads and create shadows across their faces.

They leave the city and stop at the base of the tall white trees providing a natural wall around the city. A tunnel is carved into one of the tall trees, but Lyrrel leads the group away from it.

"Meridon," he says, looking to an older man.

Meridon turns his face upwards and makes a bird call with his voice. After a few seconds, an answering birdcall is heard, and several ladders are lowered as well as a slow-moving platform.

"Those who can climb, use the ladders. If your supplies impede your speed place them on the platform. We only have time for two rides up so only those who can't climb use it," Lyrrel explains.

Anxious faces look to one another before several walk forward to place bags on the platform. Lyrrel waits to see who will ride the platform up, but none step onto the wood.

Three of the men from Eraunel climb first encouraging those in the group to follow. Tanith whines at Daniil, but he eventually convinces her to ride the platform. Once she's on, Meridon sends a different birdcall upwards. The platform shakes to life and slowly ascends.

Aya follows Jaxon up, not surprised when he places a large gap between them. Yme climbs behind her. He doesn't rush, giving her less pressure to climb.

It's a long climb before they reach a platform built into the side of the trees. They are almost as high as the tower and Eraunel stretches before them. The platforms cutting through the trees form another city of sorts. Cots are placed inside carved out trunks and torches line the walkways. There are bridges connecting platforms attached to trees leading deep into the forest.

Lyrrel and Meridon are the last to climb onto the platform and the men of Eraunel pull the ladders up. The smaller platform bearing Tanith and the supplies is locked into place before the group is allowed to gather their belongings. Once everyone is situated and Tanith is back at Daniil's side, Lyrrel takes them across multiple bridges, distancing them from Eraunel.

The bridges are well made and hold the group easily. The many branching pathways give the platforms in the trees a maze-like quality and the group is thankful for their guides.

Meridon takes over leading the group once they reach a platform forking into two paths.

As the group follows the new guide down the left path, Aya stops and turns to look back at the now hidden city. The vision is still fresh in her mind and the fear that had been gnawing at her since is too great to ignore.

Noticing her missing from his side, Yme stops and faces her. "Aya, we have to keep moving. Teron could reach the city at any moment and if we aren't far enough away, he might catch up."

"I can't leave them like this. There has to be something we can do, some way to help," Aya says.

Jaxon has stopped and glares at the two. "We have to keep moving!"

Hearing Jaxon's yell, the group stops and glances back at Aya. She shakes her head. "We can't leave them to Klaeon's men. People will die. If anything, I can heal those who are hurt. Please, there must be—"

Screams echo through the forest. They're faint, but unmistakable. The screams of those dying fill Aya's ears. Black smoke rises from the forest behind and small explosions ring out, overpowering the screams for a moment.

Without a word, Aya drops her bag and runs back the way they came, crossing the bridges and guessing at the correct paths.

Yme bolts after, managing to eventually catch up to her and grab her arm. He stops her and pulls her close. "You can't go back! They'll only kill you, too."

She jerks from his hold. His words "kill you, too" sends a shock through her body, confirming what she already feared. "We can't abandon them."

Appearing next to Yme, his cheeks flushed from running,

Lyrrel waves his hand forward. "Life Healer, please, we must continue on. If we stay too long, they may find us."

"But your home."

Lyrrel sighs and looks to Yme, then motions the elemental mage to return to the group. Yme hesitates, eyeing him suspiciously. But he acknowledges the young man's request and walks back across the bridges.

Waiting until Yme is out of sight, Lyrrel holds his hands up on either side of Aya's head. "Life Healer, may I?"

"What?"

Biting his lip and bouncing on the balls of his feet, Lyrrel glances behind Aya in the direction of Eraunel before his darting eyes lock onto her face. "May I use my magic on you?"

A pause brings the sound of more screams and Aya quickly nods her head. Lyrrel steps closer to her and places his hands on either side of her head. His violet eyes stare deep into Aya's green ones. "You have to trust me. Don't fight it."

Aya nods her head, having a little trouble with the hands on her head. "I trust you."

"Close your eyes."

She does. Lyrrel places his forehead against hers. Aya feels pressure surround her body. But this pressure is gentler than the one the Spirit of the Forest used on her. Her mind fills with white light.

Suddenly she's moving fast through the trees. So fast, she can feel the branches of the trees hitting her as she strays too close. A hand grabs hers and she knows Lyrrel is next to her. But she can't see him.

"Don't release my hand, Life Healer," Lyrrel's voice says as though he's standing directly in front of her.

The forest flashes by and Eraunel appears before them. They fly past the buildings and appear at the entrance of the city. The bridge the group crossed when they first arrived now carries several dozen heavily armored men to the city. Teron leads, wearing his red sash and handing his helmet to a man next to him.

Wynsil meets them with several cloaked Seers. But unlike when he met Aya and the others, those of Eraunel are nowhere to be seen. The people of the city are hiding in their homes, watching the strange men from small openings in their curtained windows or cracks in their partially opened doors.

The small army stops before Wynsil and his Seers. Teron's gaze moves from each person with a look of disgust on his face. Wynsil watches him calmly, waiting for the stranger to speak first.

"We're looking for a group of escaped prisoners. We've been told they entered this forest several days ago and were heading in the direction of this city. Under order of Blood King Klaeon, ruler of the lands bordering your city, you are to bring them forward."

A kind smile forms on Wynsil's face. "We don't receive many visitors here in our city of Eraunel. Your escaped prisoners included."

Teron's eyes narrow and look past Wynsil to those hiding in their nearby homes. "You deny seeing or housing them?"

"Yes. You and your men are the only ones we've seen."

Gripping the hilt of his sword, Teron shouts an order to the men behind him. Two men walk forward, a third hanging limp between them. The smile disappears from Wynsil's lips as he takes in the sight of the still body.

"Your scout told us there was a group who passed through your city not that long ago," Teron says, watching Wynsil's reaction. "In fact, he told us quite a bit about the group."

The two men holding the Eraunel scout throw him to the ground before them. Blood splatters on the white stone.

Teron continues, "It took some coercing, but eventually he

told us about the magic users who use ice and fire, twin brothers I believe he said. There was also mention of a woman claimed to be a Life Healer."

Two of the cloaked Seers start to move forward, but Wynsil stops them with his hand. They stare helplessly at the bleeding scout.

"My favorite bit of information he told us, though, would have to be that the group is, in fact, staying here in your beautiful city. Clever though they were, the distractions you had your magic users perform to keep us from finding this place were easy to see through. That's how we found your very talkative scout."

Teron walks forward and places his armored foot on the unconscious scout's head. "Would you like to rescind your statement from earlier? Or will you claim your scout to be a liar?"

The Seers behind Wynsil grow anxious. Wynsil's expression remains neutral, but his hands clench tightly at his robes.

A weak groan rises from the unconscious man's lips. Teron leans down slightly as though listening. "Seems your man is coming 'round. Should we wait to hear the words from his own mouth? Or..." Teron shifts his weight, placing pressure on the scout's head.

Terror-filled gasps echo behind Wynsil, but he remains silent.

Staring at the Seers gathered behind Wynsil, Teron smiles, showing teeth. "Search the buildings."

Teron's men run forward, knocking Wynsil to the side and several of the Seers to the ground. The soldiers kick the doors in of the closest homes, barging in as screams fill the air. Any who try to fight back or flee are killed with blades. Others are forced to watch as the men destroy their homes. Crashes are heard from inside and furniture is thrown out of the homes into the street.

Wynsil and his Seers watch with wide, horror-filled eyes. "You're killing innocents. Stop this now," Wynsil demands, turning back to Teron.

Sneering at him, Teron places more pressure on the scout's head. "Bring me the prisoners and we shall stop."

"There are no prisoners here."

"Shame." Teron places all of his weight on the scout.

Aya screams and turns away from the sight. "No! Stop him!"

"We can do nothing. These are visions of things that have already come to pass," Lyrrel says, sadly.

A white light flashes, blinding Aya. When her vision clears, she sees the tower looming above them. She turns and recognizes the training grounds. The people of Eraunel move solemnly, cleaning the debris from their streets. Destroyed stone buildings in the distance are searched by others for salvageable goods or possibly people who weren't lucky enough to escape, Aya isn't clear which.

The arena where Jaxon and Yme sparred now has rows of bodies covered in cloth laid out on the ground. A parade of people carrying bodies wrapped in cloth move closer to add to the growing numbers. Standing within the pen is Wynsil. He stares at the body in front of him. The head is misshapen, and blood has stained most of the white cloth. Wynsil's robes are fouled with dirt and blood and his face is tired, making him appear far older than he is.

One of those who remained behind carries a body and places it down in a row. She touches the covered face and weeps. Aya recognizes her as the woman who led her to the Forest Spirit's room, but she can't remember her name. A shocking revelation as she watches the young woman weep over the body. Tears swell in her eyes as she looks at the growing number of dead.

"Don't weep for us, Life Healer." Wynsil's raspy voice scares Aya and she stares at him. A Seer stands next to Wynsil with his hand resting on his leader's shoulder. His eyes are blue with magic, but Aya still recognizes him as Oswen, the teacher of the children Kylii and Daniil spent their time with.

Aya releases shaky breaths, trying to control the sobs so she can speak clearly. "I'm sorry. I wish I could help. I wish I could repay you for what you've done."

"We must all play our parts, Life Healer. Go. You must continue on. Don't let our sorrow stop you. We shall rise from this. All I ask is that you treat our people well and promise to send them home when your journey is complete."

"I promise."

The white light flashes and Aya opens her eyes. Lyrrel blinks and releases her head. They're back in the trees. The screams of the city are still echoing through the trees.

"We must go, Aya," Lyrrel says, grabbing her hand.

Aya stares back at the burning city. "But the bodies. The attack was over."

"Wynsil's words are from the near future. It took a little more of my power to allow you to see it. But trust me, we must go, now."

Hesitating, Aya nods and they rush to catch up to the group. Once together, Yme comforts Aya. The group moves on without any more interruptions.

39

The treetop bridges are extensive. Perfectly blending into the surrounding trees and foliage, the pathways lead in all directions. Separate platforms built higher in the trees provide safe places for the scouts traversing the maze to rest.

Hours pass as the group follows the guides. They reach the end of the pathways, and Lyrrel signals to two of the other men from Eraunel. They grab ladders, hidden beneath the platforms and journey down to the forest floor.

"We'll wait for Dounal and Harin before heading down," Lyrrel says. "They'll make sure we haven't been followed."

"Wouldn't sitting here allow anyone who may be following us to catch up?" Kylii asks.

"It won't take them long." Whistles from below bring a smug smile to Lyrrel's lips. "See. Down we go."

Meridon, Lyrrel, and the youngest man from Eraunel, Neall, set up a platform to be lowered. Tanith reluctantly hops on as bags of supplies are placed on with her. The descent to the forest floor begins. Many are relieved to have solid ground beneath them.

Once the platform has been fully lowered, the group grabs their bags and Tanith leaps off, rolling on the ground, appreciatively. The men who lowered the platform pull it back up as well as the ladders. Then they climb down the thick bark of the tree.

"Let's continue on. The sun will be setting soon," Lyrrel says.

The fear of nightfall and the possibility of Teron's men catching up to them push the group forward. The trees grow closer together, cutting off most of the light from the lowering sun. But it still takes several hours before the group needs to stop to light torches.

Once darkness falls the forest takes on a new life. The calm felt back in Eraunel is replaced with discomfort. The animals sound larger, hungrier.

The small circle of light created by the torches provides little comfort against the unknown shadows just beyond the reach of the light. Animals watch the group from the safety of the darkness, light reflecting in their eyes for a moment before disappearing. The cry of a night bird sends chills through the group and presses everyone closer together.

Lyrrel and the other men from Eraunel don't seem as affected by the change in the forest. But that doesn't mean they're any less tense.

Fog rolls along the ground like water. The air is cooler and strange shapes among the trees give illusions of large beasts watching the group. Aya also notices the bark of the surrounding trees darkening to an odd scarlet color. It reminds her of blood, and she shivers. Yme nudges her with his arm.

Aya shakes her head. "I'm fine. A little tired, that's all."

"Stay together," Lyrrel says, his voice only loud enough for everyone in the group to hear. "We'll continue for a couple more hours, then rest."

"Don't wander off or drag behind. Strange things happen in this part of the forest," Neall says, his hand tight on the hilt of his knife.

"What kinds of things?" Rava asks, huddling close to Mava.

Meridon moves his torch to his other hand so he can meet the sisters' eyes. "This part of the forest has grown upon ancient graveyards. Thousands are buried beneath this earth. These trees grow from the dead."

Neall nods his head and sweeps his torch towards the nearest tree, showing the dark scarlet of the bark. "They say the red of the bark comes from the trees feeding on the blood of men."

"Stop that talk," Lyrrel says angrily. "They're only stories."

Despite Lyrrel's words, the group finds itself moving at a faster pace. New trees fade into view among the taller trees. They are much smaller and twisted into painful shapes. The branches reach for the group like skeletal fingers, catching on loose clothing.

Insects scatter from the light of the torches. A small, black-furred beast hisses as the group passes too close to its nest and a member of the group shrieks as a skull comes into view. A hole in the top of the head allows a different small brown animal to peek its head out and watch the group.

The farther into the darkened forest they travel, the more regularly they spot bones hiding among the grass and under the fog. Most are of larger animals, but now and then a human skull is spotted, half-buried in the dirt.

A shiver runs up Aya's spine as they pass another animal skeleton. Daniil and Kylii walk up on either side of her, each holding a torch. Tanith's ears spin around at each sound. Her head jerks to the left or right and she hesitates before returning to Daniil's side.

"This part of the forest is full of dark magic," Jaxon says, suddenly behind Aya, Daniil, and Kylii.

Nodding, Daniil searches the darkness. "We've heard stories about forests that took root in graveyards. The trees would take sustenance not only from the bodies, but also from any magic that once belonged to the dead."

"Some say the magic would leech into the soil and bring the dead back to life," Kylii adds.

"Others say the forest would use the magic as a defense. When unwary travelers entered, the trees would fill the bones with magic. Skeleton hands would emerge from the earth to grab any unlucky traveler and pull them beneath the earth to feed the trees."

Yme turns angrily. "Stop telling ghost stories. We've enough trouble worrying about the men chasing us without you scaring the group. And you." He looks at Jaxon. "Don't encourage them."

Jaxon shrugs. "I was simply stating a fact."

"You still know better than to say anything around these two. They could transform a worm into stories of horrors."

A flying animal shrieks as it flies directly in front of Yme, almost crashing into him. Yme yelps and uses his wind magic to send the beast back into the surrounding forest.

Daniil and Kylii explode into laughter at his fright.

His face turning red, Yme glares at the brothers. "Stop that! Your stories are making me paranoid."

Trying to stifle her laughter, Aya can't contain herself with the brothers laughing on either side of her. Jaxon turns his head away, to hide the smile on his face.

Lyrrel suddenly stops walking. "Everyone, quiet!"

The serious tone of his voice silences the laughter. His head moves from side to side as he searches the darkness. The silence hits the group. The shriek from the flying creature distracted them, but they now realize they hadn't heard the sounds of the night creatures for several minutes.

From the silence a new sound echoes through the darkness. It moves towards the group from the front. Once it reaches the edge of the light created by the torches it splits into multiple sounds, surrounding the group.

"What is that?" Aya asks softly.

Leaning down, Yme places his hand on the cool earth. He waits until he's certain before speaking. "It's the earth. It's shifting."

"With earth magic?" Jaxon asks.

"I'm not sure. It doesn't sound or feel right."

The sound moves into the circle of light and the group moves closer together. The sound grows louder and closer, creating small screams of terror even though nothing can be seen.

Silence. The sound stops. Fear is palpable in the air as eyes search the darkness for movement. Aya places a hand on Yme's shoulder. He places his hand on hers but keeps his attention forward and slowly stands.

A hand explodes from the ground beneath Aya and grabs her leg. She screams, falling to the ground as she tries to escape. Yme grabs her, pulling her free with a swift kick at the disembodied hand. The hand retreats back into the earth and the sound of shifting soil returns.

"They're under the ground!" Yme yells.

40

W alls of earth surround the group, blocking their way forward and back. Shock and confusion blazes through the group. Yme and the two other earth mages run to the walls. They place their palms on the earth and try to lower them, but nothing happens.

The earth beneath Aya opens up. Screaming, she tries to grab either Daniil or Kylii, but misses them. They grab for her, but it's too late. She inhales a quick breath as the earth swallows her up. Terror fills her and she fights to keep from screaming, afraid opening her mouth will only fill it with earth. An arm wraps around her and she's forcefully pulled back. The earth opens up around her and she's pulled from underground on the other side of the walls.

Gasping for air, Aya is greeted by four men dressed in blood-red armor. The man holding her isn't wearing armor, but thin leather dyed the same red. More men in leather rise from the earth and stand around the walls. They place one hand on the walls and wait for orders.

"You the Life Healer?" the largest of the armored men in

front of Aya asks. She recognizes the armor. These men are soldiers, but how they were able to get ahead of the group, she has no clue.

She glares at him and struggles against the man holding her, hearing the confused screams coming from inside the earthen walls. "You picked me out of a group. I think you know I am."

"Lower the walls."

The men in leather step back and the walls of earth lower. The entire group is trapped in the ground up to their shoulders, preventing any mages from using their magic. The only ones not affected are Yme and the two earth mages who were able to counter the magic. Once the walls go down, they immediately face the soldiers.

"Aya!" Yme yells. Wind blows around the group, leaves flying through the air.

The sound of metal unsheathing cuts through the blowing wind and two sword blades appear under Aya's chin. The wind stops immediately and Yme takes a threatening step forward.

"Stop there or she dies!" the larger soldier yells.

Aya searches the group, relieved to see no one has been injured. But she notices someone is missing. Tanith is nowhere to be seen. *Did she escape? Or did they not think she was part of the group?*

The larger soldier steps forward, nodding his head at the leather-clad earth mages. They touch the ground and Yme and the two mages still free sink into the earth up to their shoulders.

"Send the signal," the soldier orders. "When General Teron gets here, all of you will be dragged back to Bloodfall."

Anger burns inside of Aya as one of the leather-clad mages raises a hand above his head. A flash of light shoots up and an explosion of multi-colored flashes light up the sky. The larger soldier walks up behind Aya and roughly pulls her arms behind her back, placing shackles on her wrists.

As soon as the shackles are locked, a wall slams down between her and her magic. Why any mage would choose to make anything that blocks another mage's magic is beyond her. The familiar feeling is odd, bordering on terrifying. She remembers the first time she felt this magic. Back when Jaxon was still a slave trader and she was still naïve to the ways of the Blood King. He had similar chains. She never wanted to wear them again.

The soldiers sheathe their swords and slowly walk through the trapped group. The leather clad mage holding Aya sinks her into the earth up to her thighs. He releases her arm but stands just behind her as though ready if she escapes.

Another soldier approaches Yme with a metal collar and snaps it onto his throat. A frustrated yell escapes his lips, and he curses at the soldier. The other soldiers carefully walk through the group trapped in the earth, heading for the earth mages. They place a metal collar on each, assuring their earth magic is blocked.

The larger soldier hesitates before looking back at the others. "Hey, look who's here. We got us a celebrity!" Laughing, he nudges someone with his foot issuing a frightened yelp from the man.

The other soldiers wander over to see, and their snickers send a shiver of worry through Aya. She leans over to see who they're talking about and spots Dolus's head between the legs of the soldiers.

"You've got it wrong, Len. This guy ain't no celebrity. He's a traitor," one of the other soldiers says, his hand resting on the hilt of his sword.

"Kyle's right," the larger soldier, Len says, kneeling down. "And you know what we do to traitors."

The soldiers eagerly laugh. One kicks dirt into Dolus's face, a rock hitting him in the eye. Dolus screams in pain and blood rolls down his cheek. He jerks back and forth, trying to free himself of the earth, but makes little headway.

Len grabs Dolus by his hair and pulls his head back. He smiles up at his comrades. "What do you think? Slit the throat? Or cut the whole thing off?"

Tears mix with the blood on Dolus's cheek. He whimpers loudly, shaking his head furiously.

"He's not a traitor! He's our prisoner!" a voice yells, drawing the soldiers' attention.

Leaning over farther, Aya almost loses her balance trying to see who spoke. Her eyes widen when she sees it was Rava. *What the hell is she doing?*

"Shut up!" one soldier, Kyle, yells, kicking a nearby rock at her. "Course he's a traitor."

"If he ain't a traitor, why was he walking with you without being tied up?" another soldier asks.

"Look at him," Rava continues, spitting the words out. "He's too much of a coward to be a traitor. All we had to do was threaten to break his legs and any thought of running was gone."

Len roughly releases Dolus's head and stands, sauntering over to her. "Now why would we believe that? Maybe you're trying to protect him. Which is ridiculous since even if he isn't a traitor, he's still going to be killed for letting you pieces of shit escape the Arena. It would be a mercy to kill him here. Who knows what the King would do to him?"

"How do you know the King doesn't already know about him?" Rava glares at Dolus.

"What?" Dolus stammers.

"He's been communicating with your leader." Rava leans her head back to meet the larger soldier's eyes. "How else could you have found us so quickly?"

Aya can't see Len's face, but the other soldiers look at each other with a hint of unsureness. Even the leather-clad mages shift uncomfortably.

"Our orders were to capture them. Maybe we shouldn't kill anyone until Teron gets here," one of the other two soldiers says.

"Shut it, Huk," Kyle yells, hitting the soldier in the arm. "She's just trying to save that grodun shit's pathetic life! You think he looks smart enough to be a spy?"

"What if he is and the general knows it? What if he gets here and we killed him when he might be carrying important information?"

Dolus's face blanches, realizing how thin this farce is. Aya feels bad for the former Voice of the Arena, almost wishing she hadn't convinced the others to let him come with them. It's her fault he's here. Even if the other alternative was possible death.

"All of you shut your mouths!" Len roars. He punches Rava across the face, bringing a shout from Mava nearby. "Not another word outta you, either!"

Rava moans but stays silent.

Stomping back towards Dolus, Len draws a knife and kneels down. He grabs Dolus by the hair and holds the knife high. "Whole head off it is, then."

Dolus screams, many in the group echoing him. Others turn their heads away, unprepared to watch the horrifying deed. Aya struggles in the earth, desperately trying to somehow free herself as the knife lowers.

41

A strange sound whistles through the air and an arrow stabs into the head of the larger soldier. The knife falls from his hand and his body topples to the ground, dead.

Silence overtakes the entire group as they all stare at the soldier's still body. Blood pools around his head and his eyes are still open, though no longer able to see. Dolus gapes at the dead man, confusion and horror mixing on his face.

"Who the fuck did that?" Kyle yells, drawing his sword and spinning around. The other two soldiers do the same, all three searching for any signs of who shot the arrow.

Another whistle precedes an arrow slamming into the leather-clad mage standing beside Aya and he falls to the ground. An arrow protrudes from one eye, but Aya is more interested in the fact the arrow was shot from a different direction. *There's more than one.*

More arrows fly from the forest, killing the leather-clad mages remaining. The three soldiers move towards the center of the still trapped group.

One soldier, the one named Huk, turns to Yme. "Is this you? Did you have people hiding in the trees?"

Yme doesn't answer, only stares at the soldier with contempt.

The young man kicks Yme in the chest. "Answer me!"

"Come out or I'll kill this bitch!" Kyle yells, aiming his sword at Rava. There's only silence in response.

Aya searches the surrounding trees for any sign of movement. Is it others from Eraunel? Or is this some new danger... worse than these soldiers?

The response is quick. Not the whistle of arrows, but the sound of many bows firing. The soldiers jump at the sound, but it's too late. Arrows fall from above, impaling the men. All three fall to the ground, but Huk is still breathing.

With a sudden roar, Tanith leaps from the forest and jumps onto the gasping soldier. She bites down on his throat as he screams and attempts to throw her off. Soon his screams stop, and she releases him. Raising her head, she licks the blood from her jowls.

Men appear from the forest, holding bows aimed at the group. Scarves cover their heads and mouths. Their clothing is made of light material, but leather pieces keep the cloth from being too loose. They carry few supplies, but their well-worn shoes tell Aya these people walk long distances.

Heavy footsteps walk up behind Aya and the cool metal of a blade is placed at her throat. "Who were those men?" a deep voice rumbles, reminding Aya of an animal growling.

"Soldiers of the Blood King's army," she answers, not even sure if the man holding the blade knows of Klaeon. "There are more coming. We need to leave before that happens."

"How do we know you aren't with them?"

Scoffing, Aya wishes she could move her hands, but the metal shackles prevent it. "Do we look like we were with them?

They almost killed one of us." The blade presses against her throat, causing her heart to pound loudly in her ears.

The owner of the voice and blade walks in front of Aya, giving her a good look at this new captor. The skin she can see not covered by cloth is dark. Light brown eyes, the color of wet sand, watch her curiously. With his free hand, the man removes the scarf covering his mouth, leaving it hanging below his chin.

"There are some in your group wearing the clothes of Eraunel. Explain."

Casting a glance at the group still trapped, Aya sees the men with bows still aiming their weapons at the defenseless prisoners. "Tell them to lower their weapons," Aya says.

"I asked you to explain."

Licking her lips nervously, Aya looks at the man. "We came from Eraunel. We are travelers searching for the city in the canyon beyond this forest. The men from Eraunel are our guides."

The man's face is unreadable, but he removes his blade from Aya's throat. Sheathing his weapon, he turns to his men. "Help them."

Relief washes through Aya as the bows and arrows are put away. "These shackles are inhibiting our magic. One of those men must have a key."

One of the newcomers searches the dead bodies and finds a ring of keys. He removes the collars from Yme and the two earth mages. Taking deep breaths, the three free themselves from the earth and begin helping the rest of the group. The man with sandy eyes is handed the ring of keys and he quickly removes the shackles from Aya's wrists. The familiar connection fills Aya's body with warmth and she takes a deep calming breath.

Yme cautiously approaches Aya, his attention fully on

Sandy Eyes. Seeming to sense the cause of the hesitation, he nods his head at Yme and backs away.

Yme runs to Aya and grabs her shoulders. "Are you okay?"

Nodding, Aya smiles. "I'm fine. Though I can't feel my feet."

Moving his hands to the ground, Yme inhales deeply. As he releases his breath, Aya feels the earth push her upwards. Once free of the dirt, she takes a few steps to reassure herself everything is fine. Yme stands and she places her hand on his chest, making sure the kick from the soldier didn't break anything.

Aya looks to the group. Dolus is sitting on the ground, his expression reminding Aya of a sad child. The cut above his eye is still bleeding, but Tristan and Skara are already at his side. Rava walks to them and sits beside Dolus. They speak to each other, though Aya can't hear what either says over the sound of the group thanking the strange men. Daniil and Kylii find their way to Aya and Yme, the Khorgoi watching Sandy Eyes.

"Tanith is sorry she didn't come out to help sooner. When she felt the earth shift, instinct kicked in and she bolted for the trees," Daniil says.

"We saw the flash of lights in the sky, but we didn't truly know where you were until we came across your beast," Sandy Eyes says. "She told us there were dangerous men here."

"You can hear her voice?" Kylii asks with sharpness to his voice causing Daniil to place a hand on his brother's shoulder.

Sandy Eyes ignores the hostility beneath Kylii's words. "No." He gives a high-pitched whistle and a shadow leaps from the trees. "But he can."

The shadow is another Khorgoi. He walks to Sandy Eyes and sits. His scales are charcoal gray. A dark brown mane contrasts the scales and the black horn curving from his head. He is smaller than Tanith, but his horn is slightly longer.

"This is Saunem. Your Khorgoi told him where to go and he told me," Sandy Eyes explains.

Saunem looks at Tanith with dark blue eyes and coos. Tanith bares her fangs, slapping her tail on the ground. Daniil places a hand on her head, but he can't help the small smile on his lips.

"Who are you?" Jaxon asks, he and the rest of the group approaching.

Placing a hand on his chest, Sandy Eyes bows his head. "My name is Deven. My group patrols this area for any threats from the south. Though we rarely come this far into the forest." A sudden flash of light in the sky sends a panic through the group. "You said more men were on their way?"

Aya nods. "More soldiers who are after us."

"You'll explain why these men are after your group as we walk. That light is too close for my liking."

"And where would you be taking us?" Kylii asks.

"You can come with us or you can stay." Giving a sharp whistle, Deven and his men return to the darkness of the forest.

The group's hesitation doesn't last long. They follow, catching up to Deven quickly.

"These men following you are soldiers?" Deven asks.

Aya nods her head. "Soldiers of the Blood King."

"Why are they hunting you? Did you kill their king?"

"No. We escaped from his Arena."

"Well, to be fair, we killed his best fighters and humiliated him... then we escaped," Kylii adds.

"And we escaped with his favorite slave," Daniil says, nudging Yme in the gut.

Yme flinches and moves away from the brothers. "He throws any who oppose him into the Arena in order to kill them. Some of us were a little too tough to kill."

Deven glances behind at the group, lingering on Lyrrel and the four other men from Eraunel. "So, you all escaped north."

"Surely you've had others fleeing from the Blood King pass through here?" Jaxon asks.

"We've had many fleeing for numerous reasons. But none were being followed so blatantly. There is more to you than you're sharing. Maybe you're all criminals and we should sell you back to the soldiers."

"We're not criminals," Aya retorts. "But we do aim to stop him."

"Who? This Blood King? How are you going to do that with such a small group? You couldn't even handle nine soldiers. How will you fair against an army?"

"That's why we're heading for the city in the canyon," Jaxon says. "We heard there may be an army there willing to aid us."

"You're speaking of Kellahn?"

"Yes. Do you know it?"

Deven pauses, his eyes narrowing slightly. "I'm familiar. Are you sure you'll be able to convince them to help you?"

"Klaeon isn't interested in only us," Aya says. "He's conquered all the lands to the south of the Great Mountains. Why would he stop there? His next step is to conquer the north."

"How do you know this?"

Jaxon releases an exasperated breath. "Because it's what any king who yearns for power would do. Why leave the lands here in the north to do as they please when they could one day attack him? Why wouldn't he want to control the north? Control the entire continent?"

Deven raises a hand to quiet Jaxon. "That's very nice, but that's not proof."

"We have proof," Jaxon says. "The men following us. If we capture the one in command, he can tell it to Kellahn with his own tongue."

Aya nearly stops walking in shock, but she manages to keep moving. "Are you suggesting capturing Teron?"

"Not right now. He's going to follow us all the way to Kellahn and if we prepare, we can not only capture him, but send a message back to the Blood King."

Deven laughs and slaps Jaxon on the back, startling him. "I

like how this one thinks. Fine. We'll help you reach Kellahn and even capture this man. If you're successful and your words are true, consider us your first recruits from the north."

The dense forest continues for many hours. Deven's men break apart from the group occasionally to scout the surrounding areas. They confirm the group isn't being followed by any soldiers.

Saunem, the male Khorgoi, ventures into the surrounding trees, disappearing for several hours. He appears next to Tanith and playfully nips at her. She growls and swipes at his snout with her front paw. He leaps out of her reach and runs to Deven's side.

"Looks like someone has a little playmate," Kylii says, elbowing Daniil.

Tanith snorts and lowers her head angrily.

"Be nice," Daniil says, not specifying whether he's speaking to Tanith or Kylii.

Walking next to Jaxon, Aldur motions his head at Deven. "Do you think they're men from Kellahn?"

"I can't say. They recognize the Eraunel men," Jaxon says.

"But the Eraunel men won't say whether they know these men or not," Fleance adds. "Lyrrel will only admit they've heard of groups patrolling the outer edges of the forests."

"But you think he knows more."

"I know he knows more."

Trees are fewer in number. The darkness of the forest lightens as sunlight breaks through the thick foliage. Dark red bark changes to a light brown. Grass grows higher and thicker.

The end of the forest greets the group with the sun high in the sky. Stretching far into the distance before the group is an immense plain. The grass is a stunning green, reaching ankle height.

Aya is reminded of the plains she saw on her journey from

her home to the Arena. Unlike those plains, the one she now stares at has no trees or hills. The flatness of the plain adds to the seemingly endless floor of grass.

Turning to Yme and Aya, Deven says, "We won't be stopping until we reach Kellahn. Is that all right?"

"We're fine. We'd prefer to be far from this forest before resting," Yme says.

With a wave of agreement, Deven orders the group forward. The openness of the plain is welcomed after the closeness of the forest. The warmth of the sun fills everyone with relaxing energy.

The forest disappears behind, the distant mountaintops the only reminder. The vibrant green of the grass dulls and the blades lower. Patches of dirt become visible, as the air grows warmer.

The sun descends in the sky. Weariness fills the group from the continuous travel. Even Deven and his men show signs of tiredness, wiping the sweat from their brows and slowing their pace.

"We're here," Deven says suddenly, stopping.

Excitedly, the group looks ahead. But all they can see is more plains, their visions hampered slightly by the setting sun. Abandoned towers stand great distances apart, reaching high into the sky. No other buildings are seen.

"There's nothing here," Daniil says angrily.

"I thought Kellahn was in a canyon? Where's the canyon?" Kylii asks.

Deven only smiles. Members of his group laugh knowingly at each other. "Take a look for yourselves." He motions with his arm, encouraging the travelers forward.

Aya walks ahead, realizing the ground is at an incline. The sun disappears below the horizon as she climbs uphill. Aya's mouth gapes open at the sight before her. As she climbs higher, the earth appears to split in two and a great canyon stretches in both directions. She turns to the group in shock. "Get up here!"

Everyone runs forward. Deven and his group move out of the way, watching the reactions with a touch of pride and excitement.

Gasps and words of awe fill the air. The sound of a horn cuts across the plains and Aya spots a man standing at the top of one of the abandoned towers. Another horn from a tower on the opposite side of the canyon echoes the first and soon more join in, announcing the approaching group.

Wind blows from an unknown source, stopping the group from proceeding forward. A giant bird appears from the canyon, flying high into the air. Its white feathers catch the last of the light from the sun and a man is seen on the back of the animal.

"What is that?" Aya asks. "I've never seen a bird large enough for men to ride!"

"A pelaphor. We call them pela for short. They've lived in this canyon for thousands of years. The birds build their nests into the walls of the canyon, using their thick beaks and sharp claws to cut directly into the stone. Our ancestors mimicked them, creating our beautiful city," Deven says with obvious pride in his voice.

The sudden appearance of the bird is shocking, but it only draws Aya towards the edge faster. She hears others following behind her and when they reach the edge of the canyon the sight is even more shocking.

The city of Kellahn is carved deep into the walls of the canyon, an overhang of earth protecting it from the weather. Buildings of all heights stretch far into, as well as along, the canyon. Some areas of the city reaches all the way down to a flowing river, while others are kept separate high above. Hundreds of bridges connect the city together across the canyon opening, each at different heights. Giant pillars of stone give the bridges stability while still allowing the river at the bottom of the canyon to flow uninterrupted. There are also larger pillars with multiple levels to support multiple bridges, creating a spider web-like look.

More of the giant birds fly through the canyon, their calls echoing off the walls. They fly from one side to the other or down to the bottom. Aya sees a large building where many of the birds go in and out, making her believe the building is where the birds are kept.

Circling above the group, the first large bird carefully lands nearby as Deven walks forward to meet the man leaping off its back.

"I told you I'd be back before nightfall," Deven says, embracing the man.

"I believe you used the word sundown. And if I'm not mistaken, that sun is down," the man responds. He turns to the group, his eyes moving from face to face. When he spots the men from Eraunel, he smiles a bright, white smile. "Lyrrel! Look how big you've gotten. When was the last time I saw you? Ten years ago?"

"Fourteen years, Arvid," Lyrrel says, walking up to the man and embracing him. "You're always welcome to visit Eraunel. Wynsil is starting to think you don't like our city."

"I could say the same about him."

"I'm getting the feeling you all know each other," Daniil says, waving at the men.

"Ah, yes. Sorry. I am Arvid. I guess you could say I'm the leader of Kellahn, but we don't really have a ruler," Arvid says, the giant bird he flew on nudging his back with its immense beak. He gently shoves it away, pulling food from his pocket. The bird eagerly pecks the food from his palm.

"We apologize for the deceit. The original plan had been to

meet your group as you exited the forest. But when you didn't arrive and we saw that light in the sky, we ventured in after you," Deven explains.

"You already knew we were coming?" Aya asks.

"Well, we knew you were on the way the same time you knew you were on the way." Deven nods his head at Lyrrel. "The best way to keep in touch with Seers is with Seers."

"Does that mean you already knew about our need of an army?" Jaxon asks.

Arvid's smile disappears and he turns to Lyrrel. "No. That seems to have been left out of the communications. All we were told was that a group would be arriving who needed shelter. What's this about an army?"

The group looks to Lyrrel, the young Seer appearing a bit embarrassed as though being caught having done something wrong. "There wasn't much time to send a message once we learned of the approaching threat."

"Now there's a threat?" Arvid's calm exterior slips away. "What kind of threat? Raiders? Gangs? Another wannabe ruler?"

"Something like that," Deven says. "Apparently, that little king in the south is planning to invade the north."

A moment of silence passes before Arvid snorts. "What? Where did you get that idea? He doesn't have the strength or the numbers to even attempt such a thing."

"We can get you proof. His soldiers are following us, including his second in command. If you help us capture him, he'll tell you himself," Jaxon says.

"It's true soldiers from the south are after them. We bumped into a few in the Forest of Spirits." Deven shrugs his shoulders at Arvid.

"But why would they risk angering Kellahn to get this group back?" Arvid asks.

"These two are the main reason." Lyrrel motions Yme and Aya forward.

The leader of Kellahn looks them up and down. "And who are you?"

"This is Yme Gurek, an elemental mage who controls the four elements. And this is Aya Flandeen. A Life Healer."

Arvid playfully shoves Lyrrel. "All the Life Healers were killed over forty years ago."

"Two survived and went on to give birth to a third."

"I see." Arvid's brows furrow in deep thought. "Very well. We'll assist you in dealing with these soldiers. If they can confirm your theory on a possible invasion, *then* we'll discuss the possibility of an army."

He walks back to his large bird and climbs on. "Deven, give them whatever assistance you can. I need to return below to check on the preparations for tomorrow." He kicks and the bird runs towards the edge. Leaping off, Arvid disappears into the canyon.

Aya runs to the edge, along with most of the group. Arvid is flying through the canyon, heading for a large building made of white stone, similar to Eraunel's tower.

"What's the plan to capture Teron?" Yme asks, facing Jaxon. "I assume you have one?"

"I wouldn't call it a plan. I'd call it an outline of a plan," Jaxon says. "But first, we're going to need to split up."

43

"Have I mentioned I'm not a fan of this plan?" Daniil groans.

"Yes. Five times. I think you're just angry Kylii gets to fly on a big bird, and you're stuck in this tower with me," Yme mutters, peering through the small window.

He wasn't exactly thrilled with Jaxon's plan either, but Yme trusts the former leader of the most well-known slave trading caravan knows how to plan ambushes. It came with the line of work, he's sure. In the distance, he can barely make out the fire of the faux campsite.

"GROUP A WILL STAGE A FALSE CAMPSITE A FAIR DISTANCE from the canyon," Jaxon said, nearly three hours prior. "We'll need bedding stuffed with grass, hay, anything we can get our hands on. It'll need to look like all of us are there. To ensure there's no suspicion, about ten will need to be actually present, preferably Aya and Dolus amongst that number. Fleance will lead the group."

"Why Aya and Dolus specifically?" Daniil asked.

"Aya because she's the one they'll be searching for first and Dolus because he's the most recognizable."

Dolus nodded his head, though his hands shook at his side. "I'll do it."

"Me, too," Aya agreed.

"Group B will be separated into two groups and hide in the closest towers. As soon as the soldiers attack the campsite, both groups will circle around behind, blocking Teron's escape and taking care of any mages that may be kept back from the attack. Most likely it will be more earth mages and, possibly, Teron himself," Jaxon continued. "Yme, Daniil, and Tanith will lead one group. Aldur, Deven, and Saunem will lead the other."

Turning to Deven, Jaxon pointed to a few pela flying overhead. "Is it possible to have five or six of our mages ride with your men?"

"Of course. Pela can easily bear two riders. Three if they're small enough," Deven responded.

"Group C will be Kylii, myself, and three mages. Once Group B is in place, we'll attack from above. The final group, Group D, will head into the city for safety. If all works out, Teron is as good as ours."

"How long do you think Teron will wait to attack?" Daniil asks, pulling Yme from his thoughts.

"I don't know. My best guess would be when the moon is high." Yme jumps as something presses against his thigh but is relieved when he realizes it's only Tanith squeezing between him and Daniil for warmth.

"They better attack soon or I'm gonna fall asleep," Bern whispers.

The others in the tower, two of Deven's men, agree. Their names escape Yme as he stares from one to the other. *It's been hard enough to learn the names of those we escaped with.*

"Hey, the fire's out," the gray-haired one of Deven's men says.

Peeking through the window, Yme sees the man speaks true. The campfire is out. He strains his eyes, hoping to see anything in the little moonlight shining from above.

"You think that's our cue?" Daniil asks.

"I think we need to wait a little longer. If we go too early, we'll give the plan up too soon," Yme answers.

"Right." Daniil gazes down at Tanith. After a moment, he says, "Tanith can faintly hear Saunem. Deven will give us a signal."

Yme's muscles tense at the growing suspense. He hopes Aya is ready for whenever Teron's men strike.

44

"Tell Aya what you told Skara when she tried to heal that cut above your eye," Rava encourages Dolus.

"I said I wanted to keep the scar," he responds.

"And?"

A blush rises on Dolus's cheeks. "And... I asked her if it made me look more rugged."

Laughter rises from the six sitting around the fire. Aya smiles and places her fist under her chin. "I assume she answered with a yes. You're starting to look like a real fighter."

The laughter subsides into words of agreement and encouragement for Dolus to join in some sparring matches.

A chilly breeze moves through the camp and Aya rubs her arms. *How much longer should we wait?* She wishes Teron would attack. The sooner he does, the sooner she can climb into a real bed. She wishes Lyrrel or any of the other Eraunel Seers could've helped, but somehow Klaeon's blood magic still blocks them from clearly seeing Teron and his men.

Mava leans close to Aya, keeping her voice low. "Do you think they may be waiting for us to fall asleep?"

"I don't know. Jaxon seemed to think they'd attack whether we were asleep or not," Aya says. She peers past the fire.

Fleance stands near the edge of the fake campsite, feigning keeping watch. He makes sure to only face the direction of the canyon, but she knows he's aware of the direction Teron and his men would most likely come from. The other four in Group A are "sleeping" throughout the fake camp. Now and then they shift to keep up appearance.

Aya fights the urge to look up at the night sky. She thinks she could convincingly appear to be stargazing as she tries to spot the pela flying above but doesn't want to risk it.

Another cool breeze passes through the camp, but Aya feels a tingle of magic. Her heartbeat quickens and she taps Mava's foot with her foot. Understanding, Mava locks eyes with Rava and gives the slightest of nods.

"My eyes feel like stone. I think it's time for me to turn in," Rava says. The others sitting around the fire tense, quickly covering it by stretching or yawning.

"I'm going to stay up a bit longer," Aya says, following the plan they all agreed upon. Everyone, besides Aya and Fleance make their way to their bed rolls and lie down.

Once Aya is alone, Fleance walks around the camp, moving to a position out of sight of Aya. The hope is he'll lure out the first of the attackers and be able to warn the others.

The tingle of magic rises in the air as a third breeze kills the campfire. The camp is plunged into darkness as Aya's vision slowly adjusts. A loud thud behind her makes her jump. Her instinct is to turn and look, but she focuses ahead. She searches the darkness for any movement, any sign of the soldiers attacking.

Another thud behind her is closer and she can't help but turn. Two soldiers who made the grave error of trying to attack Fleance lie behind her. However, two more have managed to subdue him. Standing, Aya screams, but a hand clamps over her mouth, silencing her. She's dragged to the ground and the man holding her struggles to put shackles on her wrists.

Aya reaches deep inside to her magic, feeling it unfurl within. Concentrating, she pushes her magic into the man. He knows she can heal... but may not know she can harm, too. She imagines the man's femur breaking, willing it to happen. She hears the crack and the man shrieks in horrific pain, releasing her.

The man's screams act as a signal and shadows appear throughout the camp. Soldiers grab the fake bodies, confusion giving Mava, Rava, and the others of Group A the chance to fight back.

Grass, hay, and torn cloth fly through the air and the soldiers, not needing to be stealthy, bark orders to one another. Aya runs to Fleance, drawing her knife and plunging it into the neck of one of the soldiers holding him. She pulls the blade free, blood nearly spraying onto her. The soldier grabs at his wound, but Aya kicks him in the knee, sending her magic into her attack. He shouts, but it comes out as a gurgle and he falls to the ground.

Fleance easily breaks the arm of the other soldier holding him before snapping the man's neck. They head for the others seeing everyone fighting the soldiers.

A symphony of screeches tears through the night as the pela dive from above. Large rocks fall onto a number of soldiers, crushing a few, stunning the rest. Small fireballs rain down, somehow missing friendlies and only hitting soldiers. Blue fire engulfs others and Aya soon hears the shouts of confusion change to screams of pain.

The fighting ends quickly, and the pela calmly land outside the fake camp. Jaxon and Kylii hurry towards Aya and Fleance. Soon everyone is gathered, and the damage is surveyed.

"How many were there?" Rava gasps, blood splattered on her face. Even Dolus has a few droplets and a small knife in his hand.

"Two dozen? Maybe more?" Kylii says. "Probably more, right?"

Jaxon searches for signs of any more men, but the night is still. "Where are the others? Yme and Deven's groups?"

"Here!" a voice hails as the groups in question walk towards the rest. Daniil and Aldur drag a soldier between them, the furious man's arms tied together in front of him and a gag in his mouth.

Aya's heart drops. "Where's Teron?"

"There was no sign of him anywhere. We sent Tanith and Saunem to check farther out, but he wasn't here," Yme explains. The two Khorgoi huff in response, grass sticking to their fur.

"But we did catch this one trying to escape," Aldur says.

Deven hits the soldier on the chest, not trying to be gentle. "I think if we get this one to talk, that'll be enough for Arvid."

"You think, or you know?" Jaxon asks.

"I guess that's up to what information this grunt has."

The soldier struggles against Daniil and Aldur, his muffled yells unable to get past the gag.

Daniil places his free hand against his ear. "What's that? You want me to freeze your hands off? Well, I guess he asked for it." He grabs the man's bound hands and ice forms on the soldier's skin. He screams and ceases his struggles.

Daniil removes the ice and shakes his head at Jaxon. "I don't know how much you'll get out of him. He's not very cooperative."

"That's fine. I'm sure Lyrrel and the other Seers can help

with that," Deven says, motioning to two of his men. "Take him to our cells. We'll chat with him in the morning. Make sure you remove anything he can hurt himself with."

The men grab the soldier, dragging him away. All three disappear down into the canyon.

"Can't say your group hasn't brought us some excitement. I think that deserves fresh beds."

Deven leads the group down the hidden path his men took into the canyon. It's steep and several times someone from their group slips on loose rocks. Luckily, the path is wide enough there's no real danger of falling into the canyon.

The path ends at two pillars signaling the entrance to the city. Figures of pela are carved in great detail into the stone of the pillars. Their eyes watch the group as they enter the city.

Entering the city, there is no discernible differentiation between economic standings. At least, not in the buildings. There are still men and women sleeping in the paved streets who gawk at the group walking through. They reach one of the larger bridges crossing the gap of the canyon and Aya is surprised at how sturdy the bridge feels as they cross.

"Rooms have been prepared for you in the west wall. The rest of your group have already been taken there," Deven explains.

As they cross the bridge, the group can't help but peer down to the canyon floor where a mighty river cuts through the surrounding stone. Homes built along the river's edge have docks stretching into the flowing water.

The pela used during the ambush fly past, heading back to their nests. There is an assortment of colors and patterns. They fly through the openings under the bridges and high in the sky. Some dive into the canyon and allow the wind blowing through the canyon to catch them before hitting the bottom.

Once across the bridge, Deven leads them up to a higher

level of the city. He stops before a large building with multiple floors. "This is where you shall be staying."

A woman appears in the lit-up doorway. "Hello, travelers."

Deven faces the group. "If you need anything don't hesitate to ask Emeka. She and the others who run this hotel will be looking after you while you stay here."

The woman, Emeka, waves the group inside. "Come in, your rooms are ready as well as the baths. The others from your group are already in bed, but don't worry. Our walls are quite thick."

Mava and Rava squeal with excitement at the thought of a warm bath and quickly walk inside.

Saunem coos at Tanith as she follows Daniil and Kylii inside. She ignores him, but the male Khorgoi only coos louder. She slaps her tail against the doorway and Deven places a hand on Saunem's head, quieting him.

"Deven. I have a request," Jaxon says suddenly. He pulls Deven to the side and speaks quickly.

Aya's curiosity is piqued, but she can't make out what the two men are discussing. However, she sees Jaxon hand Deven a slip of paper before they finish. *What could it say?*

"You coming?" Yme asks, standing in the doorway of the hotel with Emeka eagerly waiting. Aya nods and they follow Emeka to their room on the third floor of the hotel.

The room isn't as large as their room in Eraunel, but it still has a balcony overlooking the city and canyon. Unlike Eraunel, there is only one, large bed. The window is open, a gentle breeze keeping the room cool.

Aya sits on the bed, bouncing slightly on the thick mattress. "Only one bed. Hope you don't mind sharing."

Leaning against the door, Yme stares at her. "I don't mind."

Aya looks at him and smiles. "You haven't slept in the same bed as me yet. You may regret those words."

"I won't." He walks towards the bed.

"Famous last wo—" She doesn't finish before Yme's lips are on hers. His arms gently wrap around her waist, as he lowers to his knees.

Pulling away, Yme stares at her. She sees a flash of shock and surprise in his eyes, making her wonder if he truly planned the kiss or if it caught him as off-guard as it did her.

"Words," Aya says.

"What?" Yme gasps.

"Famous last words." She takes his head in her hands. "Just finishing my sentence."

"Oh. Sor—" He doesn't finish as she pulls his lips to hers.

46

Jaxon's knee bounces as he sits on the wall. He's been waiting almost an hour for Deven and Lyrrel. He's sure the building built into the canyon wall he's sitting outside of is where the captured soldier is being held and his eagerness to find out what the young man knows vibrates inside him. There's a chance the soldier doesn't know anything major, but even the smallest clue could be useful.

"I didn't expect anyone else to join us," Deven says, walking towards Jaxon. Saunem trails behind, the Khorgoi's tail swinging lethargically. Lyrrel and Meridon follow, now wearing the familiar robes of Eraunel Seers.

"If I'm not welcome, I can leave." Jaxon stands.

"You're more than welcome. I trust you aren't afraid of enclosed spaces?" Deven asks, pausing at the door. "We will be going deep underground."

Jaxon shakes his head. "We travelled two days in a cave system. I think I can handle cells."

Deven opens the door and heads inside, followed quickly by Saunem. Lyrrel and Meridon wait for Jaxon to go ahead, both men staring at him blankly. Smiling, Jaxon follows Deven inside.

Torches are the only source of light inside. The entrance hall is short, ending at a staircase leading up or down. Two men sit on either side of a small table playing cards. They glance up at the group entering, nodding their heads at Deven. One holds out a ring of keys and Deven takes it without slowing his step.

Deven climbs the stairs, not bothering to check if the others are following. Jaxon catches up to Saunem, cautiously walking behind the Khorgoi. They climb three floors before Deven leads them down a longer hallway with doors lining the walls.

Jaxon traces his fingers along the walls and over the doors, confirming a nagging thought. Magic tickles the tips of his fingers when he touches the metal of the doors.

"How many of these cells have occupants?" Jaxon asks.

"Just the one," Deven answers.

"You only have one prisoner? In a city this large?"

Deven's laughter floats back to Jaxon. "These cells were built for war prisoners. We haven't used them in many years. When we need to punish citizens who cause trouble, we put them in the nicer cells."

"Nicer cells?"

"They have windows," Lyrrel quips.

"And a bed," Deven adds defensively. "They're located higher in the city near the pela hatchery."

Stopping at one of the doors, Deven searches for the correct key on the ring he's been carrying. He unlocks the door and pushes the heavy metal open. A stabbing shriek echoes through the hall as the rusted hinges are forced open.

Jaxon winces at the noise, noticing Saunem's ears flatten against his head and the hair on his back standing on end. A low growl rises from the beast's chest and once the door is open, he slinks into the pitch blackness of the cell.

"Hand me that torch," Deven says, holding his hand out to Jaxon.

Jaxon grabs the closest torch and hands it to Deven. Deven walks into the cell, waving the others to follow. The light from the torch reveals a barren room with chains on the walls.

Sitting on the floor at the back is the young soldier. He's been stripped of his armor and his wounds have been cleaned and bandaged. Chains on his wrists are only long enough to allow him to lay down, but not move far from the wall. The soldier winces and raises his hands to block the light from Deven's torch.

Saunem stands in front of the soldier, his head low and back arched. His growls vibrate the air, and the soldier presses his back against the cell wall.

"Morning," Deven says, kneeling in front of the soldier and placing a hand on the Khorgoi's back. "I hope you were able to catch some sleep and think about your predicament. Are you ready to answer our questions?"

The soldier sneers at him. "It doesn't matter what questions you ask. I won't tell you anything."

"Well, we figured you'd feel that way. Lyrrel?" Deven stands and moves back from the soldier. Saunem snorts and moves to Deven's side.

Lyrrel and Meridon step forward. They move to either side of the soldier and kneel down. They each place a hand on the young man's shoulders and bow their heads.

"What are they doing?" The soldier tries to shake them off, but the two hold him steady.

"They're going to encourage you to be honest. We'll start with easy questions. What's your name?" Deven asks.

"I'm not going to answer anything."

Jaxon breathes in deep as the air tingles with magic. *Let's see how well these Seers can dig for information.*

"What is your name?" Deven asks again.

The soldier shakes his head, his brows furrowing and his lips pursing. "Ben... Benton Natus."

"Pleasure to meet you, Benton. Where are you from?"

Benton lowers his head, his hands clenching tightly into fists. "Stop it."

"Where are you from, Benton?"

"Madorfeld," Lyrrel and Meridon say together.

A chill fills Jaxon. Madorfeld is familiar to him. It's a small farming town located within sight of Rabhartach, the Blood King's city. When he was a slave trader, his Black Caravan passed through the town many times on their way south.

"That sounds like a very nice place," Deven says. "Why would you want to leave such a nice sounding place to chase escaped slaves across the continent?"

Benton lifts his head and glares at Deven. "It's an honor to serve our king. Those escaped slaves are criminals and traitors."

"Maybe. But these criminals and traitors claim your king wants to invade my home. Is there truth to that?"

The young soldier's eyes move to Jaxon. "I know you."

"You know *of* me," Jaxon corrects him. "My caravan passed through Madorfeld many times."

"Black Caravan."

Deven snaps his fingers in front of Benton's face. "Focus, Benton. These are the easy questions, remember? Stalling won't do you any good. Is it true? Is your King planning to invade the north?"

"Yes," Lyrrel and Meridon say.

"No. They're lying!" Benton yells.

"I don't think so, Benton. I think you are. I'd prefer to hear everything from you, but if you don't want to cooperate, I'll have Lyrell and Meridon dig deeper."

Fear flashes in Benton's eyes and he swallows. "If I tell you, I can't go home. I'll be executed as a traitor."

"You don't have to tell me. I'm offering you a chance to tell me in your own words. Otherwise, these two will have to dig to find the answers. I've heard it isn't very pleasant, but one way or the other, you will answer the questions."

Lyrrel and Meridon turn their heads so they stare directly at Benton. Jaxon can't see their expressions, but the widening of the young soldier's eyes gives the impression it isn't calming. Benton jumps and shuts his eyes, whining for a moment.

"The Blood King has been gathering power." Lyrrel and Meridon speak together, the tingling of magic in the air growing in intensity. "The north hoarding resources that can benefit the south is the leading cause. If they do not want to willingly share, resources must be forcibly taken."

"Stop! I'll talk! Just get out of my head," Benton shouts.

Deven leans forward. "Prove you will, and they'll stop."

"Our orders were to locate and kill all of the escaped slaves." Benton looks at Deven, sweat forming on his brow. "Except for the Life Healer and the man who stabbed the Blood King. We were to bring them back alive."

Jaxon raises an eyebrow. "Why only those two?"

"I assume because our king wanted to punish them himself. Though General Teron only seemed interested in the Life Healer, not whoever stabbed the king."

"I have one final question for you. After that, I'm sure Jaxon has a few for you as well." Deven kneels down to be at eye-level of Benton. "When will your king invade?"

"Right before we were sent out, all majors forces were ordered to return to Rabhartach," Benton says. "The last thing we heard before we caught up to the slaves was a timeline. In six months, the border would be breached. In eight months, the north would fall."

47

"What do you think this Festival of Magic is for?" Aya asks, standing on the balcony and enjoying the afternoon sun. She watches the people of Kellahn busy themselves with preparations, festive clusters venturing to the many squares throughout the city.

"Emeka said it's to celebrate the diversity of magic and honor the gods who gifted it to us," Yme responds from the bed.

Turning to him, Aya raises an eyebrow in surprise. "When did you ask her?"

"Breakfast. While you were eating your fifth helping of eggs."

"Excuse me," Aya scoffs. She walks to the bed and sits at the foot. "If I remember correctly, you ate five helpings, too."

Yme sits up and pulls Aya towards him. "But I can eat and listen at the same time."

"I don't believe that." She taps his head with her finger. "We should go."

"To the Festival?"

"Yeah."

"Why?"

"It sounds like fun." She frowns. "Oh, wait. You don't like fun things."

"I can think of one fun thing I like," he whispers, leaning his face towards hers.

A knock on their door briefly precedes Jaxon's entrance. He pauses when he sees them on the bed. "I hope I'm not interrupting anything?"

Yme and Aya quickly move apart, shaking their heads and Jaxon walks fully into the room.

"Good. I had a very interesting morning with Deven and you two are the only ones still here... rather, still here and conscious." He walks to the bed and sits down. "That soldier we captured spilled everything. The Blood King is gathering his forces and will invade the north in six months."

"Six months? That doesn't seem like a lot of time to prepare," Yme says.

"He also claimed that Teron knew about the ambush which is why he wasn't there."

"How could he possibly know that?" Aya asks, moving to the edge of the bed.

Yme does the same. "Why send his men into an ambush?"

Jaxon holds his hands up, shaking his head. "I don't know the answer to either question. But there's some good news. Arvid is ready to listen to our request for use of Kellahn's army *and* he'll help us contact those living in other lands here in the north."

"That's fantastic! Except for the whole possibly going to war thing, I guess." A smile grows wide on Aya's face. "You know what a perfect way would be to celebrate the news?"

Yme groans. "I think I know what you're going to say."

"Are you talking about this Festival of Magic happening tonight?" Jaxon asks.

"Don't tell me you want to go, too?"

Jaxon's blue eyes sparkle with magic and excitement. "It might be a good distraction."

Bumping against Yme, Aya gives him a look of pure child-like eagerness. She's almost bouncing on the bed.

Yme eyes her with playful annoyance and shrugs his shoulders. "If we must."

Aya squeals happily and leaps to her feet, grabbing both men by the hand. "Great! Let's go."

Night has fallen over the canyon and lanterns line the walkways, glowing with different colors, adding more magic to the city, and leading festival goers to the large squares located throughout the city.

Many lanterns can be seen now that the sun has set. They glow brightly and appear as large balls of multicolored lights along the canyon walls.

It's to the western square Yme, Jaxon, and Aya head, following the crowds of joyful men, women, and children. Those of the city greet the group of three with large smiles, some singing happily.

The square is large, maybe the largest of the city's numerous squares. Lanterns float magically in the air, platforms are spread throughout, and stands of food and trinkets circle the square. At the center, many people dance around a band of musicians playing spritely tunes.

Mixed among the crowd are others from their group. Bern and Eka are sharing food as they walk from stand to stand, staring at the amazing trinkets for sale. Mava, Rava, and

Fleance are dancing with those of the city and many more are enjoying what the Festival has to offer.

Barely containing her excitement, Aya quickens her pace to join in the festivities. Before she goes too far, she looks at Yme and Jaxon who have pulled away from the crowds. Yme, noticing her longing expression, nods his head and waves her off. She runs into the square. Having little trouble deciding where to start, she runs towards the center.

Yme and Jaxon find a row of seats built along the outer edge of the square and climb to the middle level. They sit away from the large crowd, keeping their eyes on Aya's quick moving figure.

"There's still much to do," Jaxon says, leaning back so his elbows rest on the seats behind him. "I'm sure we'll be able to convince Arvid and the soldiers of Kellahn to fight. But we don't know how easy it will be to convince the others."

Yme releases an exhausted sigh and rests his elbows on his knees. "I know."

"The easy part is over."

Glancing at Jaxon, Yme raises an eyebrow. "The easy part?"

"War is never easy. If it is, you're doing it wrong."

"Are you speaking from experience?"

Jaxon pauses before continuing. "You won't win as you are."

Returning his attention to Aya's figure moving through the crowds, Yme clasps his hands together. "What do you mean?"

"There's a reason your fire magic was taken. It's true that knowing all four elements is rare magic, but something about your fire frightens Klaeon."

"What about your fire, Blue Mage?"

Jaxon laughs. "My blue fire may be rare and stronger than other fire magic, but it has its limit."

"Maybe Klaeon doesn't like being burned. It's very unpleasant."

"Joke all you want, but it isn't a coincidence. Your fire magic is going to be an important tool and you'll need it if we plan to defeat Klaeon."

"Then the war is already over. He stole my fire. It's gone," Yme says, allowing the anger and annoyance of having to remind Jaxon of the fact to enter his voice.

Movement in Yme's peripheral vision allows him to realize Jaxon has leaned forward, close to Yme's ear. "I know how you can get it back."

The floating lanterns above the heads of the crowd shift to different colors, bathing the crowd in a magical dance of color. Some move around the square, lighting all corners.

Mages standing on the roofs or balconies of the surrounding buildings create shapes out of light and send them soaring overhead. High in the sky, men riding pela trail sparks of multicolored magic behind them and draw immense images in the dark sky. Great beasts, smiling faces, and even dancing waves fill the night sky.

Aya spins around, trying to take everything in. But there is too much to see.

A pair of festival goers appear in front of her wearing ornate masks. They dance around her before moving through the rest of the crowd. A vendor carrying a box of similar masks hands Aya a violet mask. When she places it upon her face, it magically forms to a perfect fit, not needing any straps to hold it in place.

Fire erupts from a stand close by and Aya makes her way to where a man and woman hold sticks with fire on one end. The man drinks from a jug and sprays the liquid at the flames, creating fireballs that shoot into the sky before quickly fading. The woman waves her sticks of flame in a small dance before lowering one, fire first, into her mouth.

The audience and Aya gasp as the woman closes her mouth around the flame. When she opens it, the fire remains on the stick and her mouth is unburned. She does the move again. Only this time the stick reemerges from her mouth without the flame. She does this again until the sticks in her hands are completely out. Then she bows.

Aya moves to the next platform, eager to see the next wonder. A man wearing brightly colored clothing creates small balls from nothing and juggles. He starts with two balls, then a third ball appears from nowhere. He does spins and juggles between his legs, before a fourth ball appears.

As a fifth and sixth ball appear, the juggler feigns losing control and one of the balls flies towards the audience. Shrieks rise, but quickly change to laughter as the out-of-control ball changes into a small bird. The bird flies around the crowd before returning to the juggler and becoming a ball once again. With a large smile on his face, the juggler uses not only his hands, but his feet and, at one point, his head to juggle the large number of balls.

Aya passes fire mages creating shapes from burning flames, water mages sending snakes of water through the crowd, air mages making small children float above the ground, and earth mages creating statues from large blocks of stone.

A man with a booming voice tells fantastical stories using his own voice to create the sounds of animals, stormy weather, and anything else his imagination can think of. He even performs a scene where he's on a battlefield, providing all the sounds of weapons, men yelling, and horns blaring. Amongst those watching, Aya spots Dolus, his eyes wide. She wonders if it's because he's found another who uses similar magic or if he's truly enthralled in the story.

A couple performs amazing feats of strength. They move slowly with deep concentration. They lift each other and at one point the man sits in front of the woman with his legs straight out in front of him. He raises his hands, and the woman takes them. He moves closer to her and she slowly leans back, bending at the knees. The man's arms tense, and he slowly rises from the ground. The woman leans back until her back is parallel to the ground and the man stretches his body until it's straight. The woman releases one hand and moves it above her head, elongating the line they have created. The crowd, holding its breath until the calm, graceful movement ends, doesn't react until the two return to a neutral position and stand together to bow. Applause and cheers echo loudly across the square.

Men high above the square walk across wires above the crowd. Some move slowly, using long poles or fans to help them balance, while others run back and forth.

Three men walk to the center of the wire and, one at a time, sit close together and lean forward. A fourth runs up to the three men, stopping before he reaches them, then quickly running back. He runs forward again and pauses. The only movement is his hand waving to keep his balance. After a moment he shouts a single word and leaps over the men, landing safely on the wire on the other side. He moves to a small platform at the end of the wire as the three men take turns standing to join him at the platform. They hold their hands out and cheer to the crowd. The crowd greets them in kind.

As she continues moving from platform to platform, she realizes that not all performers are magic users. Though she wonders how some of the amazing sights she's seen could possibly be done without magic.

More wonders surround the square, even off of the plat-forms. Jugglers who throw not only balls, but also discs and even flaming torches show off their skill. Men who can make puppets move with only magic interact with children and adults alike, sometimes having the puppets perch on shoulders or even tops of heads.

The night goes on and Aya feels the crowd growing larger. Music becomes louder and the center of the square is the main area for dancing. As she moves closer to the center, those dancing grab her and pull her into the dancing mob. She's star-tled at first, but as people dance with her, she laughs and joins in. She spins around in the mass of movement and closes her eyes. She feels the music fill her. Raising her hands above her head, she becomes aware of every person around her.

Her magic allows her to feel those around her, letting her know where they are without looking. She feels the blood pumping through their veins and hears their bodies moving. The realization stops her, and she opens her eyes.

A group of children standing on the edge of the dancing mob watches with longing gazes. Aya runs to the group and holds a hand out to the children. But they only stare at her. One, the oldest girl, grabs Aya's hand and Aya pulls her out into the crowd. The girl grabs one of the other children by the hand and the others follow, confused.

Taking them to the center, Aya starts dancing with the oldest, swinging her around as she has seen other dancers do. At first, the girl doesn't join in the dancing, watching Aya, confused. But as Aya spins the girl around again, a smile appears, and the girl starts laughing. The music picks up and the other children join in.

Aya dances with them for a while longer before excusing herself. She manages to reach the edge of the square where fewer people are gathered and tries to catch her breath. A gentle, cooling breeze moves across her skin and she leans against a wall.

Her eyes search across the square for Yme and Jaxon, but a small chirp from behind makes her turn. A small creature made of fire stares at her from an alley. Its body is so long that as it stands on four legs its back curves upwards. Tiny black eyes blink at Aya.

Looking around, Aya sees no one nearby. She takes a few steps closer and lowers to the ground. She holds her hand out to the flame creature. It cautiously moves forward and sniffs her hand, before bolting into the alley it appeared from.

After a second, its small head appears again, watching Aya. Wanting her to follow. Aya smiles, assuming the creature is the creation of one of the fire mages of the Festival. She follows and the creature leads her away from the Festival. It leads her down several more alleys, before stopping and turning a sharp corner. Aya rounds the corner quickly.

Rough hands grab her, one covering her mouth to stop her from screaming. A blindfold forcefully placed over her eyes knocks the violet mask from her face. She struggles, but strong arms lift her from the ground and take her away.

50

Yme lifts his head suddenly. He searches the crowd, his head turning sharply from right to left.

"What's wrong?" Jaxon waves at a man carrying food. He takes a stick with meat impaled on it and bows his head in thanks.

"I can't find Aya. I was able to keep track of her until she joined in the dancing."

Jaxon pulls a large piece of meat from the stick and sniffs it curiously before popping it into his mouth. "Maybe she's having too much fun to be found."

Yme jumps to his feet, startling Jaxon. "I feel something..."

Jaxon lowers his food, waiting for Yme to continue. The silence only grows longer until Jaxon asks, "What do you feel?"

Searching for the words, Yme narrows his eyes. He knows this feeling. It's familiar to him, as familiar as... His eyes widen when he realizes. "My fire. I feel my fire."

How is this possible? Unless...

Screams erupt at the center of the square, as though Yme's words were a signal. The crowd creates an opening and the music cuts out. Yme and Jaxon are already on the move, forcing their way through the crowd. As they emerge into the opening, the cause of the screams is revealed.

A man stands above the still body of a woman. He holds another woman at knifepoint to keep any mages from approaching him.

Yme's breath catches in his throat as he stares at the body. But the hair is the wrong color, and he doesn't recognize the clothing. He relaxes only slightly as his attention turns to the man with the bloody knife.

"Yme Gurek," the man demands.

Yme's eyes catch sight of Deven and his men moving forward through the crowd. They have their weapons drawn but stop at the edge of the circle.

Stepping forward, Yme glares at the man. "I'm Yme. Why did you kill that woman?"

"To get your attention," the man says. He throws a violet mask to the ground before Yme. Yme recognizes it as the one Aya was wearing earlier. "We have the Life Healer."

"We?" Jaxon steps forward, next to Yme.

The man carefully lifts his shirt to reveal the familiar armor of the Blood King. "Teron waits for you at the top of the East cliffs. Meet him, *alone*, or he will kill the Life Healer."

Deven and his men move forward, seeing a small opening to attack.

"Stop," Yme shouts. "Let him go."

To Yme's surprise, the men stop and move back into the crowd. Deven orders a path to be cleared and the crowd does so quickly.

"Take me to Teron," Yme says.

The man's eyes land on Jaxon. He tightens his grip on the woman, who whimpers in fear.

Jaxon raises his hands in front of him. "I won't follow. I'll even make sure no one else does. But only if you hand over the girl."

The man hesitates before tossing the woman at Jaxon. He turns his back to Yme and walks through the opening in the crowd. Yme follows in silence. Before he gets too far, Jaxon grabs his shoulder. He hands him his sword.

"Be careful. If Teron sent this man, there's a good chance he has more with him."

"Where were you keeping this?" Yme asks.

"Don't worry about that. Bring Aya back."

Yme takes the sword and nods. "Thank you." He follows Teron's man, leaving the crowd in shocked silence.

51

Following Teron's man, Yme stays a good distance away. He grips the sword Jaxon gave him tightly. He can't see any weapons on the man besides the knife he used to kill the woman. But Yme can't shake the feeling he felt earlier. He knows he felt his fire. It happened only for a moment. It can't be coincidence the man appeared after Yme felt his fire.

The two men move through the city, using the largest bridge to cross to the eastern wall. They pass many groups of people celebrating the Festival of Magic. Several try to get Yme to join in the festivities. But when they see him trailing the strange man with a bloody knife they move away.

Teron's man never looks back to ensure Yme's following him. He probably knows there's no way Yme would take such a risk. They walk through the entrance of the city and ascend to the top of the canyon. Passing the towers, the man leads Yme farther and farther along the canyon.

The sound of a struggle comes from the opposite side of the next tower. When they emerge on the other side, Yme looks past the man and sees three figures standing close to the edge of the canyon. Teron holds Aya by the throat, his arm outstretched so that she's closest to the edge. Metal shackles keep her arms behind her and Yme knows she can't use her magic. The third figure stands, waiting patiently for an order from Teron.

The man leading Yme stands on the opposite side of Teron and faces Yme. Yme stops walking, afraid moving closer would encourage Teron to do something stupid.

"Here he is," Teron says, a cruel smile forming on his lips. "The star of the Arena. I've been waiting for you."

"Yme," Aya's voice is high with fear. Tears roll down her cheeks as Teron squeezes tighter to silence her.

Yme keeps his eyes on Teron. "I did what your man asked. I came alone. Let her go."

Nodding his head at the men on either side of him, Teron pulls Aya away from the edge. The two men grab Aya's arms, allowing Teron to walk towards Yme.

Holding his hands out to his sides, Teron laughs. "Demands are not for you to give, slave. You and those other prisoners killed almost all of my men. If it hadn't been for a little black bird with a warning, you probably would've killed me, too."

"We weren't planning to kill you," Yme says. "But that's not the case anymore."

"If you want her back, you must fight me. You must fight for her."

Yme raises a hand and the rocks at his feet rise into the air. His anger reaches his eyes and his blood boils. "I accept."

Teron moves one hand to point at the men holding Aya. They move her closer to the edge, leaning her over the sheer drop. She shrieks in terror and tries to pull herself away.

"No. No magic. If you use your magic, I'll have my men throw her off the cliff." Teron glances at Aya. "I doubt you'd be able to save her in time if all three of us attack you at once."

The rocks rising from the earth stop, as Yme's breath catches in his throat. Yme drops his hands and the rocks fall to the earth. Yme grips the sword in his hand tightly. "No magic. I don't need it to defeat you."

Teron lowers his arm and the men pull Aya from the edge. She stares at Yme and Teron with wide eyes.

Drawing his sword, Teron moves closer to Yme. When he is close enough, Teron strikes, moving lightning fast. He swings his blade down on top of Yme, giving Yme only enough time to raise his still sheathed sword to block. Yme pushes Teron back, using the small opening to draw his blade and throw the sheath to the side.

Using the momentum given to him by Yme, Teron spins and slices at Yme from the right. Yme blocks again, pushing the opposing blade away, and following through with his own blade. He strikes from Teron's left side and Teron moves away. But the tip of Yme's sword catches Teron's arm, creating a shallow gash.

Cursing, Teron spins to his right, bringing his blade around to strike at Yme's right. Yme blocks, but while he is distracted by the sword, Teron kicks one of Yme's legs out from under him. Yme falls to one knee, catching himself with his sword hand. Teron raises his sword and swings it down, aiming for Yme's neck.

Instead of dodging to the side, Yme lunges forward into Teron's gut, knocking both to the ground. Teron's sword falls from his hand a few feet away. He kicks Yme off, but Yme uses the force to maneuver his way to Teron's sword. He grabs it and aims both blades at Teron. They both rise to their feet.

"Let her go," Yme demands.

Laughing, Teron raises his chin defiantly. "You'll have to kill me first."

Sneering at the man's feeling of superiority, Yme runs at

Teron, preparing to slice into him using both blades. Teron makes no move to avoid the strikes.

As he closes the distance between them, Yme feels a growing pressure in his chest. He stops inches from Teron, his eyes widening at the familiar sensation. Teron raises both hands at Yme and smiles.

Yme throws himself to the side, barely missing the flames. He falls to the ground, rolls away from Teron, and leaps to his feet. He stares at the Blood King's second in command a mixture of rage and shock filling him. "Impossible."

Playing with a small flame on his palm, Teron says, "My King gave me a gift before sending me after you. He thought it would be a fitting death, a magic user killed by his own magic."

52

Infuriated by Teron's words, Yme stomps a foot onto the ground. The earth shakes and the wind picks up.

Teron quickly points to his men, who lean Aya farther out over the deep chasm. She stands on her tiptoes, trying to remain on solid ground. The earth ceases shaking, and the wind stops, as Yme immediately cuts off his magic. He raises one sword in front of him and the other behind.

Teron shoots fire from his hands, taunting Yme. It works.

Yme runs at Teron. Teron throws small balls of flames at Yme, forcing him to change course multiple times. Yme dodges easily and slowly makes his way closer. When he is too close for Teron to risk being attacked, Teron throws up a wall of fire and pushes it, causing Yme to move back to avoid the thick flames. But once he clears the wall, Yme continues advancing on Teron. Teron tries using the wall of flames again. This time Yme doesn't move back. He uses Teron's sword to cut through the flames, creating an opening.

The heat of the flames melts Teron's sword and Yme throws the useless weapon away. He uses Jaxon's sword to attack Teron, but the man is ready to dodge. He encases his arm in fire and swings it at Yme as the blade swings past, harmlessly. He connects with Yme's side. The force of the hit elicits a gasp from Yme, and he moves away to prevent another attack.

The clothing where he was hit is burned away. Luckily, the flames didn't burn long enough to affect his skin. Teron follows Yme, both arms now covered in flames, and swings at Yme. Yme blocks Teron's swings with Jaxon's sword, surprised to find the metal more sustainable against the heat. However, the flames engulfing Teron's arms prevent the sharp blade from cutting into his skin.

Yme feigns an upper slash so that Teron blocks with his arms. But he changes the direction of his blade at the last possible second and slices at Teron's legs. Before his blade hits Teron's legs, Teron increases the flames around his arms so suddenly Yme is momentarily blinded. Staggering back, Yme covers his eyes with his free arm.

Thinking he can catch Yme unguarded, Teron sets the ground beneath Yme's feet afire. But Yme feels the flames and quickly leaps away. His vision returns and he angrily prepares to use his wind to kill the flames.

He stops when he sees Aya held over the edge of the cliff by Teron's men. She meets his eyes, and a shock runs through Yme. He takes a deep breath and runs towards Teron.

Teron throws more flames at Yme's feet, attempting to halt his advance. But Yme ignores the flames and keeps pressing forward. Teron tries to throw small balls of flame at Yme, but Yme uses Jaxon's sturdy blade to destroy the fireballs. Yme feels small remnants of the fireballs land on his arms and legs. Burns sting his skin, but he ignores the pain and continues running for Teron.

Teron covers his arms in flames when he realizes he can't stop Yme. When Yme is close enough, Teron swings his arms at him. He knocks Jaxon's sword from Yme's hand and hits him in the same spot as before. Yme winces as the flames burn his bared flesh. He yells and kicks Teron in the lower gut. Teron gasps and the flames on his arms go out. Yme grabs the back of Teron's head and pushes it down as he brings his own knee up to meet Teron's face.

A crack of bone signals Teron's nose breaking and the man instinctively pulls himself back, falling to the ground. Yme grabs the cuff of Teron's shirt and pulls him to his feet. He uses his wind magic to pull Jaxon's sword into his hand and stabs Teron through. Teron's eyes go wide and he grabs Yme's burn wound on his side. Yme cries out in pain, lowering to his knee, and bringing Teron down to the ground with him.

Pulling Jaxon's blade from Teron, Yme punches the Blood King's second in command in the gut. Teron leans forward and Yme brings his elbow down on Teron's back. Before Teron can fall to the ground, Yme uses the last of his strength to uppercut the man, sending Teron onto his back, unconscious.

Gasping for breath, Yme stands. The pain in his side almost brings him to his knees again, but Yme uses Jaxon's blade to steady himself.

Yme lifts his head to stare at the men holding Aya. They stand farther from the cliff now but both have their knives drawn and held at Aya's throat. They give Yme a threatening look, but he can see the fear hidden beneath.

Yme laughs, but it's cut short by the burning pain in his side. Taking deep, calming breaths, he approaches the men slowly. "Let her go."

The men move the blades closer to Aya's neck, almost touching skin. Yme rolls his eyes and raises one hand. Wind knocks one man away from Aya and the earth beneath his feet launches him into the canyon. His screams echo all the way down.

The second man grabs Aya's shoulder with his free hand and shoves her dangerously close to the edge. Yme bends his arm at the elbow and water from the man's jug shoots into his eyes. He releases Aya, wiping the water from his face and the earth beneath him launches him into the canyon.

Aya loses her footing and falls off the edge, but Yme's wind surrounds her and pulls her back to safety. Running to her, Yme pulls her from the edge. He tries to open the shackles, but they're locked. He storms over to the unconscious Teron and searches him for the key. Finding it, he quickly frees Aya's wrists and she wraps her arms around him.

Yme takes in a sharp breath as she hugs against his wounds.

"Sorry. Let me help you," Aya says, placing her hands above the large burn wound on Yme's side.

Yme grabs her hands in his. "I'm fine. Let's head back into the city in case more men are hiding."

Nodding, Aya hugs him again, gently this time.

Teron, regaining conscious, laughs from the ground behind them. "There're no other men. You've killed them all. Except for the little black bird." He coughs and blood rolls from his mouth. "You'll never defeat the King with this land's pathetic army. His army grows stronger every day. You will die and everyone who stands with you will die. And *you* will die, Life Healer. You will die most horribly of all."

Pulling away from Aya, Yme crosses to Teron's supine figure. He stares down at Teron, holding Jaxon's sword above the man's heart.

"Wait." Aya grabs Yme's wrist, stopping him. "We should bring him back alive."

"Why? We already have the information from the soldier," Yme says.

Glancing down at Teron, Aya releases Yme's arm and

kneels down beside Klaeon's second in command. "But he'll know more. And maybe he'll be useful in other ways."

"You might as well kill me. If you leave me alive, I'll simply burn this city to the ground," Teron says, spitting blood into Aya's face. Yme kicks him in the side, sending a shudder of pain through the man.

Aya holds her arm out, stopping Yme from a second kick. "It's not your magic. It was given to you, which means it can be taken away." Tearing Teron's shirt to bare his chest, Aya places her hands on his skin. Her magic uncurls and eagerly moves into Teron. It heads for the wound in his gut, but Aya turns it away. She aims it towards Teron's core, the warmth found in every living thing.

Surrounding it is a swirling darkness Aya recognizes. It's the same that lives within the Blood King, the living magic that feeds on others. Flames mix with the darkness, providing the magic-less Teron with fire. Aya urges her magic closer to the swirling miasma, a sudden strain growing. It wants to be released and Aya grants its wish. Her magic attacks the darkness, pulling it from the man's core.

Teron groans on the ground, sensing something wrong. "What are you doing?"

Aya ignores him, watching her magic swallow the darkness, leaving only the flame behind. But the familiarity of it to Yme's magic disappears with the darkness. Without the second magic, the flames die out, leaving nothing behind. With Klaeon's magic gone, Aya turns her attention to the wound and heals it quickly, ensuring Teron feels every restitch of flesh. The pain causes Teron to pass out from shock, but Aya feels no sympathy.

Yme quickly kneels beside her and places the shackles on Teron's wrists, his eyes moving from the unconscious man to Aya.

"It wasn't really your magic," Aya says, softly. "It was an imitation wearing its appearance. Without Klaeon's magic, it can't survive. I'm sorry."

He nods his head slowly, but she catches a look of disappointment in his eyes. "Then my fire is truly gone. And Klaeon is to blame."

53

Moving slowly through the city, Aya and Yme pass those still celebrating. Many have already started heading home, as the night grows longer. Several people watch as the two walk past, but when they see Yme's wounds and the unconscious man in shackles they quickly avert their eyes.

Yme winces as they pass too close to lit torches, his burns sending waves of pain through him.

"Let me heal you," Aya says, trying to lead Yme to a nearby bench.

Forcing her to continue walking forward, Yme shakes his head and eyes the diminishing crowds. "Not here. Somewhere less crowded. Private."

Reluctantly, Aya agrees and they move through the city. They cross the largest bridge of the city. It's wide and made entirely from thick stone. A large tower, supporting many other bridges of the canyon, marks the halfway point; stairs allow people to reach the other bridges and the top of the tower.

Aya and Yme reach this tower and pass through a doorway which leads into a large, open circular room. Curved stairs lead up or down and benches line the wall. A single couple appears from the lower level and exits the opposite doorway, leaving Yme and Aya alone.

"I'm going to heal you," Aya tells Yme, not asking. They lay Teron's limp body on the floor in front of the closest bench and Yme reluctantly sits. Kneeling before him, Aya places her hands on the large burn on his side and he inhales sharply. "I'm sorry. It heals faster if I'm touching it."

Waving his hand at her, Yme says, "It's fine. It's been... a long time since I've been burned." A shadow crosses his face. "I thought I could control it, but I should've known better."

Aya concentrates, feeling skin repair itself and dulling the nerves causing pain. Slowly raising her eyes, Aya hesitates before asking her question. "Was that truly how your fire used to be?"

Yme stares at his hand where small burns cover his skin. His eyes narrow and he clenches his hand into a fist. "I don't know. It felt like my fire, but..."

Finishing the large wound on Yme's side, Aya takes his clenched hand in hers. She smiles gently at him. "But also, not like your fire."

"It's hard to explain."

Aya begins healing his hand, as she finishes, she moves to his arms and legs, healing any burns she finds. "From what I can tell, Klaeon's Blood Magic is *forbidden* magic for a reason. No man should have this kind of power to take away magic from those who were born with it and give it to those who don't deserve it. If we're going to defeat him, we need to learn how his magic works and how to defend against it." Moving to Yme's face, Aya places her hands over small burns Yme hadn't even realized he had received.

Yme watches her work in silence. He knew the talks of war were to come. But he'd been avoiding the discussions since they escaped the Arena. Even when Jaxon tried to speak about it during the festival, Yme had avoided the subject. It seems fitting the first serious talks about the war are with Aya.

Finishing the last of the burns, Aya sits on the bench next to Yme. Snaking her arms around his left arm, she leans her head on his shoulder.

Gazing at her face, Yme can see the dark circles forming under her eyes. The tiredness weighs her body down, and she fights to keep her eyelids from drooping.

"Teron made it sound like Klaeon's army is larger than we believed it to be. Do you think he was telling the truth?" Aya asks, her gaze locked onto Klaeon's second in command.

"I do. Unlike us, Klaeon has been in one place. He's had plenty of time to gather more forces to his army. We'll need more men than this city has to offer."

"Yme! Aya!" Voices call to the two.

Aya and Yme sit up and look through the doorway leading to the west side of the city. Daniil, Kylii, Jaxon, Tanith, Deven, Saunem, and three of Deven's men run towards them. As they reach the tower, Yme and Aya stand.

Spotting Teron on the ground, the approaching group slows, tension building in their bodies.

"What the hell? Aya gets kidnapped and you go off on your own without telling us?" Kylii demands.

Crossing his arms, Daniil frowns at Yme. "It could've been a trap and you both could be dead right now."

"We're fine," Aya says, calmly.

Nodding his head, Yme eyes Jaxon. "I had no choice. Teron sent one of his men to make sure I came alone."

Jaxon raises his hands, defensively. "I tried to tell them that, even had Deven and the woman held at knifepoint explain it. But they wouldn't listen to me."

"One of our riders could've used a pela to aid you without the enemy knowing," Deven joins in.

Aya squeezes Yme's arm. "Everything's fine. Yme defeated Teron and we made it back." She nods her head at Teron. "And we've got a high-ranking prisoner now."

Deven turns to his three men. "Take him to join Natus, our other guest in the cells." The three men quickly grab Teron and carry him away.

Yme watches them carry Teron away, his fists clenching. "It's time to make detailed plans to defeat Klaeon."

54

Jaxon steps closer to Yme and crosses his arms. "I'm glad to hear those words from you. In regard to *how* you are going to stop Blood King Klaeon," Jaxon starts.

"You said you knew a way for me to regain my fire," Yme interrupts.

"Yes. I do."

"Wrong. *I* do," a voice says loudly. "Stolen fire, eh? Forbidden magic was used on this poor boy."

Yme and Aya step away from the man who has appeared standing between them. His white hair is pulled back behind his head. Thick, white stubble covers his lower face, and his pale eyes stare at Yme incredulously. His clothes are made of light material, but hug tightly to his body, showing the muscles beneath. Though at first glance, the man appears old, he radiates a youthful energy.

Instinctively, Yme moves to stand between the man and Aya. "How did you know my magic was stolen by forbidden magic?"

Sneering, the man shrugs his shoulders. "Not hard to miss when I take a peek at your source."

"Source?"

"All in good time, boy. You, snar eyes." The old man turns his attention to Jaxon.

"Snar eyes?" Jaxon grumbles, irritated by the nickname and for being interrupted a second time.

"Snar?" Aya looks at Yme, who only shrugs.

"A snar, my dear, is a furred animal, much smaller than your Khorgoi there. They're notorious for being clever, sly, and are able to camouflage by burying themselves in the ground or changing the color of their fur using dirt, mud, feces, or anything else they can find. It's said their eyes can never be trusted because they're such clever liars." The old man never breaks his gaze with Jaxon.

Jaxon's eyes grow dark with anger. "Are you saying I can't be trusted?"

"I'm saying, I can't tell what goes on behind your eyes." Finally, breaking eye contact with Jaxon, the old man sighs. "But you were the one to call me. You wouldn't be a very clever liar if you called me to help with the boy."

"Help?" Yme walks to Jaxon. "Is this what you meant when you said I could get my fire magic back?"

"Yes. Though I'm starting to regret my decision," Jaxon says.

A tug on Aya's dress pulls her attention from the three men. Tanith is gently pulling her away. Raising her eyes, Aya sees why. Daniil and Kylii have both paled. Daniil is as still as a statue. But Kylii is gripping his brother's arm tightly and moving slowly back, attempting to bring Daniil with him.

"What's the matter with you two?" Aya walks towards the two with Tanith at her heels.

Both brothers look at Aya with wide eyes. Daniil is the first to look away, turning so his back is to her. Kylii forces a smile, but it doesn't reach his eyes. "Nothing. I just want to go see if there's any food left at the festival square."

Tanith rubs her nose against Daniil's limp hand. But he doesn't move to touch her or look at Aya. Kylii turns away from Aya and tries to pull Daniil forward.

"Running away again?" the old man's voice cuts through the air like a sharp blade, freezing Daniil and Kylii. "What do you think will happen this time? There's no Arena to hide in this time."

Aya turns to face the man. His pale eyes watch Daniil and Kylii intensely.

"We weren't hiding," Daniil's soft voice responds to the old man's sharp words. There's a dark tone, unfamiliar in the usual calm nature of his voice.

Kylii turns to face the old man, but he can't bring his gaze any higher than the ground at the old man's feet. "We didn't run away."

The old man takes several steps towards Daniil and Kylii, his expression stern. The brothers visibly shrink as he approaches, as though the force of the old man's presence were pressing against them.

Aya steps between the old man, Daniil, and Kylii. "Stop it."

Looking at her for the first time, the old man's eyes move up and down her quickly, taking her in. His lip twitches and Aya believes she saw a smile.

"A Life Healer. Quite a rarity in this world."

Fear grows in Aya's stomach the longer the man stares at her. But she stays between him and the brothers. Finally, the man's lips curve upwards into a humorous smile and she sees a familiarity in his face that catches her by surprise. Her eyes widen and she looks back at Daniil and Kylii. She again looks at the man and the realization shocks her.

Crossing his arms, the man releases a small laugh. "I see you understand."

"Understand isn't quite the word," Aya answers.

"Boy, come here," the man turns to Yme.

"My name is Yme."

"Yme, boy, rare kind, they're all technicalities. But for now, boy will do. Come here."

Yme hesitates, but Jaxon gently nudges him forward.

The man places a hand to his chest. "Name's Kiphy. I can help you retrieve your stolen fire magic. But you must do exactly as I say. Are you sure this is what you want?"

Nodding, Yme answers, "I have to defeat Klaeon. I can only do that with all of my magic."

"Good. We leave now."

"Leave?"

"Yes. Your training can't be done here. We leave now."

"But what about planning our attack? How long will this training take?"

Leaning his head from side to side, thinking carefully, Kiphy makes an annoyed sound. "If we're lucky, three months."

Yme and Aya stare at Kiphy in confused silence. Jaxon, Kylii, and Daniil aren't surprised by the news.

"Three months? That's cutting it a little close, don't you think?" Yme asks.

"That's the time frame. Anything less depends on you."

"You should have enough time if you don't dawdle," Jaxon says.

Crossing to Yme, Aya places a calming hand on his shoulder. "Go with him. Jaxon, Daniil, Kylii, and I will take care of everything here. Get your fire back."

Yme meets her eyes and places a hand on her cheek. He kisses her and nods. "Fine." Taking a step towards Kiphy, he says, "We leave now."

Kiphy turns to lead Yme out of the tower. But he stops in front of Daniil and Kylii. He doesn't speak, waiting for the two to fight to meet his eyes. His face softens for a moment and he places a hand on each brother's shoulder. The touch shoots through them like lightning, widening their eyes, and catching their breaths in their throats.

"I'm happy you both made it back to me." Kiphy speaks the words softly.

Moving past them, Kiphy regains his stern expression and strident walk. Yme pauses at Daniil and Kylii to give them words of encouragement, but the strong emotion apparent on their faces keeps him silent. They manage to keep the tears back, but their choked sobs are still able to force their way past their lips.

"Boy!" Kiphy calls.

Yme pats Daniil and Kylii on the back as he hurries past to catch up to Kiphy. The two disappear across the bridge, growing smaller as they reach the east side of the city.

"Are you two all right?" Aya asks, walking towards Daniil and Kylii.

"We'll be fine," Daniil says, his voice shaking. Kylii only nods, unable to speak without making a pained sound.

Jaxon looks at Deven. "Thank you for finding him."

"We keep records of every person who travels through our city. Honestly, I didn't think he was still here. He tends to come and go without a word." The brothers make an amused sound at that. But Deven ignores them and continues, "How did you know he was here?"

"When I asked the Seers of Eraunel for information on anyone who knew how to restore magic, they eagerly gave me his name. Of course, if I'd known we were traveling with his sons, maybe I would have asked them to talk to him for you," Jaxon says, staring at the brothers.

Moving away from Daniil and Kylii, Aya places her hands on her hips. "Enough talking about that. We're wasting time. We have work to do."

"Work?" Kylii manages to choke out, regaining his usual tone. "What kind of work?"

"Too much to talk about here, where anyone can overhear. Deven, is Arvid available to meet with us?"

Deven's eyebrow rises. "Now? The festival is only just ending."

"So he's free. Let's go." Aya grabs Deven and pulls him across the bridge. Jaxon, Daniil, Kylii, Tanith, and Saunem follow quickly.

EPILOGUE

Benton Natus pulls against the shackles on his wrists. The metal is cold and hard, but he can't remember how much length there is to the chain. The pitch-black darkness of the cell surprisingly makes it difficult for him to sleep.

How long are they going to keep me here? Why don't they get it over with and just execute me already?

It would be a mercy to execute him. He can't go back home. Revealing any information to enemy forces is traitorous and the punishment for traitors is worse than death. All Benton wants is to go back to his father's farm. He misses the fields, the smell of the animals...even waking early for a long day of hard work.

The draw of the Blood King's military had been too strong and the promise of glory and money too enticing. Even when he was ordered into General Teron's hunting party for the escaped slaves, Benton believed this would be a simple task. But reality slammed into him as hard as that terrifying animal when he tried to escape.

A loud sound echoes in the dark. Benton jumps, his heart leaping into his throat. He strains his eyes in the darkness but can't see anything. He listens and swears he hears footsteps moving softly closer.

"Hello?" he calls out, terror shaking his voice.

"Your purpose is finished," a low voice rumbles in the dark. "Your King is pleased with you and you shall be rewarded."

A strong tug on Benton's chains throws him to the floor. His chin hits the stone hard and pain shoots through him. He feels blood drip from his chin, and he yells out in shocked pain.

"Who are you?" he shouts, trying to sit up. A foot slams onto his back, pinning him to the ground. "No! Please!"

The chain wraps around his throat, cutting his shouts short. The metal tightens, his breaths stop, and panic stabs his chest. He flails his legs, attempting to kick his assailant, but only succeeds in scraping his legs against the stone floor. He tries to grab for the chain around his throat, but his hands can't reach.

Benton's lungs scream for air, threatening to burst with the strain. His legs slow their kicks and the blackness somehow grows darker as the fight leaves his body.

His father's farm passes through his thoughts and he feels the warmth of his mother's arms envelop him as the cold of death takes his body.

AFTERWORD

Thank you for reading *Blood Embers*. If you enjoyed it, please post a review where you purchased it.

The next book in the Blood Magic series will be released Fall 2021.

ABOUT THE AUTHOR

J.A. Ludwig received a BA in Theater Technology and has been fortunate to work for two theaters in Southern California. She is a proud techie who feels more comfortable behind the scenes dressed in black than on the stage. Since she was young, she's been lost in her imagination or in books. If you want an insight into her mind, you can check out her blog, A Joy on the Updays.

PUBLISHER'S NOTE

Babylon Books is a division of Bernhardt Books, a family-owned publishing house founded in 1999 that specializes in showcasing emerging authors and compelling fiction.

Editor-in-Chief: Alice Bernhardt
Marketing Director: Ralph Bernhardt
Chief Financial Officer: Harrison Bernhardt